RUN FOR YOUR LIFE

BY PHILIP ANTHONY SMITH

CW01425959

GET A FREE BOOK BY VISITING:
WWW.PHILIPANTHONYSMITH.COM

INSTAGRAM: @PHILIPSMITHFICTION

CONTENTS

For my beautiful wife, Lindsey,
You are the most supportive and amazing wife any
man could ask for. Thank you for believing in my crazy
dream of becoming an author and enduring my
'book talk' until the small hours every single night.

PROLOGUE

It was my first run of 2024, and I was hoping it would be an uneventful one. The recurrent stamping of my feet reverberated the early morning air. My lungs struggled to keep up with my legs as I ran faster and faster. My heart thumped through my chest as I pushed my body beyond its limit. The adrenaline coursed through my veins like ignited petrol. The quickening pace jump-started my brain into producing endorphins in a futile attempt to deal with some of the pain. Like supply and demand, I accelerated to keep the high going, and I punished the gravel with each footstep.

I was propelled down the canal path by my legs, working perfectly in tandem. Like two great pistons in a steam engine, they fired in juxtaposition. The heat of my breath collided with the cold morning air, producing steam, leaving a trail that only dissipated minutes after I passed. Faster. The dull grind and click of my knees radiated pain up and down my legs. My chest screamed desperately for respite, but I didn't surrender. Faster. My breathing was laboured and shallow. My endpoint was in sight; I doubled down and gave everything I had in the final moments to produce more speed. I crossed the imaginary finish line and gave my body the all-stop order. My limbs fought the forward motion, and I finally stumbled to a stop. No longer being cooled by the breeze, my entire body was ablaze. I collapsed on the icy cold ground and stared up at the sky.

The gravel soaked up my body heat like a sponge. The rapid temperature change burned lightly but was so comforting. My breathing began to normalise. I took deep breaths through my nose and out through my mouth in a conscious effort to slow my heart rate. It finally started to lower. The endorphins faded, and I was finally aware of the true torture I had put my body through. The blood in my legs was replaced with battery acid, and my legs wilted and convulsed because of the trauma of the few hours. The pain was exhilarating. Every twinge and ache chipped away at my stress levels. I leached liquid anxiety into the cold ground beneath me; it pooled momentarily before it seeped into the substrate, never to be seen again.

I was rewarded with a few minutes of perfect clarity. My brain desperately tried to sort through last year's events before it became fogged again. The trees and bushes anxiously swayed in the breeze so as not to disturb my calm. The canal water faintly rippled, reminiscing of the boats travelling down it hours before. The moon appears exhausted after its long journey, ready to yield to the sunrise. My sweat drenched the ground, melting the delicate layer of frost that had formed overnight.

The sun pierced the horizon and systematically illuminated the path before me, one row of gravel at a time. The sun's rays reached me and gently warmed my face. I squinted for a moment whilst my eyes adjusted. The intensity of the light ripped me back into reality, and I stood to greet it. The perfect outline of my form remained etched into the frost like a shadow. My legs were filled to the brim with lethargy; I paced aimlessly to try and force some life back into them.

The thicket rustled behind me, and I was immediately thrown into fight or flight. I stepped back from the treeline, ready for what would emerge. My eyes darted around the greenery for a hint as to what will come. It shook again; I cemented my feet to the ground, ready for whatever will pounce on me. My knuckles are bleached white by my clenched fists. An unseen mass dropped from the tree at speed. It took my eyes a minute to adjust until I noticed a single well-fed squirrel staring back at me. After identifying me as a threat, it retreated back into the undergrowth, and the relief filled me.

"Jesus," I uttered to myself, laughing.

For a moment, I thought it was them. I laughed at my overreaction and continued walking down the path. Every mile or so, there was a bridge. They connected one side of the canal to the other, serving me as distance markers so I knew roughly how far I had run. I stopped tracking my runs digitally a while ago. I used to be obsessed with my pace and statistics, but since I run for different reasons.

I approached the next bridge, which was derelict and ill-maintained. At first glance, the graffiti underneath was unsightly, but if you pass the bridges as often as I did, you start to see the skill and beauty of it. I turned to take in the artwork as I walked underneath the bridge. There was a single can of spray paint left upright on the path; I detected the lingering trace of solvent in the air as I drew closer. I reached the can on the ground, and that's when I saw it.

A small, red, stencilled foot was spray painted in what little free space remained on the concrete. Its crude and rushed nature left thick red drips that seeped into the ground below. The sight of it froze every drop of blood in my body in fright. I reached out to touch the image; it was fresh. The paint ominously tugged at the skin on my fingertips before it freed its grasp. My fingers had taken some of the paint with them. Panic had set in, and I turned 180 degrees and looked behind me. There was nothing there. I turned forward again, but nothing was there either.

I chose flight and exploded back into motion. My weary legs resisted initially, but self-preservation refuelled them and returned them to form. My head jolted as I constantly turned to look behind me. My heart had tripled in size and was barely contained in my chest. Each beat felt like it would rip through into the open air. It forced the gallons of adrenaline into every cell of my body. Three times a second, the explosive force of my heart almost threw me into the air like a jackhammer. The gravel beneath my feet quaked deeper into the earth as I relentlessly pummeled it into submission.

My senses became infinitely more attuned. Every unexpected flap of a bird's wings reverberated in my skull. I could smell the sharp tang of the thawing ground below. The decay of the steel beams that braced the canal's retaining wall coated my tongue in rust. I diligently studied every unpredicted movement before me and behind for threats. I treated every sway of a tree or leaf's rustle as a warning. My brain ached from processing the information from my senses; I couldn't form a plan beyond survival.

I advanced towards a right-hand bend and slowed down slightly in preparation. As the path straightened, I saw a small opening in the thicket to the side. I became quickly fixated on it and slowed myself further on the approach. When I reached it, I peered into the opening with trepidation. It took some time to decipher what I saw until I realised it was the body of a lifeless man, face down in the undergrowth.

I was immediately cast in stone on the spot. I stared in shock at the corpse and begged it for answers. The man was in full winter running attire; his hood obscured the back of his head. At the centre of the massive blood stain on his back stood the handle of a knife; the blade was still plunged into him. His shoes and socks had been removed, and the soles of his feet had been meticulously slashed to ribbons. The flow of blood has ceased, but enough remains on the blades of grass around him to subtly shimmer in the fresh sunlight.

I had no idea who this man was, but I felt partly responsible for his death. He could have been running for his life only minutes before I arrived, but then he was eerily still. He had tried to fight back, and in the struggle, he had lost his life. I carefully crouched beside him and pulled back his hood. His head was turned slightly toward me; I did not recognise his face. He appeared to be in his early twenties. He had a well-groomed beard with his hair pinned back by a headband. In his right ear was a small wireless earphone. I could hear a tinny static noise coming from it and removed it carefully from his ear.

As I leant in closer to it, I instantaneously recognised the noise. It was a chilling, droning sound, almost like a mistuned radio station. It wasn't dissimilar from white noise but had a sinister undertone behind it. The exact pitches and frequencies were seared into my brain forever. I desperately searched him for the phone that was paired to it. It was housed in an armband on his left arm. I used the thumb on his right hand and unlocked the phone. A familiar app was already open.

It was the 'B-Run' app. It looked like any other exercise tracking app, but the colour scheme was black and red. The logo was prominent in the middle of the screen, and the red silhouette of a foot with drips originating from the sole was like I had seen under the bridge previously. This app had ruled my life. I swiped to see the map of where the man had run; he had only managed three miles.

I stood above him, with his mobile and earphone still in my hands. The app was currently paused. My entire body yearned for the thrill; my hands shook in anticipation, ready to start. I placed the earphone in my ear slowly. The noise reinvigorates me with energy. I filled my lungs with air and slowly exhaled, taking in every crackle and pop. The sound was turned to electrical impulses that tingled through my entire body. I hit start on the screen. A low, dull thud played through the earphone once a second. I felt it pulsate warmly through my body. I took one last glance at the man on the ground and started jogging.

I built my pace slowly this time, determined to keep my heart rate and breathing low. I concentrated on my footwork, ensuring every stride was as efficient as possible. Thud. Thud. Thud. The app kept my pace like a metronome. My heart rate equalised to the same beat, in perfect harmony with the sound in my ear. A minute or so down the path, the thud began to speed up; I responded in kind, moving slightly faster. It went quicker and quicker until I heard the distant scraping of feet rapidly hitting the gravel. I didn't turn to look at the origin of the noise; I knew exactly what was there.

They were coming.

1

NEW YEAR, NEW ME

It was 2023. That was the year I was finally going to sort everything out. 'New year, new me' season was upon us. Oh, the joys. My daily commute to work was awash with people in brightly coloured exercise gear, only for them to inexplicably disappear weeks later. 'Posers', I thought, even though I could barely run up a flight of stairs. The constant hammering of social media made you feel sick for simply existing outside a state of perpetual self-improvement. My feed was filled with so-called 'influencers' preaching about food and impossibly fit-looking people talking about how to get fit at home with little or no effort. I told myself when I reached thirty that, I would get fit before I hit thirty-five. What a joke that was. After many failed attempts, I had one year to make good on my promise. 2023 was going to be my year.

My schedule was dominated mainly by work, followed by recovering from work. I worked in a telesales job in the city. The kind of job that makes you want to smash your head into a brick wall. I didn't grow up wanting to work in telesales; I just fell into it by necessity. With every phone call, I felt my soul shrivel like a raisin. I yearned to do something meaningful, but paying the bills always took priority.

I was intelligent, but I lacked the drive and confidence to search for my passion. I worthlessly floated from one career path to the next to keep the money coming in, but living was so expensive. One of my biggest regrets was that I dove straight into work immediately after leaving school. At the time, it was fantastic; all my friends were in college or university, and I was earning money instead of racking up astronomical amounts of debt. One by one, they all got snapped up by their dream jobs, and we lost touch. I remained on the same greasy rung of the career ladder, never getting much farther than the bottom.

I met my wife, Courtney, 12 years ago on a works night out. I'd love to say it was love at first sight, but it wasn't. I was mainly interested in her long, tanned, slender legs and what was in between them. Don't judge; I was a lot younger then. I wasn't looking for anything serious, but like everything that happened in my life, I just fell into it.

Lust turned to love.

It didn't take us long to move into a small flat in the city. Life was simple. It was fun. We got married three years later, looking back, probably on a whim. Two years later, we were expecting. Dylan wasn't planned by any means, but we were both delighted. What a shock that was. My memory of those early years after Dylan arrived was scattered. The slog of sleep deprivation left us parenting entirely on autopilot. We barely survived from coffee to coffee and from pay-check to pay-check.

I was forced to take more shifts where I could at work to keep our heads above water. Me-time was non-existent; fun was thin on the ground. I had become a silent partner in my own family. The precious hours I had at home were spent half unconscious in an armchair or shovelling junk food into my mouth as a substitution for actual sleep. I watched Dylan grow up in his sleep through his slightly open bedroom door.

But this year was going to be different.

New year, new me.

We had just moved into a modest two-up, two-down just outside the city. As an estate agent, I would have described it as a functional family home decorated to a high standard throughout. We had a small garden for Dylan to play in and just enough room to be not tripping over each other. It was in a rough area, but we didn't get much trouble. Our newly built estate was filled with copied and pasted houses, stripped of individuality. We maxed out every line of credit we had to afford the mortgage.

But things were looking up. Dylan had settled into his new school; Courtney had got a job as a part-time bookkeeper for a local small business, so we had a second income again. I had applied for a promotion at work, so hopefully, we could afford for me to work fewer hours. I finally decided to make good on my promise and sort myself out. Exercise. It's a dirty word in my vocabulary. I didn't want to be one of those posers running up and down the streets, but I had to do something.

Since Dylan was born, I was terrified my health would fail, and I'd leave him without a father. It was a genuine concern; my dad died when I was young of a heart attack. Courtney constantly nagged me to go and get checked out at the doctor, but I think the actual act of finding out I was likely to have a heart attack would give me a heart attack. Still, I needed to start looking after myself for Dylan's sake and Courtney's. We sat at the dining table in the kitchen on Dylan's first day back to school after the Christmas break. The annual health kick was contagious and infected our family. We all stared down at our granola and yoghurt bowls with disdain.

"I don't know what that face is for; it's good for you," Courtney scorned, "we are cutting out the sugary stuff and all the crap from now on."

"Mum, it tastes like rocks," Dylan said abruptly. A cheeky smile spanned his face when I giggled quietly.

"Oh, come on, it doesn't taste like rocks," I said, stifling a laugh, "it doesn't taste of anything."

"Sean, it tastes better than the rubbish we usually eat, and it's much better for you," Courtney said, shovelling spoonful after spoonful into her mouth in feigned enthusiasm.

I had a knack for making her laugh when she had a mouthful of food or drink, and I stared at her with a half-smile expectantly. It didn't take long for her to crack, and she dumped the entire contents of her mouth back into the bowl, laughing.

"Oh god, it does taste like rocks." She said, wiping the expelled yoghurt from her chin with a napkin.

"I told you so!" Dylan said proudly, waving his spoon in the air.

"Listen, if Mum says it's good, then that's good enough for me; I will chow down on this entire bowl and enjoy every piece."

"If you are going to eat all that junk food, Sean, you can at least start exercising. We all need to try to be healthier."

"I've been thinking about running, and I see enough idiots doing it on my way to work in the mornings to manage it."

"Running? You?"

"Yep, it's meant to be good for stress too. And there is enough of that going around."

"Well, that's great; I'm sure you will be able to do it," Courtney said with pseudo encouragement, "when are you starting?"

"This morning, actually; new year, new me," I said ironically, unholstering my finger guns.

I pushed my bowl dramatically to one side and left the table. I went upstairs to unearth my exercise clothes. I was out of breath from just walking up the stairs and I was in no fit state to go out for a run, but I had to start somewhere. I found my moth-bitten exercising clothes in a rarely opened drawer in the bedroom. I stretched them on; they strained to accommodate my increased size. I slapped at my taut stomach in the mirror.

"All bought and paid for," I said ironically. I returned to the kitchen and gave an ironic twirl.

"Go on then, what do you think?" I joked cheekily.

"Well, you certainly look the part. Almost convincing." Courtney chuckled.

"Dad, those clothes don't fit you," Dylan said dryly.

"I know, son, that's why I am going for a run; when I get back, I am going to be stick-thin," I said, ruffling his hair with my hand, "see you on the other side."

I downloaded a free run-tracking app and placed my earphones tightly in my ears. I sketchily replicated a few stretches I'd seen athletes do on television and immediately hit the pavement at speed. Why had I waited so long to do this? It was easy. I was good at it. Just move one foot in front of the other. On second thoughts, scratch that. I barely got to the end of the street before I started feeling queasy. My rocky repast threatened to eject itself from my stomach. I toyed with returning but thought surrendering so quickly would be too embarrassing. To avoid another biting quip from Dylan, I slowed my pace considerably to a casual jog. I made my way to the canal because the path was mostly flat, and I am sure my knees would thank me.

Every ligament and tendon screamed in agony as they stretched after years of inactivity. I turned up the music in my earphones to drown it out. A stitch formed on my left side, and I started to run lopsided to compensate. It felt like the cartilage in my knees had already worn down to the bare bone. My ankles clicked to supplement the sound of each footstep. Where was that wheezing noise coming from? Was the pain ripping across my chest normal?

As I was about to give up, I spotted another runner on the horizon. Eager not to be witnessed failing by a stranger, I continued. We exchanged a brief nod and a smile as we ran past each other. She was an experienced runner and had a flawless form. Her gilded, tied-up hair almost defied gravity, floating in the breeze as she turned to look back at me. Even though she was deep into exercise, she looked flawless. For the record, I would never cheat on Courtney, but the eye candy was undoubtedly motivational. I remembered I must have looked like a breathy hog fleeing from a predator and deduced she was just being polite.

Twenty or more steps down the path, something seemingly magical happened. The stitch lifted, and everything felt better. I found my pace, and I stopped struggling as much. The pain eased and became endurable. The chilling January breeze refreshingly whipped at my hair and face. I had already passed the point I was going to turn around in my head and was running into uncharted territory. I sustained the same pace for some time, and the flow of endorphins grew stronger with every step. I felt as high as a kite. My feet didn't feel like they were hitting the ground anymore; I was floating. I hit the 1-mile mark and turned 180 degrees to return.

Maybe I would catch another glimpse of the blonde if I picked up the pace. But it wasn't worth seeing the granola again. I continued back home at the same pace, and even though I had just completed a very short run, my self-confidence was through the roof. I returned home just in time to see Courtney leaving to drop Dylan off at school and then go to work herself. She and Dylan got in the car, and she opened the window to speak to me.

"How was it?" She questioned.

"Really good; I actually ran two miles," I said between breaths.

She scrunched up her face. "Don't overdo it and hurt yourself."

"I didn't; I actually feel pretty good about myself for a change."

Courtney winked. "Well, you look terrible," she said, looking me up and down, laughing, "you better get a shower before work."

"Yes, ma'am," I exclaimed with a faux salute.

I waved them off and jumped straight in the shower. My muscles melted like wax against the hot water. I thought I would be exhausted, but I was energised and ready for the day. Today was out of the norm because I had my interview. I selected my best-looking suit that wasn't ill-fitting and ironed it to an inch of its life. I was going to smash it.

I worked at a sales outsourcer in the city called TPL. Yeah, it was as bleak as it sounded. We approached other businesses and offered them a chunk of sales for a price. It was very fast-paced and very target-driven. The staff turnover was huge because it was a terrible place to work. I was one of the most long-standing salespeople there, even though I had only been there a few years. We had various campaigns we would work on and then move on to something else. I usually worked on business-to-business campaigns; one month, you could be selling insurance, and the next, you could be selling energy contracts. As far as dead jobs go, it was perfect for me in that sense; I usually got bored quickly and moved on to the next thing.

The call centre building was a vast grey box with a flat roof interspersed with sporadic windows. The dreary utilitarian interior was almost all whitewashed and carpet tiled as cheaply as possible to cut down costs. Was it a repurposed prison? Possibly. The sound of ringing phones and droning voices fills the room of the main call centre. A sea of cubicles filled the room, each housing a

17

single salesperson tethered to a desk with a phone headset.

Like a wave, you can hear the same cold calling script making its way through the room, followed by the faint sounds of calls disconnecting. That month, we were selling card payment terminals to small shops and businesses. Fascinating stuff. I arrived at my desk at 8:50 and logged onto the system. The phones were connected to an auto dialler, so as soon as a call ended, the next one started.

My eyes rolled to the back of my head. "Hello, I am Sean from EZ Pay Credit Card Solutions. Can I speak to the business owner, please?" I droned.

"Not interested." The voice on the line sighed. The phone immediately started dialling again.

This exchange was typical of a morning in the call centre. I became impervious to the rejection after a time. Cold calling was a numbers game, and I knew the more calls per hour, the more likely someone would treat me like a human. The rejections repeated without relenting, but I only had to endure an hour of it before my interview.

I logged off the phones and made my way over to the main building. The call centre was haphazardly bolted onto the side of a much larger and nicer office building. It was often frequented by clients and had been carefully designed to ooze success and flashiness. The entire outside perimeter of the building was forged of glass and steel, allowing pure, unfiltered sunlight to drench the highly polished tiled floor. Sporadic sets of modern tables and chairs littered the open space with professional-looking people sitting at them drinking coffee. Even the air in the building tasted better. The network of exposed stainless-steel vents emitted an organic, gluten-free version of the city's air directly into your lungs.

It made you feel like you had won a competition to be here for the day. The difference between here and the call centre was stark. I barely recognised anyone walking through. It was far too uncouth for these important people to have to visit the squalor of the call centre.

My shoes squeaked on the polished floor as I made my way over to the elaborate-looking reception desk. The receptionist looked incredibly busy, her high heels clacking against the floor as she moved backwards and forwards, sorting out paperwork. Her fire-red hair sailed from side to side. She noticed my approach and stood tall, her lips parting slightly with a smile. I felt my nerves tickle slightly as her welcoming hazel-green eyes beamed at me. I was fleetingly lost in them for a moment before she interrupted my trance with her greeting.

"Hi, welcome to TPL. Can I help?" she recited.

I shuffled nervously closer to the desk. "Hi, my name is Sean Miller. I am here for an interview at 10."

"No problem! Let me check." She beamed. For a minute, I thought the run had instantly made me irresistible, but her smile slipped as soon as she felt she was out of my eyeline. She was definitely just being polite. She turned to consult the computer in front of her.

"It's with Neil on the 4th floor," I added.

Her polite smile appears again before she turns to look at me again. "I'm really sorry, Sean," she apologised clumsily, "I think it has been cancelled."

"Oh really, does it say why?"

"No, it just says cancelled; you will have to rearrange with his office."

I patted down my pockets furiously. "Hang on, I have the email printed out somewhere."

"This is the most up-to-date information, and I can see his calendar; the interview has definitely been cancelled," she said tactfully, "I am sorry I couldn't have been more help." She then returned to clacking and sorting.

I didn't know how to feel; part of me was furious that I had been dismissed so readily without reason, but mainly, I just wondered what I would tell Courtney. I toyed with the idea of kicking off and demanding to see him, but I couldn't have pulled it off. This interview was my opportunity to sort our lives out and have a shot at repairing our marriage. Neil cancelling the interview without warning was devastating. For him, it was a small, coloured block in his calendar, but for me, it was everything. The chance to be involved in my family again. The prospect of not having to spend every waking moment worrying about money.

And just to be clear, I didn't make a habit of gawping at women, but like I said, our marriage was strained. 'It's been a while' would probably be an understatement. It's not that I made advances either; there was always a pathetic reason not to. Too tired. Headache. The passion of the early days had faded, primarily because neither of us had the energy to make the effort anymore. I missed those days.

I made my way back to the slums of the call centre and returned to my post. The monotoned hum of the room forced me into a reflective state as I stared blankly at the login screen in front of me. It seemed dramatic, but I felt shell-shocked by what had happened. I glanced at the only shred of personality in my cubicle, a photograph of me and my family crudely pinned to the cubicle wall. I am dragged back to reality by a stern tap on my shoulder. I looked up to see my team leader, Maria, using her hand to signal a phone to her ear.

"Sorry Maria, I've just got back from the interview," I said repentantly.

"How did it go?" Maria said softly.

"It didn't- it was cancelled."

"Sorry, Sean, I'm sure something else will come up eventually."

"I don't think it's over," I bargained, "it will get rearranged."

"Yeah, I am sure it will," Maria said unconvincingly whilst turning back to her desk.

I'd always liked Maria; she had been the team leader since I started. When I first got the job, I thought she was a bit of a battleaxe, but you quickly warmed to her. She was a stickler for everyone being on the phones as much as possible and diligently timed every break and toilet visit. I often wondered if she clicked a stopwatch out of view when someone left their desk. She was about ten years older than me, which worked to her advantage, as most of our team members were in their early twenties. Maria projected this strict mother persona, which worked well with the younger members of the team.

I logged onto the system and repeated the cold calling script. I really struggled to concentrate on anything other than the disappointment of the morning. By the end of the day, I was at rock bottom on the leaderboard. I was even below Paul, who, and I'm not being cruel, had a pretty severe speech impediment. It was time to go home, finally. I attempted to stand, but my legs buckled under the pressure. I hadn't noticed, but the hours I sat at my desk had set my legs like concrete, and I was still recovering from the morning run. I slumped back into my chair in failure, and my neighbouring salesman, Jordan, looked at me and laughed.

"You are getting old, Sean," Jordan scoffed.

"No," I groaned, reattempting the manoeuvre, "I went for a run this morning."

"A run? I didn't know you ran."

"First time," I said, laughing, "can't you tell?"

"The first mile is always the hardest." He said motivationally.

We rarely spoke at work despite us being desk neighbours. The sheer volume of calls didn't allow for socialising during business hours, so we only ever exchanged passing comments on our way out of the building. Also, I didn't want any work friends. That would be accepting that I was going to be staying here for a while. Jordan was in his early twenties and very athletic-looking. He had thick jet-black hair and not a single grey in sight. Jordan looked after himself; he often brought a gym bag with him into the office like he had been exercising before work. He wore almost skintight shirts, presumably to show off his muscles to the women on our team. I'd often chuckle to myself when I caught him flexing when someone of the opposite sex looked at him.

In many ways, he reminded me of myself at his age; he had this full-time job pretty much straight out of school with no responsibilities, and he felt like a millionaire. I'd piqued his interest with the fitness talk, and I could see him itching to talk about it more.

"I promised Court I would sort myself out; I'm thirty-five this year."

"Well, it's really great you have started," he said almost proudly, "consistency is key."

"I'm aiming for maybe three times a week, and I'll build it up from there. I might look like you by the end of the year."

He leaned in slightly, almost telling me a secret. "What tracker are you using?"

"I don't know, I've been using some free thing on the app store," I said, unlocking my phone to check.

"They are all useless. I have a beta for a brand new app from someone at the gym that's just come out, but it's invite-only," he bragged, pulling out his phone and brandishing a QR code, "scan that."

"What does it do?" I said, scanning the code. My phone opens a web page for an anonymous IP address, simply with a black screen and a red download button.

He leans in further, beckoning me to come closer. "You won't believe it, but they actually pay you per mile to run."

"They pay… you? Why?" I said, bemused.

"No idea. They probably sell your data or something, but it will be buried in the terms and conditions somewhere." He shrugged flippantly. "All I know is that you get a pound per minute for running."

"A pound per minute? Surely not," I said in disbelief, "that's sixty quid per hour!"

"I know, mate, it's crazy," he said, laughing, "I'm absolutely hammering it before they realise how much money they are giving away."

I rashly hit the download button, and an icon appeared on my home screen. The icon was mostly black, with a red footprint as the logo. Underneath it read 'B-Run'. I tapped it, and a standard-looking sign-up page appeared. If what Jordan was saying was correct, this could have been the answer to my troubles. If I managed to run for three hours a week, that would almost make up for the shortfall of losing out on the promotion.

"The app itself is pretty basic," he continued, "it tracks your runs through your phone and pays out at the end of the week."

"I might actually give this a go."

"The only real drawback is you can't listen to music at the same time; it has this weird static noise and banging you have to keep pace with."

I made my way through the sign-up form while he was talking. It had the usual basic information on there and bank details for deposits to be made. I got to the terms and conditions; the writing was so small that it was barely legible. I scrolled up and down the document and skimmed its contents, but it was so vast that I immediately gave up and clicked accept.

"Right, I am on."

"Add me as a friend; my username is 'Jordy'; it's at the top there." he said with excitement, "when you get up to speed, we will have to go together one day."

"Done. Thanks for that; I had better get going. Courtney is expecting me."

"Catch you tomorrow, Sean. Let me know how it goes!"

I made my way back to the car, forming a scheme in my mind. If this was legitimate, it could be the answer to everything. I could earn enough money to keep us from delinquency and get fit in the process. I sat staring at brake lights in rush hour traffic, eager to get out my phone and explore its secrets. Could it be real? Jordan seemed to think so. I doubt he would have recommended it to me if he hadn't already used it. The source of the money did concern me, but we live in the digital age. If someone wanted to pay me to see my pathetic browsing history or shopping habits, go for it.

Would I tell Courtney about the promotion? No. I didn't want to worry her. I didn't make a habit of lying to her, but our marriage was strained enough. I probably could tell her about the app, but she would have thought it was a hare-brained scheme and would try and dissuade me. I'd check it out first. If it's real and you do get paid like Jordan said, maybe I would tell her eventually. I fully admit that I did have a habit of getting overly excited about these things, and I wanted to avoid 'the look' from Courtney whenever I was explaining a get-rich-quick scheme. For now, I'd keep her in the dark; as long as we paid our bills on time, she shouldn't ask too many questions.

2

RUN, RABBIT

As I put my key in the front door, I could already smell dinner cooking. Or overcooking. As I entered the kitchen, Courtney opened the oven, took two steaming hot pizzas out of it, and placed them on the countertop. Smoke bellowed out of the oven whilst she wafted at it with a dishcloth.

"Is the health kick over? Or is it healthier when it's cooked to a cinder?" I said, amused.

She aggressively hacked at the pizza. "Listen, I've had a terrible day, and I couldn't be bothered when I got home."

I approached her with my arms outstretched in a hug. "Do you want to talk about it?"

She walked past me, avoiding my grip. "Not really. How was your day?"

"Yeah, not too bad," I explained, sitting down at the table, "the interview didn't happen today, though."

I had finally captured her interest. "What do you mean it didn't happen? Did you not get it?" she said anxiously.

"No, Neil's office sent an email this morning; he had to reschedule," I fibbed, "he had an important client meeting or something. I think it will happen next week."

"That's annoying. Are you okay?"

"Yeah, my legs are killing me, though," I diverted, "I think I am going to go again tomorrow."

"Can't we talk about one thing without you changing the subject to something else?" She said with frustration.

"I'm sorry, I've had a long day too and just feel a bit deflated."

"So, when is the interview rescheduled?"

"I don't know, he hasn't said yet."

"Well, it doesn't sound good, does it?"

"Not really, no."

"I can always ask Frank for some more hours. Or look for something else?"

"I don't want you to have to do that."

"I know, but needs must. We got more final demands today, Sean. They are racking up."

"I've seen them. Can you leave this to me, please?"

"Fine, I better go and give Dylan his dinner."

What a fun evening we were about to have. Courtney left the room, and I unlocked my phone to find the app still open. The logo pulsed smoothly above the start button. I pressed the menu button, and some options appeared. I idly went through the options until I hit the leaderboard screen. Some of the top runners were already well into triple figures so early in the month. My eyes converted the minutes run into pound signs as I scrolled further down. The bonuses tab was where I realised how much potential it truly had. There were different bonuses for running before sunrise or following specific routes. Courtney returned to the room, and I quickly locked my phone. She noticed and looked slightly vexed, then lifted her head to make eye contact.

"Are you eating with us?" she asked.

"Yeah, sure, I'll head in shortly."

"You never moved your sweaty clothes either; they are still on the bathroom floor."

"Yes, ma'am," I whispered.

We made our way into the living room, and Dylan was sat on the sofa with his eyes transfixed on the television, paying little attention to the plate of charcoal pizza on his lap. Courtney sat with him, also watching the television intently. It was the newest iteration of some 'reality' based talent show with people embarrassing themselves for a shot at fame. Courtney used it as an excuse not to talk, which was fair enough. I didn't feel like talking, either. I stared down at the burnt pizza, and my appetite crumbled to dust. I managed a single slice before placing it on the table in front of me.

"I think I am just going to head to bed; I am exhausted," I said wearily.

Courtney barely moved her head to look at me before nodding slightly. She barely concealed an eye roll before turning to Dylan.

"You need to finish your dinner, Dylan; it's almost bedtime, and you have school in the morning." She ordered.

"In a minute mum, we are watching this." He declared indifferently.

I feigned a jovial punch to Dylan's arm as I left the room, and he responded with a distracted smile. I had always struggled to connect with him. He seemed to look at me as the strange lodger that would be around sometimes. He was growing up so fast, and I got most of what I knew about him second-hand from Courtney. Looking back, we were never ready for kids. Well, Courtney was. They say that parenting comes naturally, but it didn't feel like that to me. I definitely didn't have the most conventional upbringing; I felt like the intuition you are meant to mysteriously acquire on becoming a parent was missing.

I turned on the shower and stepped inside. The shower had become a safe place for me in recent years. Courtney used to complain that I spent too long in there, but I think she understood why. Ten minutes without having to deal with the world outside of the cubicle was sacred to me. The warm water felt good on my aching muscles. I scrubbed away the feeling of failure I had been left with, and my skin could finally breathe again. Sufficiently rejuvenated, I left the shower. My sweaty pile of running clothes stared up at me from the floor. I kicked them to one side.

I entered our bedroom and laid back on the bed to set my alarm in the morning. I was tired, but I couldn't resist rechecking the app. The leaderboard section lit up in red and green like a switchboard, and I was eager to get started. I felt guilty being in bed when I knew so many others were out there. I was excited. But I needed to get some sleep to prepare for my little experiment the day after. I wondered if Blondie was on there. No, I thought and gave myself a little imaginary slap on the wrist. I fell asleep like I usually did, with my phone in my hand, in a puddle of drool.

I woke up a few hours later when Courtney came in, pretending to be quiet but intentionally attempting to wake me up. She was being loud enough to make sure I woke up but quiet enough to have plausible deniability. Classy. She never liked to go to sleep on an argument, whereas I was stubborn enough to continue it indefinitely. Her approach was what kept our marriage together for so long. She put her arm around me and held me softly from behind.

She leaned in gingerly to whisper in my ear. "Sean, are you awake?"

"Yeah, is everything okay?" I responded hoarsely.

"Yeah, I am sorry for arguing," she said tenderly, "I am just so worked up about money, and I wish you didn't have to work as much. I had a shit day, and it just brings everything up."

"I don't want to argue either," I whispered whilst turning to face her, "everything is going to be okay, you know. I've got this."

"I hate arguing about money. It isn't us at all, and I know we will be fine. It's just stressful. I had so much hope pinned on your promotion, not just for the money, but I was looking forward to having you around more."

"I know you did," I admitted, "One way or another, I am going to make it happen. If this doesn't work out, I will look for something else."

"You do work really hard, and I want you to know we appreciate what you do for us."

"I'm really struggling with Dylan at the moment," I confessed, "he looks at me like an outsider most of the time."

"He is too young to understand yet, but he will. You are keeping a roof above his head."

"I know, but that isn't enough, is it."

"He will have to do the same for his own family one day, and he will remember what you did."

"I suppose."

"And he talks about you all the time; he looks up to you."

"It doesn't always feel that way. I don't think I'm a very good role model."

"You are Sean. But it's tough."

"I know."

"Listen, it's really great you are starting to look after yourself too," she said, "I will always support you. I am sorry for being dismissive sometimes."

"And I'm sorry for being so evasive all the time," I confessed, "I am so tired, Courtney."

"Me too. When are you next thinking of going for a run?" Courtney said faintly.

"Tomorrow morning."

"Isn't that a bit too soon? Won't you need time to recover?"

"No, I'll be fine; I just need a good night's sleep. Jordan from work recommended an app to me today; I want to check it out."

"As long as you don't overdo it. We better get to sleep then. Good night."

"Good night."

I kissed her on the cheek and turned back around. I lay awake for what felt like hours. Although the passion had faded between us through the years, I still loved Courtney. We had a strong connection beyond the physical. Sure, the physical side was important, but we had built a life together. Or tried to. Yeah, the foundations were a bit cracked, but we would make it.

Even though we bickered and squabbled, Courtney always knew the right thing to say. The olive branch had lit a fire in me and doubled my determination. I still held out some hope for the promotion, but Maria's face when she spoke to me made me think she knew something I didn't. It was the expression on her face. I can't overstate how much we needed this promotion. It was part of the plan. I wrestled with my anxieties until they finally submitted and allowed me to fall asleep.

I had set my alarm for 6 am the night before, feeling brave, but actually waking up was grim. I had about an hour to get as much running done as possible. The financial rewards almost made me forget that I was a novice runner and that I was attempting something way beyond my fitness level. My creaking knees mirrored the creaking floorboards of the bedroom. I crept not to disturb Courtney; as soon as I got out of there, I threw my running gear on in the bathroom and got ready to leave. I whispered goodbye to Courtney, and she affectionately grunted in her sleep before turning away from me.

I left through the front door, and the cold air hit me like a train. I was severely underdressed for the occasion; the fine rain outside made it difficult to see any actual distance. The morning was as miserable as I was. But I reminded myself why I was out here, the experiment. The excitement thawed my freezing limbs. I walked briskly to the end of the street in warmup, window shopping the bonuses section of the app to see what was attainable.

I reached the canal path, and my finger hovered above the start button for a moment in hesitation before pressing it. My phone showed various permission warnings about using GPS and tracking my movements. I clicked accept. My wireless earphones started playing the bizarre droning noise Jordan had mentioned. It complemented the fine rain striking the surface of the canal water beside me. In total coordination with my heartbeat, there was a dull thudding noise booming into my ears. I started running slowly, and then the timer started.

Yeah, my heart wasn't in this. Or my legs. Or anything, really. The rain was freezing against my face, almost pushing me backwards as I battled through it to reach some kind of sustainable pace. I must have stopped ten or fifteen times before I truly got going. It would be hard to find the motivation when the weather was that bleak. But this experiment wasn't about self-improvement or health; it was about wealth. I was sick and tired of scraping in the dirt for loose change. If this didn't work, I'd have to find something else. I started to get a rhythm going; every minute that passed, I imagined a pound coin dropping into my bank account. It was enough to keep me going, for now.

I had never been on the canal at this time in the morning. It was eerily quiet; the sound of every footfall bounced back and returned to me as I made my way down the gravelled pathway. We were hours away from sunlight, and the moon gave everything a macabre glow. The canal water twinkled in the moonlight, accenting every fluctuation in the water's surface. The fine rain faintly disturbed the flow of liquid as every drop fell. I noticed my reflection in the canal. I saw how my body moved in the third person, and I barely recognised the man in the mirror. I looked good, strong, even. Maybe Blondie wasn't just being polite.

I timed my foot strikes to the sound of the thumping beat in my ears. It produced a pleasant but steady pace that kept me from overexerting myself. I periodically checked my phone whilst in motion and I had managed about 8 minutes without stopping. My self-imposed target seemed so achievable when I started, but I felt myself slowly floundering. The thudding kept me in check as I told myself I could make it. As I went underneath the next bridge on the canal, the path turned from gravel to poured concrete. I mourned the loss of the loose stones as I felt my knees take the full force of my feet hitting the ground.

But I continued despite the pain. That's the odd thing about running. I had lived a sedentary life for many years, and it made me claggy and slothful. Not just physically but mentally, too. Yes, I was a novice runner, but with every step, I could feel my whole outlook on life-changing. Before I started, my mind was clogged up with the plaque of everyday stress that had built up over the years. With every thump of my heart, I felt the blood flushing it away, allowing me to truly think clearly again. It was a form of meditation for me; I discarded a lot of my worry and insecurities on the path as I ran over it.

It was addictive.

I spotted an old chimney stack from an old derelict factory in the distance. I lied to my body that it was the halfway point. The mind was still willing, but the flesh was failing. As the chimney stack drew closer, I noticed the slight increase of speed in the thudding, and my feet fell slightly out of time. I trusted in the noise and sped up to keep in time. I looked to the next bridge, unable to see the path beyond it. A lit-up car crossing the bridge briefly interrupted my isolation as I advanced further. The beat's regularity increased and decreased erratically; I struggled to keep up with its changes and abandoned trying. I reached the bridge on the horizon and moved persistently towards the next. I checked the app on my phone, and I was almost halfway.

I kept checking my phone for my progress. There must have been something wrong with it. I felt like I had been running for hours, and time had no meaning. The run was much more difficult than I anticipated. No amount of money bought a single second of time. That was true, but when you have money, you get to choose how you spend your time. As gruelling as it was, I couldn't lose sight of why I was doing this.

The next bridge was a small level crossing for cars in the middle of a moorings for canal boats. The canal boats swayed delicately in the water. Each of them meticulously decorated, sporting different names in ornate hand-painted writing. I squinted through the rain to try and read some of the names at a distance. Maybe there was a funny one I could tell Dylan later. It was a welcome distraction from the sheer stress my legs were under, carrying me down the path.

The thudding grew quicker the closer I got to the crossing. I wondered what it signified and dismissed it as a weird bug in the app. I briefly looked either way before crossing the road, but once I got to the middle, I was instantly illuminated by high-powered headlights. I ceased moving like the proverbial rabbit and stared at the source of light. The car roars into speed, travelling directly at me. At the last possible moment, acting in instinct alone, I tumbled out of the way, and the car missed, coming to a screeching stop on the other side of the crossing. My arm was badly scraped as I landed, and I cradled it gently as I returned to my feet and faced the culprits.

I had no idea what to expect after. I had done my fair share of late-night joy rides when I was a lot younger and a little less stupid, but it was almost 7 am. Although I couldn't exactly make out the car, it looked way too expensive to be packed full of teenagers on a bender. They also hadn't tried to drive off, which would have been my first instinct. Instead, the car just sat there, unrepentant for almost taking my life.

The initial shock had passed, and now I was angry. They obviously didn't feel the need to flee from me; I took a few steps towards the car with my arms outstretched as a show of dominance.

"Hey!" I shouted.

The car remained immobile; its inhabitants were unknown. The longer the lack of movement continued, the braver I got, inching closer to the vehicle. I took the absence of a response as an insult. I only really wanted an apology, and I would have been on my way.

Suddenly, it all felt very sinister, like it wasn't an accident. I suddenly started to panic like I was about to be mugged or worse. I took a few steps back. The driver revved the engine harshly, and the exhaust popped and spluttered under the strain. I took it to be a definite threat and walked back a few paces, waiting for whatever came next.

I looked down the path I had just travelled. I didn't know if I could run down it again. I had exerted all my energy just getting here. If I had to escape, would I be physically able to do it? My arm stung sharply as the sweat started to soak into it. I didn't think I'd be able to fight either, and I hadn't had a fistfight since I was in high school. I was an easy target, frozen in indecisiveness, waiting for the outcome to be made for me.

3

THE COOKIE CRUMBLES

The car continued to sit completely dormant, about 20 metres away from where I was standing. The wet tarmac glowed red with foreboding from the SUV's brake lights. Its exhaust spewed vast amounts of gas into the air around it, partially obscuring the vehicle.

It turned threateningly in the road and then remained idle, menacingly pointed in my direction. The headlights were blinding, and I raised my uninjured arm to my eyes to protect them from the beams.

"What the hell are you playing at?" I screamed at the car, throwing my arms in the air.

Each of the four doors opened almost in unison, and from each, a single figure emerged. They stood in front of the car headlights in silhouette; the driver stepped forward from the line and pointed what looked like a baseball bat in my direction. What was going on? The man slowly walked towards me, whistling a menacing tune as he got closer. The rest of the figures followed him at a distance. Unable to process what was in front of me, I remained perfectly still as he became closer and closer.

I had to snap out of it, and my instincts kicked in; I surged to sprint back the way I came. I was still cradling my scraped arm, which knocked me off balance. I turned to see the man in fast pursuit. The gravel shattered in all directions from my feet like shrapnel, shredding the water's surface as it hit. Water from the pooling rain on the ground dove out of the way of my feet as I zipped through them without concern. I reached the previously passed footbridge and grasped the handrail clumsily to slingshot my way through it.

A sixth sense became active. I was convinced the man was almost breathing down my neck, and every time I turned around to check his progress, it hampered my own. I resisted the urge to look; instead, I continued as fast as I could in my escape. I could almost feel the wood grain of the baseball bat rubbing against the base of my skull. My chest was expanding and contracting violently as I struggled for each breath.

The dull thudding in my ear continued and slowed the further down the path I travelled. The slight suggestion of sunrise illuminated the clouds, gifting me a slight increase in visibility. I turned my head to check my attacker's progress, but he was nowhere to be seen. The thudding in my ear returned to its starting pace, but I continued at full speed. Whatever the men wanted, I didn't want to find out. No chance.

I reached the final bridge on my journey and expelled last night's half-eaten pizza straight over the handrail. I had run way faster and further than my fitness allowed. I was terrified but also exhilarated, my body trapped in the opposites of the emotions flooding through it. My eyes remained locked on the bridge in the distance for a few minutes, expecting the menacing figure to emerge from underneath it, but it never happened.

I jogged up the steps to cross the bridge, nursing a stitch, frantically checking for signs of life. I reached my front door, and the entire street was still. I fumbled for my keys and unlocked the door, locking it behind me. I slumped on the floor behind the door in exhaustion.

"Exercise completed. Unlock for summary." The app boomed in my ears, the unexpected intrusion almost sending me into cardiac arrest.

The droning sound had stopped, and the thumping concluded. I reached for my phone in my pocket and unlocked it to find a summary of the run I had just completed. It displayed a map of the route I had taken along with various stats on pace and distance. There was a pounds and pence total at the top of the app that increased as the app continued to speak.

> *Total run time; 34 minutes, 16 seconds.*
> *First run above 30 minutes. Bonus; £20.*
> *Survival. Bonus; £50.*
> *Total earnings; £104.26*

As the app so eloquently put it, I had survived my first run. The next screen displayed the leaderboard, and my username, 'Millertime', jumped up a few places before returning to the home screen.

I let out a nervous laugh when I saw the total, and for a moment, I had forgotten I could have been beaten half to death by those men or worse. I had earned a day's salary in just thirty minutes, and the sun hadn't even risen yet. The panic I felt minutes earlier turned to euphoria. Not only had I run faster and longer than I had ever done in my life, but I had also escaped a gruesome beating.

But what did they want with me? Surely, they mistook me for someone else. Or was it a random act of violence? Maybe I goaded them with my reaction, and they decided to scare me. I knew we lived in a rough area, but I didn't think it was that bad. One thing was for certain: I needed to be more careful in the future.

I removed the earphones and used the small console table in the hallway to aid me in standing. The sweat on my arm seeped into the wound and burned like acid, and I immediately rushed into the kitchen like a wounded animal to clean it. I delicately brushed away at the dirt and debris stuck in the open wound; it looked pretty gnarly. The stairs creaked as Courtney made her way downstairs in her dressing gown. I could tell by her stamping that I had prematurely woken her up. I expected her to be annoyed, but she spotted my arm and rushed over to inspect it.

"What the hell happened, Sean?" she said, panic-stricken.

"Some lunatic almost ran me over at the canal crossing, and I had to dive out of the way."

"Are you alright? Did they stop?"

"Yeah, he stopped, then he got out of the car holding a baseball bat."

"Oh my god, you could have been mugged!"

"I know, but I ran away. I didn't even have anything valuable on me."

"You have to be more careful! You shouldn't be running down there at this time in the pitch black!"

"I was just unlucky, but I managed to get away. I think it was just some nutter."

"You better ring the police. Did you get a licence plate?" Courtney said, calming down into practicality.

"No, I couldn't make it out."

"You have to report this. They could do it to other people!"

"I will, but I have to get ready for work."

She leaned in to hug my uninjured arm tightly before walking over to the kettle to put it on the boil. She started to look increasingly agitated and pulled her phone out of her dressing gown pocket and made a call.

"Police, please." She said assertively.

"Courtney, I will call them. It isn't that big of a deal. They are long gone," I pleaded.

"Yes, my husband has been on a run this morning and was attacked. They tried running him over and then beating him with a baseball bat." She explained, nodding whilst listening to their response.

"No, he managed to escape— No, it is an emergency— This evening? That's ridiculous. Fine- it's 37 Buchan Road, the new build estate— Thanks." She argued before ending the call with a huff.

"Useless," she uttered to herself, "they are going to send an officer round tonight to talk to you."

"Fine, but I don't see what they can do about it," I dismissed, "I better get a shower. I am going to be late."

Courtney started aggressively stirring her cup of tea whilst I retreated from the room slowly. The unsaid words ricocheted in her mind like stray bullets. She turned slightly, poised to speak, but thought better of it. It was too early for a lecture, thankfully. But she was right, of course. I felt like the less I said about the incident, the better. I didn't want to mention the app. She would have prevented me from using it altogether.

I chalked the entire incident up as random and unrelated to me, so it wasn't relevant to mention. I had a quick shower and prepared for yet another day of cold calling. My shirt caressed my scraped arm like a fresh sheet of sandpaper; it served as a painful periodic reminder of the attempted attack.

The incident played over and over in my head on the commute to work. I should have stayed and fought them.

I might have got a few good punches in. Then again, they were armed, and there were four of them. I concluded I did the right thing in the end. Courtney was right, too; I should leave this to the police. I was never a fighter and would have likely gotten myself killed if I had responded in any other way. I felt like a coward. The replays in my mind prodded and poked my fragile male ego.

But who were they? Courtney's reaction made me think I was underreacting. There was a dramatic flair to the attack, the amount of time they waited before leaving the vehicle, and the slow movement towards me. I could still hear the man's menacingly cheerful whistling. I tried to put it from my mind.

I arrived at work and found Jordan already sitting at his desk mid-call. He looked at me and smiled eagerly as I sat down, clearly waiting to hear if I had used the app he recommended. I was glad he was busy- I didn't feel like talking about it. There was a small handwritten note in Maria's handwriting simply saying 'see me when you get in' stuck on my computer screen. I stood to go to her desk, which was on the other side of the room.

"You wanted to see me?" I questioned.

"Good morning, Sean. Neil called, and he wants to see you as soon as possible." She said, barely looking up from her computer.

"Oh great, is it the interview?"

"I'm not sure. You better get over there." She said indifferently.

I bounced back to my desk with a grin on my face. It was the lift I needed after the chaotic morning I had. Maybe I wouldn't have to use the app after all; I did feel uneasy about it after the attack. If I secured the promotion, at least I would have options. Being a team leader would certainly be the safer option compared to running through the night.

I stopped in the bathroom to straighten my tie and tidy my appearance. I didn't anticipate the interview being rearranged so soon; I looked like I'd been dragged through a bush, which wasn't too far from the truth. I briskly made my way over to the main office building, and the same red-headed receptionist as the day before was there. She shot me the same warm and welcoming smile for a second before vaguely recognising me from the day before when it fell from her face.

"Hi, me again. I believe Neil wants to see me?"

"Yes, he is expecting you. Go straight up to his office."

I made my way beyond reception to the lift behind it. Neil's office was on the fourth floor. I pressed the button, and the lift whirred into action. The fourth floor was mainly home to medium-sized offices for middle and upper management. Neil's office was at the back of the floor. I reached his office door and knocked; a muffled voice instructed me to come in. Neil was sitting behind his desk on the phone with his finger pointed in the air, signalling me to wait.

Neil had a reputation down in the call centre for being a bit of a lech and an onanist. That was a fancy word for wanker. He sporadically charged into the call centre, seemingly at random, to deliver a trademark group rollicking. There was talk he had got a girl's number from her personnel file and was sending her indecent messages, but nothing was ever proven. I wasn't scared of Neil as such, but he was erratic and hard to read. He also held the key to my happiness in his greasy palms, so I had to play nice.

The back wall of his office was a huge sheet of glass, allowing the views of the city to flood into the room. It was split into two parts, a conventional office on one side and more like a sitting room on the other. A muted television played the news channel on repeat. For show, obviously. As if he cared about anything else, other than himself. The wall to the left of me was full of glass shelving, filled with seemingly unrelated items and trinkets, presumably mementoes from clients we have sold for over the years. He finished his phone call and started typing on his computer one-handed, with his finger still in the air. I stood in front of his desk, staring at him. He turned to look at me and leaned back in his chair slightly.

He clapped his hands together once. "Sean, thanks for coming in."

"No problem. Is this about the interview?" I said, my hand outstretched, waiting for a handshake.

"No, it isn't. Please take a seat," Neil said, ignoring my outstretched hand and gesturing to the seat behind me. The sleight annoyed me slightly, but at least I didn't have to touch his clammy mitt.

The unexpected turn the conversation had taken made me perspire lightly, too. The scrape on my arm started to singe, which stole my attention slightly. He returned to operating his computer for a moment, clicking and typing assertively. I was sure it was a put-on, some weird façade to exercise his power over me. I stared at him with a blank expression on my face, not knowing what to expect.

"This is actually about your sales record, specifically yesterday." He said, leaning in.

My face crumpled in confusion. "Sorry, Neil, I had something else on my mind and had a bad day."

"What did you have on your mind?" He said fastidiously with a slight shrug.

His line of questioning replaced my nerves with frustration. "Well, I was meant to have an interview, but it got cancelled," I said facetiously.

"Oh, where?"

"Here… with you."

"Right. Well, we aren't here to talk about that," he says firmly, "we are here to talk about your sales record, and it isn't good reading."

"Neil, I had an off day, it won't happen again."

"I understand that, but unfortunately, we are going to have to let you go."

"What?" My fists clenched underneath the desk, out of view.

"Client cutbacks, I have to let some of the worst performers go, and you were at the bottom of the list." He explained, devoid of expression on his face.

Is he joking? He had to be joking. I had seen him 'fake fire' people before in a public setting. He probably picked up the tip from some cringeworthy online management seminar he attended. I started to smile to test the water, but his vapid facial expression confirmed that this was real.

I couldn't believe what was happening. Only a few days ago, my prospects were finally starting to turn around, and now, I was going to be made unemployed. This pathetic man in front of me had such little foresight he couldn't even be bothered to look beyond a bad day that he had caused. I gripped the injury on my arm tightly. I felt it begin to bleed through my shirt, but the pain restrained me from acting impulsively.

"Neil, with all due respect, I am one of the longest-standing salespeople on the floor, and because of one bad day, I am getting the sack?" I spat with venom.

"It's just the way the cookie crumbles," he said, shrugging, "we are offering you a moderate redundancy package in respect of your years of service." He slides a letter across the desk to me, "The details are in here."

"You can't do this; I have a family," I pleaded.

"Well, with all due respect," he said mockingly, "you should have thought about your family yesterday whilst you were on the phones, then we wouldn't be in this position."

Neil stood from his chair and started pacing the office nonchalantly for a minute, avoiding eye contact. He strode with both arms behind his back whilst glancing around the room. He moved towards me as I remained seated and loomed over me to my right.

"If you check your contract, you will find we are more than within our rights to do this," he began, "when you signed it, you agreed to meet certain standards that just aren't being met. Of course, you can try and fight this, but you'll lose."

The rage bubbled and simmered in my stomach at first before slowly starting to claw its way up my throat. Every muscle in my body tensed and seized in ire. Every gush of blood pulsated my neck violently as my fury reached boiling point. I broke eye contact and stared desirously at a large ornamental glass cube on Neil's desk. In a single moment, I weighed up every repercussion of picking it up and cracking his skull open with it.

The emotions of the attack in the morning broke through and added to the anger. The pressure in my head reached bursting point, and I began sweating profusely. My heartbeat grew louder, urging me to act on impulse. I breathed exclusively from my mouth like a rabid dog, eager to pounce on its prey.

I resumed eye contact with Neil. The moment had passed. My inaction diluted my wrath as it receded to my stomach and dissolved in the bile. The familiar self-resentment and cowardice replaced it, forcing my eyes to drop to the floor. Neil looked over me triumphantly, the clear winner of the dispute. He towered over me, knowing he had me on the ropes but poised to deliver the knockout blow.

"If you do fight this," he sneered, waving the envelope in my face, "this goes bye-bye. Think about it. You have a family, after all."

I raised my hand to receive the letter, and, in a final display of dominance, he pulled it back slightly. Like he was dangling a treat in front of a dog's nose, he wanted me to reach for it. I didn't know why he despised me so much. I had never been disrespectful to him in any way. But he wasn't doing it for that. The scoffing grin across his face said it all. He actually enjoyed this. The rabid dog had turned into an obedient puppy, and he slowly placed the letter in my open hand.

I gripped the letter and left his office without a further word. The corridor's silence was broken momentarily by the sound of Neil slamming his office door victoriously. There was a piercing ringing in my ears, a hangover from not releasing the anger I had just felt. It swelled in my stomach like poison, eating away at my insides. My feet stamped against the polished floors in meagre protest. I returned to the lift and scowled at myself bitterly in the mirrored walls.

I agree. It was definitely the correct decision to leave the ornament where it was. I know that. It was the first time in my entire life that I had even thought about responding to something with such violence. There was something deeply animalistic about even thinking about doing it, though I wondered what I was truly capable of. Part of me regretted not doing it, to see if I could and to watch the smile be wiped clean from his face.

But at the very least, I could have mustered a more compelling argument. I wondered if there was some combination of words that I could have used to convince him otherwise. But what's done was done, and then, I had to live with the consequences.

4

LUMINOUS GREEN

I saw my cubicle from the entrance. A small brown box had been left on there. I knew what it was for. I plucked the only possession I left here, the family photograph, from the cubicle wall and placed it in my pocket. Jordan looked at me with a solemn expression on his face.

"Sorry, mate." He said empathetically.

"These things happen," I uttered bitterly.

"I meant what I said about that run, we need to arrange–"

I hear the faint sound of a call connecting in his earpiece, and he starts reciting the script. Maria gave me an earnest look as I made my way out of the call centre for the last time. There was no fanfare or uproar. I quietly walked through the desks the same way I came in. Those brown boxes were a common sight in there, anyway. I wasn't Neil's first victim, and I wouldn't be the last.

Right outside the call centre was a bay of slightly bigger parking spaces reserved for the most important people in the company. And there it was. Neil's ridiculous bright red convertible. He was far too important to have to park with the common stock and have to walk the rest of the way to work. It was so shiny that it made me nauseous. It was a true reflection of his sickly personality.

I put my hand in my pocket to locate my keys and gripped them so hard they almost bent under the stress. Screw it. As I walked past his absurd vehicle, I left a deep scratch from bow to stern. A little something to remember me by, I thought to myself. I lifted my head in the general direction of his office window, expecting some kind of reaction, but I didn't receive any. He had probably already forgotten that I had existed and was moving on to the next pointless sacking.

I returned to my car and throttled the steering wheel, screaming at the top of my lungs. It released just enough pressure in my skull for me to regain some modicum of composure. I didn't feel any better for damaging Neil's pride and joy; if anything, I thought it was pathetic. For my own sanity, I just needed to do something, no matter how pitiful it was. He destroyed my life with no regard, and I gave him a minor inconvenience. Hardly proportionate, but it was the best I could come up with at the time.

I became totally preoccupied with what I was going to tell my family. We were just getting to where we needed to be financially, and in the space of an hour, all my plans had collapsed. I urged the tarmac to swallow me and the car whole rather than face the rest of the day. There was no way I could look Courtney in the eye and tell her what happened. The understanding and supportive Courtney would buckle under the pressure. It could even collapse our marriage. I didn't see a way out.

Devoid of any purpose, I aimlessly started driving. My jaw clenched tightly as I drove through the city; my fists gripped the steering wheel in failure. I looked down every street, searching for an answer to my troubles as my brain tortured me with the events of the day on a loop. My body was so tightly wound that every gear change made it feel like I could rip the car in half.

I desperately continued to dwell on Courtney and what I would tell her. The thought of the look of disappointment on her face made my stomach turn. Pins and needles pricked at my spine as I quickly descended into a panic attack, carelessly speeding through the city, attempting to get my breathing under control.

I pulled the car over and fell into a complete breakdown. I was pathetic. If I couldn't hold down a dead-end job like that, there was no hope for us.

With each tear, the panic attack eased slightly. I gripped my head in my hands to squeeze out every drop. I began to calm down and stared at the letter, sitting on the passenger seat. I had to get myself together. I picked up the letter and ripped it open.

I gazed at the number on the letter in pounds and pence and laughed hysterically. Was that all I was worth? My worth was neatly summed up in a four-figure settlement. I must have made TPL a fortune, even in my relatively short tenure. The number on the paper was an insult. I should fight this, but what Neil said was right. I would lose. We needed the settlement, no matter how insulting or small. It gave us some runway, but I had to find something else to do and quickly.

The day gave way to night, and I started to drive in the general direction of home. I arrived a little later than I usually would. There was a posh-looking car parked in my space. Perfect. I parked further down the street and walked back. I still had no idea what I would tell Courtney. My mind was so desperate I could barely hold onto a thought for more than a few seconds. Deep down, I knew I should just be open and honest with her, but I couldn't. I didn't have the capacity to form the words.

I entered the house, and a man sat on the couch sipping a cup of tea, and he turned to greet me. He was a little older than me, sporting a shaved head and greying stubble. His oversized peacoat swayed as he stood with his arm offered out in a handshake. I had completely forgotten about the police coming. I didn't even expect them to follow up.

"Mr Miller, I'm Detective Sargeant Tony Banks with city police. Your wife was just telling me you were in an altercation this morning." He said, placing his half-drunk cup of tea on the table beside him.

"Yeah, someone tried running me over and jumping me," I explained, "I'm fine now though."

"You aren't fine. You could have been killed!" Courtney interjected from the other side of the room.

"I'm glad you are okay, but we take things like this very seriously, Sean," he started, "this could be part of a pattern of wider incidents across the city, so we have to investigate everything. Is there anything you can tell me about the perpetrator?"

"I didn't see much. It was dark," I began, "I think it was the driver who chased me with the baseball bat. The rest just stayed with the car."

"The rest?" Courtney interrupted.

"Sorry, yeah, there were four of them in the car."

"You made out like it was one man this morning, Sean. You didn't say four!" she snapped.

"Four men in the vehicle changes things, Sean," DS Banks added, "It looks more like a coordinated attack than an isolated incident. Is there anything else at all you can tell me?"

"They were dressed in black, in a black SUV-style car. That's about all the information I have. I don't see how I got targeted. I was out on a run, and I didn't tell anyone I was going or where."

"Can you think of anyone you have upset? Anyone who might have a reason to hurt you?"

"No."

"I can tell you there has been a spate of attacks like this across the area, so we will compile the evidence from other cases and get back to you if we find any links." DS Banks said whilst standing up.

"Sorry that I couldn't be more help."

"I'll see myself out," he uttered, "thanks for the tea, Mrs. Miller. We'll be in touch."

He left, and I sat down in the armchair with a huff. Courtney's reaction to the finer details made me question my own. Maybe I had trivialised it, but I had so much going on. We both sat there in silent reflection for a minute before she went to lock the front door. The attempted attack had obviously rattled her; we rarely used the mortice lock and chain, but she wasn't taking any chances. She slumped back down on the sofa and sighed as she looked at me. This was it. Make or break. If I chose not to tell her about what happened at work, it would make it even worse down the line.

"How come you were late back from work?"

"Neil had everyone stay later to hit quota," I lied.

"How does that even work? Aren't you ringing businesses? Aren't they shut?"

"Yeah, but you know what he's like."

"How is your arm?" she sighed.

"Not bad. It's just a graze, really."

"It's no wonder the country is in the state it's in when the police don't even do anything."

"I didn't give them much to go off."

"I know, but go to the scene of the crime or something. Can't they look for fibres or DNA or something?"

"Court, I scraped my arm. They aren't going to send the murder squad down and close off the entire canal."

She shot me a disapproving look, upset with my sarcasm, and stomped out of the room. I had told a lie to her, and as far as lies go, it was a pretty big one. For me, at least. I felt grimy; our family was plummeting into financial free fall, and she didn't even know. Her top concern at the moment was the scrape on my arm and my indifference to it all.

"Where is Dylan?" I asked.

"In bed."

"Sorry, I didn't realise what time it was. I was looking forward to helping with bedtime."

"Well, maybe you should have said 'no' to Neil instead of staying at work late."

"Fair."

We sat in front of the television for the rest of the evening, barely speaking a word to each other. She must have known something else was wrong, but I never found the courage to tell her. I mindlessly scrolled up and down on my phone, seeing the same nauseating motivational posts about exercise and self-improvement. My phone beeped, and I received a notification from the 'B-Run' app.

> *Hi mate, do you want to meet up*
> *for a run tomorrow morning?*
> *Hit me back. Jordy*

"Jordan from work has invited me to go on a run tomorrow with him," I mumbled, "I don't know what to say."

"Sean, you can't go. It's obviously not safe." Courtney protested.

"It's safer with the two of us, surely."

"What about your arm?"

"I'll use my legs to run tomorrow instead."

"Funny. Do what you want. You always do. I'm going to bed." She conceded before leaving the room again.

I felt for her; I really did. There shouldn't have been any secrets between us, but it was a slippery slope. I kept telling myself I was doing it to protect her, but in reality, I probably just couldn't be bothered regurgitating it all up again. I struggled to keep track of the outright lies and lies of omission. I hadn't told her about the app, but that was hardly grounds for divorce. Sure, I downplayed the attack, but that was out in the open now. I definitely lied about the promotion, but to be fair, I did hold out some hope it would happen. But not telling her I got sacked, I can't explain that one away.

I could measure the distance growing in the marriage with every dishonesty. I physically couldn't tell Courtney about me losing my job. I was terrified our marriage couldn't handle the strain. I felt forced to continue to lie,

I was desperate to sort everything out before the time came that I would be forced to tell her.

The answer in the short term was obvious to me; it was staring me right in the face. My side hustle had just become my only source of income. The experiment was technically a success. Of course, I almost got killed, but that wouldn't happen again. The money from the run had already been deposited into my bank account. Real money that we can use for bills or shoes for Dylan. I replied to Jordan, agreeing to go for a run with him the morning after and told him to meet me on the canal.

Convinced that I would randomly confess I was being dishonest in my sleep, I decided to sleep downstairs that night. I imagined her crying upstairs, but I lacked the communication skills to make her feel better. Recently, I just seemed to make things worse.

My alarm woke me the next morning, and my injured arm was sealed to the leather on the armchair overnight. I carefully peeled it away and got ready to meet Jordan on the canal. I already had a message from him telling me he was on his way; he was so eager to go, but I had slept terribly. If I hadn't arranged it with him previously, I probably would have given it a miss. My mouth was so dry I tottered to the kitchen and chugged glass after glass of water to stifle the dehydration that had grown overnight.

I made my way back to the canal path, where we agreed to meet. Although it was still dark, the weather was clear that morning, and I had more visibility. It looked like a different world, and I felt safer knowing that I could see everything around me. I hadn't realised the attack had rattled me so much, and I started to realise why Courtney was so upset about it all. I was so preoccupied with the sacking I hadn't really stopped to think about it until right then.

I spotted Jordan stretching against the bridge railing on the canal. His nauseatingly luminous green trainers were visible at a distance, even in the early morning darkness. He notices me approaching and turns to me, jumping in the air, full of energy and clapping his hands chirpily. The joy.

"Morning, Sean!" he shouted enthusiastically.

"Morning," I said wearily.

"What the hell happened yesterday?"

"I got the sack because of my sales figures."

"What did your wife say about it all?"

I did contemplate just making something up, but I needed to tell someone what I'd done. Who knows, maybe Jordan would have given me some wisdom on how to proceed.

"I haven't told her."

"Deep. When are you going to tell her?"

"I don't know if I will. I am hoping these runs will replace it while I look for another job."

"Risky, mate."

"I know, but I haven't got a choice."

"Neil is a prick anyway," he assured, "did you know he was sending dodgy pictures to Fiona?"

"I heard something about that."

"That's why she left, you know. They paid her off, apparently. He is old enough to be her dad."

"Scumbag."

"Anyway, you will get another job, mate."

"Thanks. It wasn't so much the sacking; he enjoyed it," I started, "he actually said, that's the way the cookie crumbles."

"Yeah, he is on a mad power trip. He came down to the call centre later and just screamed at everyone for no reason."

"I did contemplate smashing his face with an ornament, so I suppose it could have gone worse."

Jordan paused for a second before he threw his head back in awkwardly forced laughter, clearly choosing to believe I was joking. He started to bounce up and down on the spot before spotting the scrape on my arm and stopping suddenly.

"Hang on, what the hell did you do there?"

"Slipped over yesterday in the rain, it's not as bad as it looks."

"Nasty," he grimaced, "are you ready to hit it?"

"Yeah, sure," I said unconvincingly.

We both got our phones out in unison and opened the 'B-Run' app. A prompt appeared on our screens asking us to pair our runs together for an extra bonus.

"Sweet, you get a bonus for running with someone else," Jordan exclaimed.

We both hit start, and I started jogging down the path. Jordan shot off at speed, looking perplexed as to why I was so far behind him. He remained jogging on the spot, waiting for me to catch up with him whilst shrugging. For the first five minutes, Jordan didn't stop talking whilst I was fighting for every breath. He seemed satisfied with my grunts, posing as a verbal response for a while. The effects of sleeping in the armchair became apparent. I was very weak and clearly struggling. The thud from the app in our ears did little to encourage my pace to quicken. I noticed that he started to get progressively more agitated by my pace, and he turned to look at me with pity.

"Sorry, Sean, I don't want to be a prick, but I think I am going to go a little bit faster for a while. I'll catch you on the way back. Is that alright?" he requested.

"Fine," I spluttered between laboured breaths, "go for it."

With my blessing, he turned forward and sped up to a pace I couldn't even fathom running at and quickly disappeared into the darkness. With the lack of distraction, I regained my focus and got my pace in check. The thud of the app forced me into an obedient, steady pace. With the passing of each bridge, I expected to see Jordan bounding back towards me, but he was nowhere to be seen. I hadn't even asked him how long he wanted to run before he sprinted off. I approached the canal crossing, and the thud remained in a constant rhythm. I reduced speed slightly to scope out the area carefully. I stopped at the curb and looked down either road but saw no one lurking in the darkness. Happy I wasn't going to get attacked, I crossed the road at speed with my eyes almost closed, still expecting a repeat of yesterday. Nothing happened, and I felt relieved.

I had never travelled this far down the path before, and the shrubbery was less maintained. Balding trees arched onto the path as I ducked to avoid them. The path meandered beside the canal, turning into a dirt track. The next bridge was made of huge stones, connecting one side of a farm to the other. The thudding in my head sped up, and I responded in kind, lengthening my stride. It got quicker and quicker. It willed me into a sprint as I almost reached the welcoming cold stone of the bridge before me. I finally reached it and placed my hand on one of the stones, leaning against them to catch my breath. My body decided this was the halfway point in my run and declined to run any further. The thudding was so fast in my ears that it was almost a vibration. It was interrupted by a loud splashing noise coming from beyond the bridge.

"Jordan?" I gasped quietly.

I cautiously made my way underneath the bridge; the path was narrow and treacherous, without a handrail. I took every step deliberately, avoiding stepping on the moss-ridden retaining wall and splitting the land from the water. The canal was totally undisturbed, apart from a large mass floating in the water. I was unable to make out what it was at this distance and jogged closer to get a better look. When I neared the object, I recognised Jordan's luminous green trainers floating near it. Panic-stricken, I sprinted closer still to the mass to discover it was a shoeless Jordan floating in the canal.

On sheer impulse, I plunged into the freezing canal water. The rapid temperature change drove every molecule of air from my lungs by force. I thrashed towards Jordan, who wasn't moving and gripped him underneath his neck. My entire body convulsed in the icy waters as I returned with him to the water's edge. I dragged him onto dry land and tried to shake him awake. His face was pale and lifeless, and my violent response did nothing to snap him out of it. A long, thin slice on the front of his throat started to ooze blood down his neck and soak into his t-shirt.

5

THE TUMBLE

The sun had barely risen when the ambulances arrived. The flashing blue lights danced on the surface of the water. I stood, covered in Jordan's blood, completely detached from the reality and chaos surrounding me. Time had slowed; the jolts from the defibrillator left Jordan hanging in the air for minutes at a time. The paramedics scrambled around him in a desperate attempt to stop the bleeding between shocks. Uniformed police officers swarmed the canal, attaching tape to every surface like spiders spinning webs. A small gang of onlookers hung over the old stone bridge all holding their phones pointed at us. A uniformed police officer was trying to speak to me, but his words never reached my ears. The dull thudding rhythm continued in my ears, blocking out all other sounds.

I was shaking violently from the cold, but I barely noticed it. My bones had turned to ice, and the silver blanket the paramedics gave me did little to stifle the penetrating cold. The constant shivering made it difficult to focus on anything other than Jordan's lifeless body being worked on from all sides. I glowered at his body intensely, willing him to burst back into life with a mighty inhale. All of the paramedics' body language seemed to change when an arbitrary time limit had been reached. The lead paramedic checked his watch lamentably whilst the others covered his body with a sheet. He was gone. If only I were able to keep up with his pace, I could have somehow prevented all this from happening.

A familiar figure made his way down the steps from the bridge with his hands in the pockets of his grey peacoat. He had a brief conversation with a uniformed officer, and they were both pointing at me with distrust. DS Banks slowly made his way over to me, removing his hands from his pockets only to remove my earphones. I was snapped out of my trance and raised my gaze from the sheeted Jordan to meet his eyeline.

"Sean?" He loudly said.

"Yes?" I said absently.

"What the hell happened here?"

"I don't know."

"You are going to have to do better than that, son. There is a dead bloke over there, and you are covered in his blood," he scolded, "you need to tell me right here and right now what happened. This is really serious, Sean."

"I don't know!" I pleaded, "he was running ahead of me, and I heard a splash. When I got there, he was face down in the canal."

"How far ahead of you was he running?"

"I don't know; he pulled away a few miles back."

"Did you see anybody else on the path, anyone at all?"

"No, we were alone. Once I got him out of the water, I realised his throat was cut, and I rang for an ambulance."

DS Banks looked dissatisfied with my response and turned to speak with the other officers at the scene. The paramedics lifted Jordan's body into the gurney and wheeled him towards the bridge. The grass had flattened where he lay, decorated with various plastic wrappers and packaging from the paramedic's attempts to revive him. My eyes remained locked on the gurney, which made its way up the hill towards the bridge. DS Banks stared at me intensely, trying to decipher every emotion on my face. He trudges back over with his hands back in his pockets.

"Listen, Sean, I've got to caution you, and we will have to question you back at the station."

"I get it."

"Sean, you do not have to say anything. But it may harm your defence if you do not mention something when questioned, which you later rely on in court. Anything you do say may be given in evidence. Do you understand?"

"Yes, I understand."

"Now, I'm not going to cuff you. Do not make me regret that decision, yeah?"

"I'm innocent, Tony."

"Follow me. We are going to need your clothes and phone."

DS Banks shepherded me up the steps for the bridge to the large police van above. Inside were two anonymous officers in paper suits waiting for me. They looked at me expectantly, but I was still in shock and not sure what they wanted from me.

"Please strip down to your boxer shorts, Mr Miller." One of them said coldly.

I had left my inhibitions at the water's edge. What would usually be a humiliating thing to do, I did with apparent ease. When I looked down to start removing my clothes, I realised how I must have looked. My right side was almost completely stained red. The hair on my arms was matted against the skin with the drying blood. It had been sat there undisturbed for so long it had become slightly tacky. I started to swipe at it in delirium before one of the men stopped me with a single hand gesture. The other took out a large camera and started taking pictures of everything. They gestured for me to continue.

Each piece of clothing I removed was taken from me and treated like toxic waste, diligently placed into sealable plastic bags with a set of steel tongs. My off-white t-shirt was a dirty cherry colour now, almost immaculately dyed in my ineffective efforts to resuscitate Jordan. I started to sweat profusely, partially thanks to the heat in the van but largely due to my growing awareness of the grim reality I faced. The sweat forced Jordan's dried blood out of my pores, rehydrating it as it ran down my arms.

The officers diligently took photos between every step and layer removal before throwing me a towel offhandedly when they had finished. Its fibres swelled red as it absorbed the cocktail of blood and sweat from my skin. The towel was then taken from me and placed in a final sealable bag before they handed me a grey tracksuit to put on.

Although I was innocent, the misplaced remorse I felt was magnified by their treatment of me. They lifted my phone and earphones from the side carefully and placed them into another plastic bag. They asked for the pin to unlock it, and I gave it to them. I had nothing to hide apart from my deep shame of not being able to prevent what happened.

On the way to the police station, Jordan and I travelled the same route before splitting off at a nearby junction. Again, I watched Jordan depart as the distance between the vehicles increased. The ambulance still had its lights on, but the siren was silent.

Sure, I conceded Jordan was slightly annoying, and I barely knew him, but I felt like this was the start of a friendship. I didn't know if he had a family. He never mentioned having any kids or even a long-term girlfriend. He didn't deserve this. He had plenty of friends at work and had time for everybody, which was more than you could have said about me.

DS Banks intermittently glared at me in the rear-view mirror, carefully investigating every subtle body movement and micro-expression on my face. The guilt I felt quickly turned into self-preservation. He clearly liked me for this; I was the only one there and covered in blood. I needed to get my head screwed on, he was going to be asking me some very serious questions, and I didn't have the answers to many.

"Are you okay, Sean?" he empathised, "for the record, I don't think you did it, but we have to bring you in for questioning. It's standard when there is a body involved."

"His name was Jordan."

"We know, I'm sorry. Listen, is there anything else you can tell me?"

"Honestly, I didn't see a thing."

"I shouldn't tell you this, but someone further down the canal saw someone running from the scene to a car. Did you see them?"

"No, it was dark."

"Well, we are checking the CCTV for the area to see if we can pick up their trail."

We arrived at the police station; it was a drab-looking building with a line of people chain-smoking outside. What little greenery outside seemed to wilt in the plumes of second-hand smoking drifting by it. There must have been a sale on cheap grey tracksuits; they were a popular fashion choice in this neck of the woods. We were met outside by two more officers who ushered me through the automatic doors. The doors closed behind me with a hiss, signifying the start of my confinement.

I was taken through the booking procedure and left in a cell. I barely remember the questions they asked. The cell was made entirely from painted grey breezeblocks and a springy blue rubberised floor. There was a small cot attached to the wall that posed as a bed. I was offered breakfast- a slice of lightly buttered brown toast and a prepackaged yoghurt. I picked up the toast initially but noticed the red crust underneath my fingernails and lost my appetite.

I lay on my back, glaring at the ceiling. The fluorescent lights flickered faintly, highlighting every imperfection in the walls. I locked my eyes on the camera in the corner, and it rotated every time I made a movement. I had been locked away from time itself. Every minute lasted hours. A million thoughts raced chaotically through my mind. I knew I hadn't killed him, but it didn't look good. How would I explain this to Courtney? Would I ever see Dylan again? My insecurities thrashed at my disposition; I had no answers. But there would definitely be questions.

An eternity passes, the cell door clumsily clunked open, and DS Banks appeared in the opening.

"Ready for a chat?" he said.

"Well, I'm not doing anything else," I said sarcastically.

He led me out of the room to a small interview room. It had enough space for a table and four chairs. On the table was a large recording device that DS Banks was setting up. I sit down on the opposite side of the table, and a long, monotone beep fills the silence. The police-issued grey sweatsuit started to irritate my arm as I shook in anticipation. DS Banks shuffled some papers in front of him when the beep subsided. He looked at me with his game face on.

"Okay, this is a police interview with Sean Miller with DS Tony Banks in attendance. We are investigating the murder of Jordan Davis. The time is 11:42 on the fifth of January. Sean, you are waiving your right to a solicitor. Is that still the case?"

"Yes–" I gulped, "–that's still the case. I'm innocent, so I don't need a solicitor. I am happy to help."

"You are being treated as a witness at this time. Can you tell me in your own words what happened this morning?"

"I met Jordan for a run in the morning. We set off running, but he wanted to go faster than I did, so he pulled away. He was meant to meet me back on the route on the way back home, but I never saw him. I got to the bridge where he was found and heard a loud splash. When I went beyond the bridge, I saw him in the water."

"Then what did you do, Sean?"

"I thought he had fallen in, so I jumped in after him. When I got him out of the water, I noticed he had a cut on his throat and immediately rang for an ambulance."

"How did you know Jordan?"

"Up until a few days ago, he was a colleague."

"Why up until a few days ago?"

"I got sacked."

"I'm sorry to hear that, Sean. Did you notice anything else at the scene? Or anyone else on the path while you were running down it?"

"No, we were totally alone."

"You were involved in a separate incident a few days ago on the canal. Can you tell me about that?"

"Someone tried running me over, and I nearly got jumped."

DS Banks started sifting through the papers in front of him until he selected a large black and white still from a CCTV camera. He looked at the photograph for a moment before carefully rotating it and placing it in front of me.

"For the recording I am showing Mr Miller evidence item '14D'. It is a black and white photograph taken from CCTV on Lodge Road. Do you recognise this car, Sean?"

"It looks like the car that tried running me over," I peered at it carefully, "yes, that's the car. Have you found them?"

"No, enquiries are still ongoing."

"But you think this car is linked to what happened to me?"

"Enquiries are ongoing," he affirmed, "is there anything else you can tell me about what happened on either occasion you may have forgotten at the time?"

"Not that I can think of, no."

DS Banks started shuffling through the papers again and selected another photograph; he placed it on top of the photograph of the car and tapped it lightly.

"For the recording, I am showing Mr Miller evidence item '12A', which is a screenshot of Mr Miller's phone. What can you tell me about this?"

"It is an app we were using to track our run."

"Why does it have a payment amount at the top?"

"It's new. The app pays you to run."

"Sean, I have done my fair bit of exercise, and I have never heard of an app that pays you to exercise. The boys in forensics couldn't find any mention of this app anywhere on the net. How did it end up on your phone?"

"Jordan said it was invite-only; he had a copy and invited me."

"Jordan didn't have the app installed on his phone, only you."

"But he showed it to me before we set off. He definitely had it."

"Well, it isn't there now. Did you access Jordan's phone at the scene?"

"No."

"Tell me about the feet, Sean."

"The feet?"

"Jordan's feet?" DS Banks leaned in slightly, trying to force the correct response from me.

"I have no idea what you are talking about."

DS Banks rifles through the papers once again, producing another photograph.

"For the recording, I am showing Mr Miller evidence item 6C, a forensically taken photograph of Mr Davis' feet. What is all this about Sean?"

He pushed the colour photograph in front of me and slammed his hand down on it. It was a photograph of Jordan's feet, but they had been slashed multiple times. There was no pattern to the cuts, seemingly random and frenzied.

"What the hell is this?"

"Are you telling me you don't know about this?" DS Banks said with finality.

"No."

"Okay. I have no further questions at this time, and I will be terminating the interview there. The time is 11:46."

With that, DS Banks leaned forward and pressed a button on the recording device. He leant back in his chair with a sigh, staring at the documents spread in front of him. The high of anxiety in the recorded interview passed, and I got the impression that he didn't think I had anything to do with this. Maybe I was in the clear.

Even though I knew I was innocent, I couldn't shake the idea that they could have somehow found something that made me look guilty. I suddenly realised my mouth was insatiably dry. I drank the clear plastic cup of tepid water that had been left for me and looked at DS Banks, waiting for his next move.

"Listen, Sean," he grumbled, "you are being treated as a witness here, but don't go leaving the country or anything. You should be able to go home today."

"Thanks, Tony. I appreciate it," I said in relief.

"It's DS Banks. If you think of anything else when you get home, please give me a call. We will get your belongings together."

He led me back to the front desk, and I was handed a clear plastic bag with my phone in it. My clothes were being kept as evidence. When I finally got outside, the winter sun was in full force. The rapid change in lighting made me squint like a bear leaving hibernation. I unlocked my phone to ring a taxi. The 'B-Run' app was still open but had paused due to inactivity. The summary was displayed.

Total run time; 38 minutes, 46 seconds.
Run with a friend. Bonus; £30
Sole Survivor. Bonus; £75.
Total earnings; £143.76

I didn't receive the mood boost of the day before. The app had placed a pounds and pence value for Jordan's life. I felt sick having earned this money. I was perplexed by the 'Sole Survivor' bonus. I prodded at it with my finger, expecting an explanation, but none appeared. I called for a taxi and sat on the wall outside the police station, waiting for it to arrive. Several second-hand cigarettes later, the taxi driver turned up and took me home. I didn't say a word on the journey. My mind was totally scrambled, but one thing I knew for sure: Courtney couldn't find out about this. Too much had happened already this year.

I arrived home just before Courtney was due back from work and sprinted up the stairs to get a shower and get changed into my usual work attire. The police-issued tracksuit got dumped straight in the bottom of the outside bin before she could see it. I wearily made myself a coffee and collapsed into the armchair in exhaustion.

My thumb hovered over the app icon, ready to delete it. It shouldn't have been a difficult decision, but stupidly, I elected to keep the app. Right then and there, I made a promise to myself that I wouldn't go running early in the morning again and that I would at least wait until sunrise. Now I was unemployed; I had plenty of time during daylight hours to get my earnings in. At the time, it felt like an appropriate precaution in light of what had just happened.

I had barely touched my coffee before I heard Courtney trudging through the front door holding several bags of food and shopping. She nearly had a heart attack when she saw me, not expecting me for at least another few hours.

"Bloody hell, why are you home so early?" she gasped breathlessly.

"That's some welcome Court," I replied sarcastically.

"Sorry, I didn't think you would be back so soon from work. Are you all right?"

"Yeah, I didn't feel well, so I came home. I think it's a stomach bug," I feigned, patting my stomach.

"I missed you this morning after your run, too. Did you even make it to work?"

"Yeah, I left at lunchtime."

"Did you get to work late?"

"Christ, what is this, question time?"

"It's just unusual, Sean."

"Sorry for snapping. I just feel dreadful."

Courtney slumped on the couch, dropping the shopping bags at her feet with a sigh. She gazed into space, amping herself up to say something. I looked at her intently, waiting for it. We were due a big chat, and for good reason. Surely, she knew I wasn't telling her the truth. It was written all over my face.

"We need to have a chat. I feel like I don't know what is going on with you." She said with her voice breaking.

"What do you mean?"

"We've had a crappy start to the year with the attack on the canal and the promotion. You've barely spoken to me about it; you are just like a zombie. These things have happened to me too, you know."

"I know."

"Also, Dylan is getting to the age now where he realises you aren't around that much."

How dare she. The last thing I felt like doing was arguing with Courtney in the middle of the day, but she had poked a nerve. She was totally unaware of the struggle I felt keeping the family together and making sure there was food on the table. She knew this would provoke me to anger and wouldn't even make eye contact. My eyes pierced the side of her face, waiting for her to turn and face me.

I couldn't explain what had been going on because I had lied at every turn. The awkward silence forced her to turn and look at me for a response. The tears pooled in her eyes and started to run down her cheek. I loved Courtney. I got lost in her chestnut eyes and dreamt of a world where I could tell her everything that had happened, but it was fantasy. I needed to insulate her from all this; it would break our family in two. My anger subsided; her response was a rational one. I reached into the void for an honest, empathetic response.

"I've got to work, Court," I mustered.

The floodgates opened; she had given me an opportunity to be honest, and I had rejected it. In just a few words, the cracks in our marriage became a chasm. Her eyes streamed disappointment. Her bottom lip quivered in grief. She inhaled deeply in strength, and the stream slowly dried up. She stood in silence and stood in the doorway.

"Dylan and I are going to stay at my mum's for the weekend." She said bitterly. "You need to think carefully about what you want to do here."

I was left again in the sitting room on my own. I gazed through the slats in the blinds and saw Courtney get in her car and drive off. Part of me wanted to chase after her, but it was already over. What would I even say if I stopped her? She was completely right. I needed to clear my head and sort this out. It wasn't fair that I was keeping her in the dark; she did as much for this family as I did. More, even. But would she understand? I sat in that armchair for hours, wrestling with my demons. I kept checking my phone for a text or a call, but it remained silent.

The four walls of the sitting room started to feel like the cell at the police station. I yearned for freedom from the imprisonment I had placed myself in. Every piece of curled wallpaper and stain in the room grated at me. I had to get out of here; I needed the release from the self-inflicted torture. My heart thumped in rhythm as I reminisced about my first run. The freedom I felt, the euphoria. It was the source of all my problems but also the only coping mechanism I had. With nothing to stop me, I put on my running gear and left the house.

The sun hung low against the horizon, painting the sky with purple and crimson. I must have had at least another hour of daylight left. My legs trembled like an addict waiting for their fix. As I neared the canal path, my anticipation grew. My breathing grew faster in excitement. I hit start on the app and began in a jog. The euphoria was instantaneous. With every step, my jumbled mind sorted itself gradually. The blood flowing through my veins flushed away the tension as I became preoccupied only with forward movement. I studied the path before me and closed my eyes for minutes at a time, finally alone in my own thoughts. Bliss.

With each dull thud in my ears, a piece of me was left on the path. It continued until I felt almost weightless. I glided down the path at speed, my feet barely disturbing the stones below. Every time I closed my eyes, I was reminded of cherished family memories like I was flicking through a photo album. Every refreshing breath of cold air extinguished the lingering anger and resentment.

I ruminated about Courtney when we first met. Her curled brown hair bounced effortlessly whilst she danced to the music in the nightclub. Her olive skin shimmered in the lights as she turned to me in slow motion. Then, the smile. I looked longingly into her chestnut-brown eyes across a crowded dance floor. Maybe it was love at first sight, after all. A smile crossed my face as I ran. If we could get back to that feeling we had for each other, we would be fine.

I had no idea how far I had run, but the sun had become a slither behind the silhouette of the city in front of it. My shadow lengthened quickly behind me. The darkness infected the path like a plague, consuming everything in front of it. The corruption reached me, which sent a cold wave throughout my body. My perception of the metronome in my ears changed the tone to become menacing again in the absence of the light. I stopped dead and looked into the shadowy abyss forming in front of me. I could just make out Jordan's bridge in the faltering sunlight, the discarded police tape fiercely flapping in the breeze.

It didn't take much to convince me I shouldn't be here. I had outstayed my welcome. I turned 180 degrees without pause and started running in the other direction. I struggled to keep up with the fleeing sun, but it accelerated way beyond my top speed. My peripheral vision faded to black as I was enveloped in the dying light. The thud grew louder and faster. It shattered my tranquillity like glass. I became a nervous wreck. I didn't know what I was thinking; I should have turned back a long time ago. The thudding relentlessly crushed pensive state to atoms. The thudding came faster. My legs accelerated way beyond their comfort zone and almost into a sprint.

I saw the level crossing in the distance. It was brightly lit by street lighting like a beacon in the black. Only yesterday, I was terrified of this place, but the illuminated road was a safe haven from the dark vacuum I was running from. I intensified my efforts to produce more speed and reach the safety of the light. The thudding responded in kind, speeding up with every step I took. I lengthened my stride to cover more distance; my balance suffered as I struggled to keep my footing against the ground.

My stride was violently interrupted by something getting caught on my leading foot. I was suddenly propelled into the air in freefall. I spent minutes in the air trying to process what was happening; my foot was still ensnared by the unknown. I crashed into the ground at full speed, rolling a few times before becoming stationary with my face in the dirt.

I stayed there for a few moments, face down in recovery. The thudding raced into a frenzy before stopping in complete silence. In the absence of the noise, I heard a scraping sound on the path in front of me. I lift my head to look. I see a figure slowly walking towards me, dragging a baseball bat through the gravel. Before I can muster the energy to lift myself up, the figure delivers a swift blow to the back of my head.

"Exercise completed. Unlock for summary," I hear in my ear before dropping into unconsciousness.

6
FIGHT OR FLIGHT

I opened my eyes; for what use it did. I had been bundled together in what I thought was the dark boot of a car, my wrists and legs tied together. I was clearly travelling at speed, and every imperfection on the road buffeted me from side to side. I had been gagged; the fabric in my mouth sucked every drop of moisture from my tongue. My nose desperately searched for air, but the nauseating smell of petrol filled the cavity. The blood from the back of my head had stuck me to the carpeted interior, and I wriggled to set it free. I used every bit of energy to try and free myself from my bonds, but ended in failure.

In pieces, my memory returned; I had been taken. The baseball bat and suit were too much of a coincidence; it had to be the people on the canal days before. They must have even been responsible for Jordan's death, too. I tried to shout for help, but the gag in my mouth muffled it into silence. I lay there like a caged animal, patiently waiting for whatever was going to happen next.

The car started to slow, which gave me a second wind. I ineffectively writhed, trying to release my tied wrists to no avail. It creaked slowly to a stop, and I awaited my fate with bated breath. I heard muffled voices from outside that grew louder as they approached me. The boot door flung open, and four masked men stood in front of me in black suits and balaclavas, staring down at my tied-up body. They looked at each other silently, and one produced a bag that was thrown over my head.

I kicked and squirmed as hard as I could, but they quickly got me on my feet and dragged me on an unknown journey. I felt like a walking corpse, being marched to my own death. I went through every stage of grief in an instant and was left with the image of my family. I focused on every detail of their faces. I wondered what their lives would be without me. I bitterly regretted every choice I had made.

I was thrown onto a chair, the gag and bag from my head removed. Directly in front of me was a high-powered light, blinding me. I heard shoes slowly clacking toward me against the floor behind the light. This was it. The end.

"Do you know why you are here, Sean?" Echoed a male voice behind the light.

"What the hell is all this? Where am I?"

"Do you know why you are here, Sean Miller?"

"How do you know my name?"

"That is irrelevant. Do you know *why* you are here?" the voice said, getting agitated.

"No, I don't," I said submissively.

One of the masked men emerges from the light and bends down to start removing my shoes and socks. I kicked at him initially, but he silently held a knife up threateningly, and I allowed him to remove them. The knife slices through the laces like butter, and they are thrown into the unknown behind him.

"You are here simply because you didn't run fast enough." The voice laughed mockingly. "We didn't anticipate having to work this hard for someone so far down the list. But here you are."

"What list? What are you going to do with me?" I quivered.

"Whatever I want to. We do own you now, after all. I know you have a lot of questions, and unfortunately, they will go unanswered."

"I don't even know who you are–"

"–and you will die not knowing who we are. But not tonight, so cheer up," He said forebodingly, "get him ready. We start tomorrow."

Once his footsteps had receded into the distance, I was dragged up by my arms and walked beyond the light. Now that I am outside its influence, I can see the room in which I am being held captive. It was a vast warehouse with filled racking from floor to ceiling. Unmanned forklift trucks lay dormant on either side, collecting dust.

The low-hanging yellowed lights sway gently in the draught, manipulating our shadows on the concrete floor. My feet became blocks of ice; I could barely feel them being dragged through the dust.

I am hastily shoved around a corner towards a small, prefabricated office and forced inside. The inside of the enclosed building almost resembles a doctor's surgery. Stainless steel trays housed a variety of polished metal tools inside them. A piece of medical equipment makes a periodic high-pitched beep. There was a steel foldaway chair in the corner, and I was thrust into it, and my hands tied to the back of it.

"You don't have to do this; I have a family," I pleaded.

My words did little to affect the men tying me to the chair; they barely skipped a beat. They obviously had done this before; I was treated like a piece of meat rather than a person. I thoroughly inspected each masked man, trying to find some distinguishing features between them, but they were totally anonymous. Their breath penetrated the wool of their balaclavas like sulphur in the cold air. They walked out of the room in silence, locking the door and leaving me alone.

I desperately looked around the room for something that I could use to escape. Everything of utility was too far out of reach. Even if it was within my range, my constrained arms and legs would be useless. I consciously breathe in and out slowly to try and control the frenzy. I remembered every decision that I idly made that landed me in this chair. I wriggled desperately to at least loosen the chair's grip on me, but I was fatigued to failure.

The futility of my struggle became clear. I had given up. I sat there peacefully, accepting what was about to happen. There was something to be said for accepting your fate; knowing I had no other options took the panic out of my predicament somewhat.

My out-of-focus eyes pointlessly glared at the whitewashed wall ahead of me. I noticed something etched into the wall crudely. I squinted to try and make it out; it was a hastily carved foot in the plasterboard next to a steel gurney in the opposite corner. It was at that moment it had all clicked into place. Somehow, these psychopaths had hacked the app to track my movements and target me for these bizarre attacks. It's what killed Jordan. It's what was about to kill me.

The knowledge reinvigorated my will to escape. My acceptance mutated into anger. I wouldn't let those bastards do this to me. The rope on my wrists found a slight edge on the chair, and I started rubbing my restraints against it fiercely. I felt the threads splaying one by one, succumbing to the friction, bringing me closer to freedom. They finally relent, and I have my hands back. I quickly untied my feet, leaving me totally unrestrained but imprisoned in this macabre room.

A world of opportunities had opened up to me with two clear options: fight or flight. I noticed my phone sat idle on a desk in the room and instinctively picked it up to make a call for help. Before I could even unlock it, my attention was drawn to the arsenal of sharp implements before me. I had no idea what they were specifically for, but it was clear their purpose was to inflict pain and injury on me. I stood with indecision. Fight or flight. My focus flitted between calling for help or fighting for my life.

Was I capable of killing someone? Even in self-defence? It isn't a question you think you will have to answer. I felt myself listing the pros and cons in my head, all the while thinking it was ridiculous. Self-defence is normally a spur-of-the-moment thing; it must be rare that you get more than a few seconds to weigh up this kind of decision. The weight was huge. I stared at the instruments on the table in front of me, imagining sinking one of these pieces of steel into another person.

My hands tremored violently; I didn't even know if I was capable in the moral sense, but I started to doubt if I could even do it in the physical sense. I touched the cold steel of the tray, willing it to give me the answer, but it remained shtum. The familiar burning of the anger in my stomach started to dissolve through the lining. There was a part of me I didn't know existed. If I let it out, it could save my life.

The time for internal debate was over. I heard heavy footsteps on approach to the door. This was my chance. I had been indecisive and weak my entire life; I had never fought for anything. But my life was worth fighting for.

My family's happiness was worth fighting for. I needed to choose. The indecision swelled in my brain, forcing something to physically snap. A part of my brain awoke from dormancy. Neurons fired sparsely at first, building into a magnificent crescendo, sending electrical impulses to every corner of my body.

I chose to fight.

My body became a well-oiled machine. My heart purposefully pumped blood, fuelling every muscle. My lungs efficiently stripped every molecule of oxygen from every breath to keep my breathing slow and focused. My eyes detected every single flicker of the lights and sent it to my brain for assessment. I was in a composed frenzy, my animalistic rage keeping me grounded and calm. The footsteps reached the door, and the handle turned slowly with a squeak.

I grabbed a scalpel from the tray beside me and put my phone back in my pocket. I stood behind the door so I would be obscured from view. The door creaked open slowly. One of the masked men casually entered the room, his face still hidden by the balaclava. He turned towards the now empty chair and threw his head around in panic. I locked eyes with my foe through his obscured face, holding the scalpel, prepared to stick it into him.

Time froze, or at least my perception of it did. It gave me a few extra seconds to calibrate my moral compass. Was this the right decision? It was too late. The flight option had expired, and he physically stood between me and freedom. I had no other choice. I remembered all the injustices I had suffered. Every single bitter regret empowered me. A switch flicked. In a flash of pure, unadulterated rage, I plunged the blade directly into his neck.

He remained standing but completely stationary. The blood came immediately. First, a drop. Then, a deluge. It soaked into the white of his shirt like a sponge. The shirt reached full capacity, gave way, and the blood started to pool at his feet. The slight incline of the floor allowed the flow of red to gush in between the grout lines of the tiles below. The stream grew into a river, bursting its banks, and consumed everything in its path. It reached my bare feet, and when I stepped back to avoid it, the man plummeted to the ground as if it had been removed from under him.

I loomed over his body, waiting for his response. None came. I squatted slowly to remove his balaclava. I don't know what I expected, but he just looked like a normal guy. The astonished expression on his face had been made permanent by his death. I would have felt better if he had a forked tongue and horns, but it was him or me.

I didn't expect the emotions that came next.

I thought I would be disgusted by what I had done, but I didn't. I didn't even feel any remorse. Maybe I couldn't feel it anymore. Something dark had awakened inside of me, something I had kept locked away. The years of letting people walk over me provoked it, tortured it, nurtured it. I gave it a glimpse of freedom and ended up standing over a dead body.

I stayed there for a few minutes before I realised this wasn't the end of my escape but the beginning. There was at least another 3 of these men walking around. I had no idea where I was beyond some dusty warehouse. I had to get out of there. I skulked out of the now-open door and looked left and right for threats. I didn't see any.

My bare feet smacked against the concrete as I ran through the warehouse, trying to find an exit. I felt like a rat scurrying through a maze of shelving and boxes. I noticed a fire exit at the back wall of the warehouse and ran towards it. When I reached the door, the sound of a single gunshot shattered my eardrums, bouncing off the concrete walls. I turned to the source of the sound, clasping my ears to see the remaining three masked men running towards me. The lead man was banging his baseball bat ferociously against the racking as he passed.

I chose flight.

There was no debate this time. I couldn't take out three of them. I pushed through the fire exit and immediately started running. My feet are made bloody by the cold tarmac, but I barely feel it. I heard the screeching of tyres in pursuit and threw myself over the chain link fence to avoid it. The roars of the car engine become distant for a minute as they make their way around the fence and through the exit by road. I find myself in an unfamiliar industrial estate, looking around frantically, begging for a route that will take me off-road.

The car catches up with me quickly and begins flashing its lights and beeping behind me furiously. The man is hanging out of the passenger side window, banging the baseball bat against the chassis. I spot a path to my left interspersed with bollards and run down it; the car comes to a screeching halt. I stop and turn to look at it. They are no longer in pursuit and start reversing back down the path. I continue aimlessly walking down the path; the soles of my feet feel like they have been worn down to the bone.

I unlocked my phone to try and find out where I was. The 'B-Run' app was already open on the screen, and it started reading out the summary.

> *Total run time; 32 minutes, 54 seconds.*
> *Survival. Bonus; £50.*
> *Escape. Bonus; £150.*
> *Total earnings; £232.90*

I held down the app logo on my home screen and hovered over the delete option once again. I could walk away from this; this could be the end. I had that option. But the something that had awakened in me lingered in my consciousness. It wasn't just about the money anymore. This tiny square on my phone was the only lead I had of finding these people and delivering justice.

What justice looked like, I didn't know. Surely, I hadn't become a murderer overnight, but I couldn't go to the police. I had just killed someone. I had chosen my path, and I had to walk it.

I memorised every tiny detail of the path I took home, planning to repeat the journey and find out who these people were. The sun rose hesitantly, and I felt safer in its glow. My bare feet selflessly carried me the entire way home; they didn't hurt anymore. The trauma they had gone through the last few days left them numb to everything. They had that in common with my mind, battered and bruised by the events. I turned the corner onto my street, hoping to see Courtney or at least her car, but her parking space was vacant. I unlock the door and collapse behind it.

The sheer exhaustion of the night knocked me out almost immediately. I fell asleep for a few minutes or hours; it was impossible to tell. When I woke, I noticed a small, folded piece of paper sitting on the console table in the hall. I stretched to reach for it and opened it.

Sean,

I came by the house last night to talk, and you weren't there. You obviously had somewhere better to be. I don't know what is going on with you, but you have changed. We have changed. We used to tell each other everything, and now I barely get a few words from you.

Dylan and I are going to stay at my mum's house for a while. I'm not coming back until you are honest with me.

Courtney

I broke down. I may have escaped with my life the night before, but my family was slipping away. What was the point of any of this if they were going to leave anyway? The house was painfully quiet without them. My instant gut reaction to the letter was to get in my car and go and find them, but I couldn't. It wasn't safe. I had to assume if the masked men knew my name; they knew where I lived. I couldn't put my family in that kind of danger. The whole thing felt to me like it was a game to them, but by killing one of their own, I had made it serious. I couldn't even go to DS Banks for help.

The man's blood had dried on my hands and started to crack slightly. I stumbled upstairs to get a shower. The hot water felt like a coal walk against the abused soles of my feet. The blood on my hands and feet stained the water pink. I scrubbed my hands for hours, trying to remove every trace. I couldn't tell if my skin was still covered in blood or just red raw from the scrubbing. The shower was my sanctuary, and I had defiled it. Was this what my life had come to?

I just wanted to earn a bit of extra money for my family and me, but I never thought I would be doing this.

I was too tired to deal with it. Between the combination of the pure adrenaline over the last 48 hours and the sheer distance I had covered running, I was almost ready to collapse. I finally reached the bedroom and threw myself face down on the bed. I gave in to the exhaustion and immediately fell asleep.

7

BAIT

I was awakened rudely hours later by the sound of the front door being almost knocked off the hinges. They had somehow found out where I lived. I hobbled downstairs quickly and armed myself with a kitchen knife. With the chain still on, I opened the door ajar to see DS Banks standing there with his hands in his pockets.

"Mr Miller, I hope I haven't disturbed you." He said, looking me up and down.

"Sorry, DS Banks, I was asleep. Can I help?"

"Can I come in for a chat?"

I looked behind me and covertly placed the knife in the console table drawer. "Sure," I said hesitantly.

I opened the door and made my way slowly to the kitchen, being followed by DS Banks. I put the kettle on and leaned against the kitchen counter. This was the last thing I needed: another arduous and awkward conversation with the police. He had a look on his face that seemed to see straight through me, always watching every movement as if it would prove some kind of guilt. DS Banks took a seat at the table and sat down.

"Are you alright, Sean? You are limping."

"Yeah, I'm fine. I just overdid it running. Tea?"

"No thanks, it's not a social call."

"Oh? And I thought we were starting to become friends."

"No. We had an ANPR hit on the suspicious vehicle last night. Do you know anything about it?"

"No. Why would I?"

"Where were you last night at around 7 pm?"

"Home."

"And your wife will confirm that?"

"She would, but she isn't here."

"Where is she? I'd like to speak with her."

"Her mum's house, we've had a bit of a falling out," I confessed.

"What about?"

"Do I have to answer that?"

"No, not really."

"In that case, it's personal."

"Fine," he sighed, "have you remembered anything else about either incident that can help with our enquiries?"

"No, sorry."

"Fine."

"Listen, I understand you have a job to do, but I am starting to feel a bit neglected here. I am a victim, and I am sick of being treated otherwise."

"Why do you feel like that?"

"A car drives past a camera, and you are here asking me if I have an alibi."

"I just asked the question, Sean."

"It's Mr Miller."

"Fine, Mr Miller. I have a lawful duty to investigate crimes when they are committed. And I have to ask questions as part of those enquiries."

DS Banks stood from the table and placed his hands back in his pockets, looking around the room casually, unbothered by my change in tone. He knew I was holding back, but he was patient. He had a knack for finding a weakness in you and then poking it with a stick until something fell out. He was starting to annoy me at this point. I felt like I was under the spotlight when, in reality, I was just a victim. If only he had done his job and actually investigated the crimes properly, I wouldn't have been in this mess.

"Fine, whatever. Is there anything else I can help with, Tony?"

"It's DS Banks," he reminded calmly, "I just can't shake the feeling you know a lot more about this than you are letting on. I don't think you are guilty, but you know something. We can help Sean."

"You can't because that isn't true."

"Well, you know how to get in touch."

"I do."

"I'll see myself out. Take care of yourself, Sean, yeah?" he said soberly.

I heard the front door click shut, and I sat down at the table with my head in my hands. These people clearly weren't going to stop, so I had to continue to take matters into my own hands. I had already taken one of them out, and maybe I could get the rest. It didn't take long to find the industrial estate where I was kept captive on the internet; the building was listed for sale. I decided my only lead was to send an email to the agent requesting a viewing of the property the following day. They wouldn't be able to attack me if there were witnesses there, and it was the perfect cover.

I started searching for any mention of the 'B-Run' app on the internet. DS Banks was right; there wasn't a single relevant result. It was a ghost. I'd heard the term dark web before, but I knew nothing of that world. It certainly wasn't an app that was widely available. My sleuthing was interrupted by the letter box opening and something softly hitting the floor. I staggered over to the front door, and a white envelope lay face down on the mat. I struggled to reach down and grab it. The front of the envelope simply read 'Sean'. I opened the letter expecting another note from Courtney, but it wasn't.

'Can't wait to see you again, Sean.'

I bust through the front door to find no one there. The streets were awash with parked cars as usual, and I scowled at each in turn, looking for some clue of who posted this through my door. It had to be the masked men. I ran back inside and double-locked the door. They definitely knew where I lived. Where my family lived. It confirmed what I had already thought: I needed to get to them before they got to us. Our lives were on the line.

I barely slept a wink that night. I lay in bed clutching the letter with one hand and the kitchen knife in the other. I writhed in a cold sweat, stuck in the limbo of extreme exhaustion and adrenaline-fuelled anxiety. My mind started to play tricks with me; every indistinct noise sounded like the front door being picked open or someone prying open a window to gain entry. The only solace was the fact that Courtney and Dylan weren't in the house.

I watched dawn break through my hastily half-closed curtains. Time had no meaning anymore; I was in a perpetual state of paranoia. The masked men were creatures of the night, and hopefully, the light would protect me. Lurking in the shadows, devoid of motive, simply existing to try and destroy my life. They were just trying to scare me, of course. And even though I knew that, it had worked spectacularly. I no longer felt safe in my own home. I first thought they were just tracking me through my phone, but this marked an escalation.

I had received confirmation from the property agent that I could view the property that morning, so I got ready to leave the house. I got in my car and winced as I started the engine. It started without a bang, and I laughed nervously. I had convinced myself it was going to explode when I turned the key. Farfetched, right? But I didn't know what they were capable of.

The paranoia continued; I had become a nervous wreck. At every junction and red light, I felt like I was going to get attacked. I had the resting heart rate of a debut skydiver, plummeting towards the earth without a chute. I had made a home in the sweet spot between cardiac arrest and hypertension. I hated what they had done to me; the constant threat of violence hung over my head by a thread, ready to drop at a moment's notice.

But then I remembered my actions the night before. Maybe, in some bizarre twist, they were actually scared of me. The letter they had left was terrifying, but it also could have been a last-ditch attempt to try and control my emotions. The alternative perception of it made me smile slightly, relieving some of the apprehension. At the very least, I was doing something about it and making a positive first step in trying to find who these people are.

My drive continued, and I started to feel some kind of twisted enjoyment from what I was doing. It was a game of cat and mouse, and I wasn't going to end up being the mouse. If they wanted to kill me, they could have easily done it the night before. I had to be as unpredictable as they were. So far, they had been ahead of me at every turn; if I wanted to come out on top, I had to bury the fear and think like they did.

A beautiful brunette woman waved at me as I entered the car park and approached my car to greet me. Her eyes were dark, outlined by thick-rimmed black glasses. Her long, flowing brown hair framed her face elegantly, showcasing the flawless makeup she had clearly spent hours preparing this morning. She was obviously the closer- used to lure in sales with her appearance, but she wouldn't be making a sale today.

"Mr Jones, lovely to meet you. I'm Carla, and I'll be showing you around this fantastic property today." She gleamed professionally.

"Nice to meet you, Carla. Shall we get started?" I said, in character.

"Well, it makes sense to start in the car park. As you can see, there is ample parking and three loading docks backing onto the warehouse itself."

She starts walking towards a large set of double doors with 'Reception' written above them, beckoning me to follow.

"We will be entering the reception area that has recently been remodelled," she said, pushing the doors open for me, "all the furniture can be included or not included. It's entirely up to you."

I hadn't seen this room; it was a large reception area with leather couches and coffee tables. There are clean, wooden floors throughout, with a brand-new reception desk at the focal point of the room. It was so nice; I almost put an offer in there and then, before remembering it was all a ruse. Method acting was clearly my forte.

"It looks perfect!" I enthused.

"Wait until you see the actual warehouse area; there is so much potential."

She led me through another door behind the reception counter and through to the actual warehouse. I couldn't believe my eyes; the entire room was completely empty. All the racking was bare. I turned left and right, looking for another section or room, but there was nothing. Somehow, they had managed to clear the entire building in less than 12 hours. Whilst I was thrashing in my bed, panicking, they were cleaning house.

"Is this it?" I said, breaking character.

"This is the main warehouse area, yes. It has an impressive square footage. Plenty of space for all your products. What does your business do again?"

"Erm- shoes," I mustered hastily.

"Okay, you could fit a lot of shoes in here, Mr Jones. The sellers are very motivated to sell the property quickly."

"Do you mind if I have a wander around on my own for a bit?"

"Sure, I'll go back into reception and make some calls. Come and get me if you have any questions."

I wandered around the warehouse, and there was a big gap in the racking where the room I had been held captive in sat. I could make out the colour difference in the concrete like a ghost, the horrors of what had happened in that room permanently etched into the floor. I walked past seemingly miles of racking and noticed the dints made by the man with the baseball bat. This was the place, but the occupants had done a moonlight flit and left.

I didn't know how to feel. It partly confirmed my suspicions that they were scared I was going to come after them. The other part of me was furious that they had evaded my lame attempt to find out who they were. They remained a few steps ahead of me. I returned to reception to find Carla sitting on a leather sofa, making calls. She smiled brightly and signalled me to wait a minute before quickly finishing it.

"I have a few questions."

"Excellent. Is there anything I can do to help?"

"Can you tell me anything about the sellers?"

"The sale is being arranged by liquidators, so they are highly motivated for a quick sale."

"Yes, you said. But what about the previous tenant? What did they do here?"

"I'm not entirely sure. I can certainly try and find out, but beg my pardon, why is that relevant?"

"Listen, I was here a few days ago," I said, abandoning the character entirely, "this warehouse was filled with boxes and equipment; where did it all go?"

Carla looked visibly anxious by my sudden personality change and edged nervously towards the door, holding her phone in her hand. If I was going to get any information from my little field trip, I needed to be more direct now. This woman clearly wasn't involved in my capture, but she might have vital information that would help me find them. But my sudden abandonment of my character had unnerved her.

"Mr Jones, if you aren't interested in buying the property, you will have to leave."

"I just want to know who was here before, that's all."

"You have to leave, or I will call the police."

"Okay, I'm sorry. I'll go."

I walked past Carla as she backed into the corner of the room and briskly retreated to my car. Maybe they had gone, and the danger was over. I thought about the letter, and maybe it was a warning not to speak to the police. It did arrive shortly after DS Banks left. By the time I had arrived home, I'd convinced myself I had beaten them. I don't know if I believed it or not, or I just told myself that to prevent a mental breakdown.

I might not have to meet that dark part of me again, after all. I couldn't tell if I was relieved or disappointed. I wanted this to be over definitively. But the way it was over wasn't satisfying to me. I needed to see these people in cuffs or bleeding out on the floor to truly know it was over. The disappearing act they pulled only added to their mystery.

I opened the front door, and another envelope sat ominously on the mat. What an idiot I was only moments before; I hadn't stopped them. I picked it up and ripped it open. It was simply another piece of paper that read, 'Let it go, or we will be back.' I couldn't live the rest of my life looking over my shoulder or chasing these ghosts. I screwed up the paper and launched it aggressively into the bin. I wouldn't let these scum bags dictate to me how I live my life. They needed to pay for what they had done. If I couldn't see them in cuffs, I would have to see them bleeding out on the floor.

I got dressed in my running gear, with the thickest pair of socks I owned to cushion my destroyed feet. I fished out the small lock knife I had bought on holiday years ago. If I couldn't find them, I would just have to let them find me. In my exhausted state, the only plan I could formulate was to use myself as bait to draw them in. Stupid, I know, but I didn't have any other leads. Hopefully, they were as exhausted as I was after lugging all those boxes out of the warehouse through the night.

I waited until nightfall in an almost meditative state, preparing for the battle ahead. This felt different; I knew what was coming, and I was prepared. The dark corner of my mind was responsible for me still being alive, pulsed in expectation. It had already taken one of them out. I walked out of the house feeling almost invincible. As soon as my battered feet touched the gravel of the canal path, I broke out into a sustained jog.

Every step I made with intent, each drawing me closer to my prey. The thud of the app resounded in my ears like battle drums, filling me with assurance. I clutched the knife in my hand tightly, ready for them to strike at any moment. The cool evening breeze kept me centred and focused. The gravel tremored in my presence. The canal water shivered in fear as I cruised past. Stray branches and leaves receded back into the thicket in terror.

I remained light on my feet, ready to be pounced on. At every opening and bridge, I gripped the knife tighter. I used the straights to practice opening and closing the knife as I ran. I took one earphone out to listen for a sound. Nothing could be heard apart from the stealthy patter of my feet lightly milling against the ground.

I reached the level crossing, expecting the inevitable ambush, but no one came. I rotated myself in circles, still in forward motion, trying to see in all directions. Everything was calm and tranquil; no ambush had been set. I focused on the path in front of me, scanning for traps or trip hazards set by my tormentors. I reached Jordan's bridge and calmly placed my hand on the cool rock as before. Only scraps of the police tape remained. No surprise attack; the only sound was my own breathing echoing back from the stone.

I was disappointed. I was ready for them. My heart rate slowed back to rest, maybe for the first time since this all began. I sat with my back against the soothing cold indifference of the bridge for a minute. They didn't get to disappear like nothing happened; I would carry these events for the rest of my life. Jordan's family would carry them, too. I wandered beyond the bridge, staring at the patch of grass where Jordan lost his life. His contour was still visible in the flattened grass. I was upset, and I wanted justice for him and for myself. I leaned over the retaining wall of the canal and stared at my reflection, looking back at me. I barely recognised the man in the ripples. What was I even thinking going after them?

I set off back at a disheartened pace, lost in my own thoughts. I remembered why I started this journey in the first place before it was commandeered. I was working on myself. I had become much fitter and ticked the box of 'New Year, new me.' Sure, I had lost a lot of myself along the way, but it was a tainted silver lining to this entire nightmare.

I would be able to repair my marriage with Courtney; I just needed to be honest with her. Maybe I could get a better job, and I could finally be there for Dylan as he desperately needed. My legs dutifully carried me as I remained in self-reflection. Although the way I found it was grisly, I had fallen in love with running. In a way, I was addicted to it. I had flirted with the darkness within, but it was time to put it back in its cage. It was the only thing that terrified me more than the masked men. It was one thing to use it to defend my own life, but now I was out, actively seeking them for revenge.

I was almost back home, and I just wanted to see Courtney and Dylan. A smile breached my frown for the first time in days, and I felt alive and eager to repair the damage I had caused. The masked men became a distant concern; surely, I had done enough to scare them off for good. The darkness within me began to slowly recede. It was there behind bars if I ever needed it, but I wouldn't actively seek it out. Not anymore.

I detected a slight variance in the thudding in my ears, which made me stop dead. My blood turned to ice in my veins. It was only slightly faster but had definitely changed. I walked in sneak, and with every stride, it increased slightly. They were waiting. I knew it. I broke into a slow jog, the knife still nestled in my fist. The penny dropped as the beat quickened; all this time, it had been a warning. It urged me to speed up, but I ignored it, remaining at my persistent pace. The calm logic I had felt only minutes before was quickly discarded. I opened the cage to release the darkness again. It was needed.

I reached the bridge leading to home and stopped to survey the scene. I had to go underneath the bridge to access the steps and go over it. The bait had worked; a small cloud of breath floated from beyond the bridge and dissipated in the breeze. I unlocked the knife as I slowly made my way underneath the bridge in complete silence.

I carefully stopped the app before I reached the end. A loud notification noise from a phone beyond the bridge impaled the silence. I heard the sound of running feet and saw one of the masked men sprinting down the path beyond the bridge.

The shoe was definitely on the other foot. They had always been a step ahead of me metaphorically, but now they were only a step ahead of me physically. I gave chase at speed, almost catching up to him within seconds. I hadn't realised but I had been training for this very moment. I took the encounter at face value: an ambush gone wrong. It didn't even cross my mind that it could have been part of a larger trap. I didn't care. My bloodlust blocked all other senses. I was only capable of chasing him, clutching the knife, and staring at the back of his head. He didn't stand a chance. He threw the baseball bat into the canal in an effort to reduce his weight and garner more speed. His pace began to erode, and I crashed into his back at my top speed, sending us careering down the embankment towards the farmer's field beside the canal.

I found my footing quicker than he did, and I stood over him, wielding the knife. His leg was clearly broken from the dive. He wasn't going anywhere. He remained on his back in complete submission, and I could almost see the pure dread through the balaclava.

"Take it off," I said, pointing to my own face.

"Sean, you don't have to do this. We just wanted to scare you."

"Take it off, now."

He removed the balaclava and stared up at me in complete terror. I was struck by how young he was, maybe in his early twenties. His golden blonde hair was matted against his face by the sweat. The panic radiated from his eyes, begging me for mercy. I looked at the knife, and it shimmered gravely in the moonlight. It was begging for me to use it, to end all this. Surely, there was no way it would continue if I took out another one. The hunter had definitely become the hunted.

The darkness grew in me like a plague, begging me for autonomy. It infected every cell in my body. I could stick this knife in him right now, and it would be over. In my head, the baseball bat set him apart as the leader. Without him breathing, the rest would likely give up. But this was different to the night before. It was in cold blood. I brawled with choice but felt my conviction wavering. He was just a kid.

"Please don't do this. I was just doing my job."

"And what is your job, exactly? Torturing people? You deserve everything you get."

"I do deserve it! I do. But I'm just a guy. I can lead you to them."

"Lead me to who?"

"The people doing this to you."

"You are just stalling."

His face dropped. "Do it, then, you coward."

He called my bluff.

I couldn't do it. It didn't feel right. The last time was in pure self-defence, but this felt different. I was terrified of the masked men, but they were just normal people in costume. I heard Courtney's voice in my head, begging me not to end this boy's life. I found a part of myself that I thought I had lost forever. I locked the blade back in the knife and took out my phone to make a call.

"DS Banks, I've found one of them."

8

DARK REFLECTIONS

The police swarmed the canal once again. I smirked triumphantly at the man as they handcuffed him to the gurney. It took six officers to drag him up the embankment. DS Banks stood at the top in his signature pose, hands in his pockets. He made his way over to me as they were loading him into the ambulance. He looked a little taken aback by my expression, but this was a cause for celebration. Sure, they weren't all in cuffs like I wanted, but the baseball-bat-man with a broken leg was a good start.

"So Mr Miller, three violent incidents on the canal, and you in the centre of all of them. Anything to say?"

"They came after me again, and I got the better of them."

"I see," he said, sucking his teeth, "why do you keep running here if you keep getting jumped?"

"I like the scenery."

"This is serious, Sean. I have to keep reminding you."

"I know."

"Am I free to go?"

"Of course, but you should get checked out."

"I feel fantastic."

"You don't look it, Sean. You should really get checked out."

"Sorry, DS Banks, but I should speak with my wife. I need to let her know I'm okay."

"Fair enough. We will need you to make a statement about this at some point, though."

"Sure."

"Look after yourself, Sean. Maybe get a treadmill. I don't think you are cut out for this."

I laughed, "Maybe."

I made my way through the rabble of police and walked over the bridge, still holding the knife in my pocket. I thought I had made the right decision. I wasn't worried about the dead body I left in that warehouse either; it would have been taken care of. A piece of work like that wasn't going to talk to the police either, not after what he had done. I saw the whole thing as a message to the masked men: I am not to be messed with. Hopefully, they would abandon their sick little game and move on.

I did think about taking the knife and hurling it into the canal. I needed to get rid of it; I could almost feel it vibrating in my pocket. It came so close to tasting blood, but in the end, I was glad I managed to regain control. The sheer amount of police littering the canal made it impossible to get rid of now anyway. I had banished my darkness back behind bars. I didn't want to feel it again. The ordeal was over, and I felt some semblance of normality. I was capable of far more than I ever thought possible, but in the heat of the moment, I made the right decision.

My mind was taken back to that first run, the morning sun gracefully playing on the water's surface. Every breath tasted sweeter than ever before. I could finally get back to living my life. I just wanted to see Courtney and Dylan. Absence makes the heart grow fonder, and it couldn't have been truer. I could finally put aside the gruesomeness of the last week and concentrate on what was important. Family. I remained on the bridge for a few minutes, watching the police do their work. I hoped that somewhere, the remaining masked men were witnessing this, and they knew what would happen if they came for me again.

I decided that I was going to tell Courtney the whole dreadful truth. Once I had told her, it was up to her how she reacted. I strolled back to the house, and her car was parked on the curbside. I broke into a jog, excited to see her. For a moment, I had forgotten the rift between us, but I felt like I had enough energy to jump it. I would make this right. My heart felt full. I burst into the house to find Courtney carrying bin bags to the front door.

"Courtney, I was just going to ring you!" I beamed.

"Convenient. I'm just here to collect some things."

"I am ready for the big chat; I love you, and I want to fix it. Whatever you want to do, I'll do it."

She sighed. "Go on then, do your worst."

"Listen, Court, I know I've been distant for a while, and it isn't your fault, but I'm ready to talk about it."

"It's too late."

"Of course, it isn't too late. We can fix this."

"No, we can't."

"I'll tell you everything, I promise."

She looked at me in disbelief but decided to give me a chance. "Two minutes."

"I couldn't tell you, but I got sacked from TPL. That's why the promotion didn't happen. I know how stressed out you've been about money, but we don't have to worry about that anymore. I've found something else."

"Some…thing?"

"Yes. It is going to sound crazy, but there is this app, and I've been earning money while I run. That's why I have been going so often. It's the way out."

She looked at me and rolled her eyes. "Some… thing? Not someone?"

"What are you talking about?"

"You just can't tell the truth, can you?"

"This is the truth, Court. Look, I can show you."

She calmly put her hand in front of mine, stopping me from taking out my phone. "Don't bother."

"What?"

"You aren't telling me the truth. You're lying right to my face. After everything. I can't take it anymore, so I'm done."

"You don't mean that Court."

"Stop calling me Court. I'm gone."

She pushed past me with the bags, leaving me standing in the doorway, looking out at her in sheer confusion. Why wouldn't she believe me? Even if she didn't believe me, she wasn't even vaguely interested in what I had to say. I thought what I had already said would have at least made her think enough to want to sit down and talk. I wanted to pour my heart out to her like she wanted, and she rejected it callously.

"Courtney, please just come back inside. I promise I am telling you the truth."

She dropped the bags and thundered back up the path. "I know about her, okay?"

"What? Her? Who?"

"The one leaving you little love notes."

"Love notes?"

She pointed at the console table to the flattened note that had been pushed through the door the night before. Stupidly, I had left it screwed up on the table, and she had found it. I didn't immediately understand the connotation of it, but it dawned on me when she turned it to me and angrily jabbed at it with her finger.

"Can't wait to see you again, Sean? You are totally unbelievable. You have thrown away your family for some stupid fling."

"That is not what it looks like."

She leaned in closer. "Okay, well, tell me, right here and right now, what does that note mean?"

I hadn't planned on telling her all the gruesome details of the past week. I didn't want her to feel like I did the night before. I wanted her to feel safe. I thought by telling her about the app and the sacking, it would be enough, and she would finally understand. She had found the note from the masked men and misunderstood what it meant. The only way I could exonerate myself would be to tell her every single detail of what had happened. It would mean confessing I had been lying to her. It also would mean confessing to killing someone. I stood at my front door at a crossroads, knowing where each path led. This was the second and probably final opportunity that she would give me to be honest. I wanted to speak the words, but others came out in their place.

"It's not what it looks like."

"Fine. Then it's over."

She looked at me and had no tears left to give; the well had run dry. She picked up her bags and walked to the car, throwing them in the boot carelessly. Dylan peered at me from the back seat, barely understanding what was happening. He performed a confused wave at me, and I stood there like a statue in response. I watched her drive down the street from the front gate and merge onto the main road.

They were gone.

I stood at the front door in total shock. I had no idea what the way out was. When I started this, I just wanted to do right by my family, but it had run away from me. Everything felt meaningless, and the toils and tribulations I had overcome still led me to this very point. I closed the front door and screamed from the bottom of my lungs until I fell to my knees. I crushed the letter that ended it all in my hand, squeezing all the life from it. I had survived the ordeal, but I had still lost. I had lost everything that I fought to protect.

I had mistreated Courtney and Dylan and underappreciated them. And this was the consequence. I was so close to getting my life back and getting my family back. But they were plucked from me by the hands of the masked men themselves. But were they really to blame? No, this was my doing. I had handled an awful situation terribly. If I had just been honest, maybe she would have been more receptive.

I sat down in the bottom of the shower for hours, letting the water hammer at my scalp. I pleaded for it to wash away my sins and get my family back. My skin pruned up as the constant flow of water drowned my pores. I was desperately struggling to plan on how to get them back, but there was no plan. I had already screwed it up beyond repair.

I left the shower and tried calling Courtney incessantly. She ignored the calls; I left message after message. I couldn't stay in the house any longer. I don't even think I locked the front door when I stumbled out of the house; I was in a state of total oblivion. I staggered to the canal bridge where each of my runs started and leaned over the wall, looking into the water. All traces of the police had been eradicated, and it was finally serene and peaceful.

I stood on my tiptoes, looking into the eyes of my alternate self in the reflection of the still water. Me, the killer. The liar. The man who ruined his family for a few extra quid. I was beset with profound guilt. I wanted to drop down into the water and strangle the dark reflection in front of me. I didn't know who was worse, me, masquerading as a good father and husband or the killer below.

The truth is, I was a coward. Always had been. Maybe not in the physical sense, but certainly emotionally. Courtney's needs had evolved in the 12 years we were married. At first, it was all about fun, but now she needed something more substantial. I knew this deeply. More than anything, she craved honesty, and I had been starving her of it. I could count the number of times I had seen Dylan this year on one hand. I should have made more of an effort. Perhaps I wouldn't have been in this position if I had.

I stepped up on the wall with both feet and continued looking down. I was only a few feet higher than the bridge level, but the wind lashed against me, knocking me slightly off balance. Would a fall this high actually kill me? I lifted one foot over the edge, and it would take such little effort to hop off it and into the freezing water below. I looked around to see if anyone was watching, but there weren't any witnesses. Not that it was just a cry for help, but I could have done with someone there to talk me out of it.

Would Courtney and Dylan be better off for it? Probably, I thought. Before all this, the death of my father was the most traumatic time in my life. It was recorded that he died of a heart attack, but me and my mum knew the truth. He had drunk himself to death. Every can and glass contributed to the massive coronary episode that took him from us. I missed him. Not that he was a good father. I barely knew him. Sure, he worked hard but could only find relaxation and happiness at the bottom of a bottle. I had spent my life desperately trying not to be like him, to be better. But I was following the same path, racing to the same end.

It wasn't just the emotional ramifications, either. Not to be pragmatic at a time like this, but they would have to move to a smaller place. I don't think Courtney could cope with the debt we were in, either. As small and pathetic as those concerns were in the cold light of day, it was still a genuinely valid consideration.

I chickened out and dropped back onto safe ground. I kicked and slammed my fists into the wall in frustration. I felt worse for even contemplating it. But I needed a way out. I had already gone to some pretty extreme lengths to get us out of this situation; hopping off the canal was trivial in comparison.

My episode was interrupted by a slow clapping sound behind me. I walked to the other side of the bridge, and the two remaining masked men stood on the path below me, mocking me with each handclasp. I didn't react. I didn't give chase. It didn't fill me with dread. I simply stood there, waiting for whatever they were about to do. They just continued to clap ominously, their rhythm barely interrupted by my attention.

"Just finish it. Please," I requested softly.

The clapping stopped. They stood completely stationary for a minute, their recessed eyes inside the balaclavas twinkling almost imperceptibly in the early moonlight. They didn't look human, two intimidating sentinels watching me mentally implode. They had planted the seeds of this every time they invaded my life, and this was the time to harvest the spoils. The bigger of the two took one single step forward, lifting his index finger in the air and moving it from side to side, gesturing 'no'. He tutted in time with his finger movements before stepping back into line.

I saw some small rocks at my feet and picked them up to throw them. They remained completely stationary, even when the occasional rock impacted them with a thud. They looked devoid of emotion, unable to feel even pain.

"Just finish it!" I screamed.

They both shook their heads in unison, not moving from their position. They were clearly here just to scare me, but for the first time since all this began, it didn't work. I parodied their stance wackily in a desperate attempt to goad them into coming up to the bridge with me. They didn't move a muscle. I started laughing manically. There was something menacingly comedic about what was happening. The longer we were in that bizarre stand-off, the more comical it became for me.

"Are you upset that I stuck that knife into your friend's neck?" I taunted sneeringly. The smaller of the men broke formation for a second before the larger put his arm in front of him to stop him from moving. At last. A reaction.

"Oh, and Goldie Locks is cuffed to a hospital bed with a broken leg. That was me, too!" I continued. The men both looked at each other as if they didn't know that information. I had my hooks in them now. It wouldn't take much more to provoke them into coming for me. I stopped laughing.

"You two are next, you know? I've got nothing else left to lose. I'm going to find you."

My attempt at being threatening had the opposite effect. The men regained their composure and resumed their sentinel-like state. The bigger of the men pointed at me slowly, took the same finger and swiped his neck, gesturing he was going to slit my throat. Both men then turned around, and I watched them walk intimidatingly down the path out of view. I meant what I said to them. I didn't have anything left to lose.

I felt more dangerous than I had ever felt in my life.

In a bizarre twist, the masked men probably stopped me from taking my own life. My hatred for them was stronger than the contempt for myself. I had a renewed sense of purpose. Every time I had fought for something, I had won. The stakes were higher than ever, but I needed to fight. I needed to get my family back. I needed to end the threat that was putting us in danger.

I walked back down the street to my empty home. I was holding myself tall and powerful. I knew what I had to do now. I was wrong to put the darkness within me under lock and key too soon. Together, we would bring this to its inevitable conclusion. I found DS Banks standing at the door, waiting for me. I know what I must have looked like, hobbling towards him out of the darkness. He looked at me with a mixture of pity and suspicion.

"Long day?" He joked.

"Yes. Do you want that statement?"

"We do, but it can wait. I was just checking to see if you were okay. You've been through a lot. Can I come in?"

"Sure. Why not."

I opened the door and realised the state of the house. In Courtney's haste, clothing and toys were everywhere. You could barely see the floor for the mess. We stepped over the items to get to the sitting room, where I collapsed on the couch. DS Banks remained standing, looking around at the mess.

"What happened here, Sean?"

"Erm, marital dispute."

"Sorry to hear that."

"Yeah… me too."

"Does she know about what happened last night?"

"No. And before you ask, it's because I didn't tell her. And I'd appreciate it if you didn't either."

"Fine, but you should speak to someone about it, Sean. You have been through a lot."

"How is he?"

"Who?"

"The scum bag with the broken leg."

"I wouldn't know. He isn't much of a talker."

"I didn't think he would be."

"I may as well take the statement now if that's okay with you. What happened out there?"

DS Banks stood there with his notebook cradled in his hand. I didn't know what I could say. I wanted them to nail this guy for his part in what had been done, but I couldn't implicate myself. I needed to thread the needle with the truth and somehow come out clean on the other side.

"One of them was waiting for me, ready to jump me, but I noticed him and chased after him. He fell down the hill and broke his leg. That's when I called you."

"But why?"

"Why what?"

"Why was he waiting for you? And then why did he run off? Surely, if he was going to jump you, he would have just done it. We recovered the baseball bat from the canal. He could have just hit you with it."

"You are asking the wrong person."

DS Banks tapped his notebook with his pen in frustration and stepped back a few paces, finally slumping down on the armchair behind him with a sigh. He smiled and exhaled sharply through his nose.

"Come on, Sean, there must be more to this."

"There isn't."

"But you must have some kind of idea why they are chasing you."

"Fine," I began, "I've just seen two of them before you arrived at my front door."

"What?" He exclaimed, poised to write in his notebook again.

"Yeah, two of them stood on the canal where it all happened. They threatened me."

"What did they say?"

"They didn't say anything. One of them ran his finger across his throat. I assume they didn't want me talking to you."

"Why did you think that?"

"Well, why else would they be threatening me."

"So, in your initial statement, you said four men attacked you. We have one in custody, and you've just seen two more. Where is the final one?"

"Maybe it was his night off."

"Sean, this is serious."

I started to get very agitated with his questioning, and I just wanted him to leave so I could try and pick up the pieces of my broken life. As well-intentioned as DS Banks was, he had largely been useless in catching these people. If he was better at his job, maybe I wouldn't have had to resort to such unpleasantness.

"You are right. It is serious. And so far, DS Banks, the only reason you have caught one of them is because of me. You should be thanking me for calling you. I nearly-—"

"Nearly what, Sean?"

"–didn't."

"Fine. Listen, you need to report everything that happens. When it happens, it's in your best interest to do that."

DS Banks shut his notebook and stood up, looking around at the carnage at his feet.

"You should speak with your wife too. Sort out your differences. Life is too short."

"How much do I owe for this session, doctor?"

"It's all part of the service. Take care, Sean."

DS Banks left the house, sitting in his car for a few minutes before driving off. I hoped I had done the right thing by telling him about the second encounter with the two remaining masked men. The last thing I needed was another investigation involving me. But I wanted them to feel the pressure. The same pressure I was under. I wanted them to think the sky was falling down on them. I didn't care what justice looked like anymore or where it came from.

It didn't matter to me if they got their collars felt by the police or by me. I just wanted them rotting in a cell or rotting in the ground.

9

BLONDIE

Straight to voicemail. Maybe she was busy; try again. I tapped the green call button on my phone on repeat, hoping there was a secret number of times I had to call before she answered. It was amazing the things you will tell yourself when you don't get the outcome you wanted. Months passed like that. Our marriage was left in tatters. You couldn't see one side of the chasm between us from the other. We barely spoke, only infrequently communicating out of necessity because of Dylan or something to do with the finances. She rebuffed every attempt to try and fix things, citing that she needed time. But how much time?

I didn't receive any divorce papers or any more 'love notes' from the masked men. They were totally silent. Hopefully, they were on the run. The last exchange I had with them on the canal was seared into memory. I spent the weeks after it searching for them on the internet, trying to find out who owned that warehouse. All I had to show for it was a corkboard nailed to the wall filled with the names of shell corporations and dead ends. It was more a testament to my mental health rather than evidence of some kind.

The scrapes and slashes on my feet slowly turned to scars, and I had more or less physically recovered from the ordeal. My redundancy package was almost depleted, and the job search proved to be fruitless. Again, I was left with no choice but to continue earning through the app. But this time, it felt different. No, I wasn't stupid. I would avoid running in the dark and would try and change my routes. Part of me wanted to see if they would take the bait again and come back out of the woodwork.

DS Banks gave me regular updates on the baseball-bat man. He largely gave 'no comment' interviews, but they were holding him on remand. He was confident they could secure a charge. The hunt for the other two was ongoing, but I hadn't heard from them. To my relief, there was no mention of the man I killed. He was probably in some shallow grave somewhere, concealed by his accomplices.

During the first few weeks of my solitude, I would wake up in the middle of the night in a cold sweat, remembering every detail. But as time passed, my recollection of it faded. I certainly didn't feel any remorse. It would have been me in the shallow grave if I hadn't acted like I did. The man I killed became just another blurry memory in a string of memories that made up the worst time of my life.

With Courtney and Dylan gone, me being unemployed, and the trail of the masked men cold, I didn't have anything to fill my days. Being alone in my thoughts, day in and day out, was tough. No, I haven't had any more self-destructive tendencies beyond pretty much living exclusively off microwavable meals. I tried to channel my despair into determination. I still hadn't given up on Courtney, not by a long shot. But I was fatigued. I didn't know what else to do to get her back. I had hoped if I gave her the space, did the time, she would come back- but I was growing impatient.

I hungered for the release of the run; it was the only thing in my life I could truly control. Every day that passed, I prodded at my feet, waiting for the pain to subside. But the day finally came when I was ready to go again. Maybe if I cleared my head, I'd find a way of getting my family back. I was willing to try anything, really. I'd exhausted everything else.

I walked to the canal path in my brand-new running gear, itching with excitement. The path was unfamiliar. Spring had arrived. It was teeming with life: people fishing in the canal, dog walkers struggling to keep up with their companions. Birds eloquently whistled in the thicket, delicately jumping from branch to branch. I started off slow, taking it all in. Muscle memory kicked in; I was worried I had lost some fitness in my sabbatical, but I actually felt strong. Well rested. Other canal users greeted me with smiles as I jogged past; it was nice.

Wildflowers blossomed on the grass verge and delicately trembled as I pushed past.

Despite the beauty all around me, I felt empty inside. There was no rush, no euphoria. Disgruntled, I marched onwards, increasing my pace. Faster. The endorphins refused to release. I felt impervious to their effects. I accelerated until I was almost sprinting, but I still felt the same. In seemingly no time, I had reached Jordan's bridge. The grass had forgotten what had happened here and grown back. Still not satisfied, I ran beyond it. Constantly pushing myself into the unknown, demanding the rush at every step. I felt cheated. My own body was withholding what I so desperately needed. My heart rate casually drummed; I was barely breaking a sweat. Something was missing.

It occurred to me that I had been overstimulated by the treacherous events I had survived. I had produced enough adrenaline to last most people their lifetimes. Even my extended break from running did little to reignite the fire I once felt. I was actually bored. At first, the money I was earning was enough, but like an addict, I needed more. The absence of threat had made it monotonous.

I turned a corner and saw a figure running away from me in the distance. I was gaining on them, gradually. I had an idea. I started to imagine I was chasing my attackers; a few drops of adrenaline were released. Hungry for more, I increased my speed to breaking point. The closing distance between us built the rush. As I got closer, I noticed the figure was a woman running. Her ponytail flicked to the side, and she turned around to look at me. I slowed down to not cause her alarm, but she stopped at the next bridge in front of us. As I approached her, I instantly recognised her. Blondie. She was half crouched with her hands on her knees, staring up at me as I arrived with a breathless smile.

"That's some pace you were running at; I was almost worried you were chasing me!" She smiled.

"Sorry, I was in my own world."

She stands tall and walks closer. "Do I know you from somewhere?"

"I think I've seen you running before."

"That must be it. Hi. I'm Kathryn."

"Sean. I'd shake your hand but, you know, sweaty."

"I don't mind that. Me too."

She gripped my hand lightly, just for a second longer than what felt comfortable, causing a bit of an atmosphere. She released her grasp and undid her ponytail, releasing a cascade of golden blonde hair that flowed weightlessly in the wind. She smiled almost provocatively, readjusting her tight-fitting clothes from top to bottom, simultaneously highlighting all her assets to me at the same time. She then raised her foot on the fence to the side and leaned into a deep stretch, accentuating every muscle in her legs and buttocks. I was definitely leching, but Kathryn was putting on a show for me. I was that out of practice. I didn't know if it was flirting or totally innocent.

I had barely spoken to anyone in person the last few months, let alone a beautiful woman like Kathryn. My heart pounded in my chest faster than any run gave me. Was my forced celibacy making me misread the situation? I became very self-aware of my gawping and picked my jaw up off the floor.

"What's the matter?" she said innocently.

"Er... nothing."

"It's really important to keep limber when you are running, Sean."

"Yeah, it is."

"Do you run here often? Sorry, that's such a cheesy line." She said, laughing.

"I do," I giggled, "maybe I'll see you around?"

"You will. It's nice to meet you, Sean."

I retreated from the exchange, smiling as I left. I turned back a minute or so down the path, and she was still looking intently at me. I replayed the chance meeting in my head, and I couldn't believe I giggled. I felt my cheeks flush red. How embarrassing. But it was certainly a confidence booster, and I felt good about myself for the first time in a long time.

The boost turned sour and curdled into guilt. Surely, I could be forgiven for a bit of light flirtation, given my circumstances, but I wanted to stay strong for Courtney. I made myself feel slightly better by telling myself it was another fleeting, superficial encounter and didn't mean anything. I can't be blamed for my own thoughts, right?

I arrived home and decided to call Courtney in an attempt to get somewhere with her. I don't really know what my motive was, but I was genuinely trying to sort things out. I just wanted to see if she somehow knew about me meeting Kathryn already. I was so paranoid about every misstep. The exercise summary was displayed.

Total run time; 48 minutes, 38 seconds.
Back on the horse. Bonus; £20.
Total earnings; £68.63
One new friend suggestion.

I clicked the notification, and a profile came up for someone called 'KittyKat,' It was Kathryn, it had to be. My thumb hovered over the 'add friend' button, wondering if this was a step too far. Before I could go further, a new notification appeared saying Kathryn had added me as a friend, asking if I would like to accept. Screw it. Accept. What harm could it do? Almost immediately, a message arrived.

Hi Sean, I didn't know you were on here. Meet me where we first met tomorrow morning. We have lots to discuss. xxx

I wasn't sure how to feel about it; she obviously had something to say about the app, and I was curious. It had essentially ruined my life, and I needed to know as much about it as possible. She might have had similar experiences with it, and it might even give me more insight to help get the masked men responsible for the attacks convicted. I accepted her invitation. It wasn't just because I wanted information from her. In truth, I wanted to see her again. I probably just misread the situation grievously and she was being friendly, but I was excited, nevertheless.

I called Courtney, and she sent me straight to voicemail. On my second attempt, she answered the phone but didn't speak for a few seconds. I could hear her sighing and building up to talk to me.

"What?" she uttered abruptly.

"Court, I just want to talk."

"Well, I don't want to talk. Not that fun, is it?"

"I get it, I really do, but I am trying here. You do know there isn't anyone else, right?"

"Sean, if you just tell the truth, we can both move on with our lives. But you insist on just telling me lie after lie."

"I'm not lying."

"Sure. Any more love notes?"

"It wasn't a love note. I don't know how many times I have to say it. Just come home, please."

"I can't."

"Why not?"

"I can't bear to be around you, Sean. Stop calling me."

The call ended. Truthfully, I felt a little less guilty for the liaison I had arranged for the morning after. The irony wasn't lost on me. Like a self-fulfilling prophecy, I was being pushed towards someone else. But of course, I knew it was my fault. As much as the situation frustrated me, I still loved Courtney. I would have done anything for her, apart from telling the truth, which was the one thing that she needed from me to return home.

The morning after, I woke up excited about meeting Kathryn again. I don't know what it was about her. Probably because no one ever really spoke to me or looked at me like that. Not for a good while, anyway. She made me feel good about myself, with little or no effort on her part. I didn't have any expectations; I just wanted to see where it went. My obsession for the masked men had faded in the weeks prior, too, but this had reignited them. Comparing notes with Kathryn could produce more leads, and I could finally end the threat once and for all.

I ran back to Kathryn's bridge, and she was waiting for me, leaning against the fence with a cheeky smile and a wave. It felt good to have someone smile at me again instead of a scowl. Her eyes glistened in the morning sun, locked on mine intensely. Her full lips separated slightly as her smile grew bigger.

"Hey, Sean. Fancy seeing you here."

"Hi Kathryn, what a coincidence."

"Call me Kat."

"Okay, Kat."

"Listen, business first. How long have you been on 'B-Run' for?"

"Since the start of the year."

"So not long then. Has anything weird happened to you whilst you were using it?"

"Yeah, but not for a while."

"Let me guess. Masked people chasing after you with baseball bats?"

My face said it all; I didn't even have to reply to her. They weren't just doing this to me. They had hacked into the app and were using it to find victims. It was a miracle Kat hadn't been taken yet. I thought they had become inactive, but they probably just moved on to the next victim. At that moment, I realised we shared a bond. We had likely both gone through hell using this thing, and I was keen to find out what she knew.

"Yes," I uttered.

She moved closer, touching my arm lightly. "What happened?" she asked.

"Well, some guys hacked the app and were somehow tracking me. They tried running me over one morning. The next time I went on a run, I got kidnapped, but I escaped. The last time, I managed to corner one of them and rang the police."

"That's awful. I've had people chasing me, but I've always got away. At first, I thought it was random, but I started suspecting the app was somehow involved. How did you get away when they kidnapped you?"

"Barely."

"I am so sorry that happened to you."

Kat leaned in and tenderly hugged me, gripping me tightly. It was the first time in months I had felt the warmth of another person. My eyes closed in contentment. I suddenly felt so relaxed. The coconut and vanilla aromas from her hair strutted sensually into my nostrils. She leaned out of the hug and clocked my left hand.

"Sorry, I didn't know you were married."

"Yeah, 12 years. Separated. We are going through a bit of a rough patch at the moment."

"Does she know about everything?"

"No."

"Why not?"

"We've got enough problems without bringing all this into it."

She walked back over to the fence and sat on it, deep in thought. She looked at me and smiled slightly, "I'll help you stop them." She whispered.

"They are gone."

"They aren't gone, Sean. I literally got chased last week. When I met you, I thought you were one of them."

"No, they are gone. The police are involved, and they have the leader in custody."

"The police don't know anything. They will keep coming."

I was clearly living in denial. If what Kat was saying was true, these people were still going out and attacking people, under the radar. DS Banks had no idea, or he would have been round to question me further. I didn't know what to make of Kat, but she seemed like a genuine, nice person. But why did she want to help me so desperately? I didn't like the thought of the masked men chasing her with murderous intent and me refusing to do anything about it. But the whole thing felt off to me. We didn't even know each other's last names, and she wanted to go out on a murderer hunt?

She looked at me, patiently waiting for my decision. She had a dangerous air about her, her bright blonde hair billowing in the wind. Her allure was strong, but it was just one more thing I would have to lie to Courtney about. I had to tread carefully where she was concerned, and I didn't want to do anything that would upset her further. Kat would just be someone else I had to worry about, and I didn't have the capacity for that.

"We can go to the police and tell them everything," I pleaded.

"So, you haven't told them everything already?"

"No."

"What haven't you told them?"

"They don't know about the kidnapping."

"Why not?"

I paused for a moment. I wanted to tell her how I escaped, but how would she react? I felt as if I could trust her, and we had formed a bond of some kind. We had lived parallel lives for a few months, and we had a shared experience. I also wanted to scare her. She needed to know how serious this was. It wasn't shenanigans. Lives were being destroyed. I decided to take the plunge and tell her.

"Because I killed one of them."

"To escape?"

"Yes. And they killed my friend, Jordan."

"Hang on, they are killing people? I thought they were just trying to scare runners."

"Yes, they are killing people. I barely escaped with my life. That's why you need to stop using the app and go to the police."

"Sure, but you can't go to the police. You will get put up for murder."

"It was self-defence."

"Maybe at the time, but why have you waited so long to tell them? You will look guilty," she argued, "and why are you still using the app if it's so dangerous?"

"I need the money."

"More than your life?"

"No, but I can outsmart them."

"But you don't need to stop using it. We can find them together."

"I just want to sort my life out, and I'm no vigilante. Sorry, but no. I'll see you around. Go to the police, please."

I turned away to start running back the way I came. She stared at me in disappointment, shaking her head slightly. It was stupid of me to share everything I had done with a stranger, but even so, I was worried about her. She needed to know how serious this was. She didn't know what they were capable of. Hopefully, she would listen to my advice and go to the police about it. The thudding restarted, and I plodded along to the beat at a casual pace; it felt dull. My legs slowed not out of lethargy but boredom. I puffed air out of my cheeks, not having any inclination to carry on. I stopped on the path and turned around; I could still see Kat propped up against the fence in the distance.

Suddenly, the thudding in my ears accelerated rapidly. I quickly turned backwards and forwards, looking for the danger, but none was apparent. There was a road running parallel to the path beyond the bushes, and a car raced down it, slowing the thud as it departed. It stopped at the bridge where Kat stood, and I saw the car doors open.

It was them.

The masked men were back and out for blood. They had found me and Kat. One of them leaned over the bridge, looming over her, but she was completely unaware of the danger, which was only a few metres away. They skulked down the steps slowly, trying not to draw her attention to the danger coming. My first instinct was to run, but I felt compelled to help her. She didn't deserve whatever they had planned for her. I started running as fast as I could towards her, waving my arms frantically to try and get her attention.

10

HAVE FUN WITH THAT

I screamed, "Kat! Behind you!"

The masked men noticed me before Kat did. They rushed down the steps to try and reach her before I arrived. I sprinted back at top speed, trying to reach her before they made their way down the steps. She finally heard my warnings and noticed the car parked up. She started to run towards me, and one of the masked men gave chase. Mine and Kat's paths collide before the man reaches us, and I turn to follow Kat, continuing down the path at speed. The man didn't let up and closed the gap. When we reached Jordan's bridge, she ducked around the wall out of sight.

"What are you doing?" I said frantically.

"We can take him." She asserted.

"No, we need to carry on running."

"No, we can take him."

I joined her next to the bridge. The man emerged from the opening underneath, and we caught him by surprise. Kat pulled a small black box out of her back pocket and stuck it to his neck. The taser buzzed fiercely as he fell to the floor, yielding to the voltage. He was a big guy, and the taser did little to incapacitate him fully. Kat frenziedly clicked at the buttons, trying to produce another shock, but it had failed or ran out of charge.

Instinctively, I jumped on top of him to prevent him from standing, and the darkness busted out of the cage to assist. There was no time for internal debate. No pros and cons. I just started relentlessly punching him with my fists. He resisted at first, but with every strike, he reacted to it less before becoming completely static on the ground. This didn't stop me. I continued ruthlessly pummelling his face into the dirt before Kat pulled me away. We both stood over him, the balaclava exuding blood into the floor below. Kat grabbed my arm for comfort tightly as I struggled for breath. She walked beyond his beaten body to check the path beyond the bridge; her lack of reaction assured me it was clear. She bent down and felt around for a pulse in his neck.

"Is he dead?" I gasped.

"Yes. We need to get out of here. Do you live nearby?"

"A few miles down the path."

"Wash your hands in the water, and let's go before somebody sees."

My body count was increasing. This one felt different. We could have gotten away, but he couldn't have run far with the getup the masked men wear. But I made a conscious choice, under Kat's influence, to wait for him and end his life. I stared at my bloodied hands, expecting the flood of remorse to drown me, but it didn't. I felt incredible. The rush was indescribable. Every breath of air tasted of pure pleasure. The adrenaline I had been chasing returned to me in droves. I was struck by lightning, and it re-energised every cell in my body instantaneously.

"Sean, we have to go. Right now!" Kat exclaimed.

I rinsed my hands in the grubby water, and we started running. It was the first time since I started running again that the endorphins surged through my veins. The euphoria I felt was incredible. The morning breeze lightly stimulated every patch of skin exposed to it. I inhaled and exhaled deeply as I ran, wallowing in pure ecstasy. My eyes remained fixed on Kat's body running a few metres ahead of me. I could see every muscle tighten and swell through her almost painted-on clothes. Both of our bodies were separate but performed together in unison. She occasionally turned to look at me with an enamoured look in her eyes. I no longer felt like I was running away from them but running towards her. I overtook her to lead her the rest of the way without saying a word. The unspoken chemistry between us thickly hung in the air as we continued down the path. We reached my front door, and both ran inside.

She paused for a moment in silence and thrust me against the wall, pressing her full lips into mine. My hands glided over every inch of her athletic physique as she kissed me with a lust I hadn't felt in years. She clawed at my clothes as she pushed me up the stairs and into the bedroom. Her sky-blue eyes turned red with desire as she forced me, willingly, onto the bed. I struggled with the juxtaposition of the emotions I was feeling at first, but I quickly didn't care. All that mattered to me at the moment was continuing to feel it.

My eyes opened hours later to see the mess of blonde hair on the pillow next to mine. I didn't recognise it at first, but then I realised it was Kat. I stayed there, staring at her, trying to make sense of what had just happened. She turned slowly with a smile and gave me a passionate kiss. I was no longer under the influence of the ecstasy of hours before and could think clearly. I didn't react to the kiss as she wanted, and she scrunched up her face slightly in confusion.

"Are we going to talk about what happened?" I asked softly.

"You were amazing."

"I didn't mean that."

"I didn't either."

"Kat, I just killed a man. With my bare hands, and then we did that. It isn't normal."

"He was trying to kill us. Let's just enjoy ourselves. I've never felt so alive."

I did feel good. In a way, I was just waiting for permission to enjoy it. I'd realised that I wasn't addicted to running; I was addicted to the chase. The thrill. Kat was now part of that. She felt the same way, I could tell. Normal people would have walked away from all of this at the first sign of danger, but the danger is what drew us to it. I was concerned about my own reaction to the beating. I kept telling myself that it was him or me. But I didn't need to do that. I *wanted* to. Maybe I had crossed a line that I couldn't walk back from. The darkness within me sniggered at my inner conflict, still satisfied from its last meal.

In a twisted way, Kat knew me better in 24 hours than Courtney had in 12 years. I felt sick thinking about it. Kat had seen the darkness inside of me and still embraced me for it. More than that, she was attracted to it. I hadn't felt wanted like this for a long time. I felt ten years younger.

"Anyway," she began, "have you thought more about my proposal?"

"A bit soon for that, isn't it?" I joked.

"Funny. No, about finding these people."

"Well, it'll be hard to explain away what just happened to the police. I guess we have no other option. The masked men will just keep coming for us, won't they?"

"The masked men?"

"Sorry, that's what I've been calling them."

"I like it. Accurate." She nodded.

"About... the other thing we did."

"The other thing?" She said innocently.

"You know what I'm talking about."

"The sex? You are an adult, Sean. You can say it without getting in trouble."

"It was incredible, it was. But did you just do that because we'd escaped?"

"No, Sean. I find you attractive. We are adults. I like fun. Do you find me attractive?"

"Yes, obviously."

"And did you have fun?"

"Yes. Obviously."

"Well, what's the problem then? We are just two adults having fun. Just because we are being chased by murderers, it doesn't mean we can't enjoy it, right?"

"That's one way to look at it."

"You need to lighten up, Sean. I thought it was incredible, too. Both parts."

"Good."

"Listen, it's been crazy, but I have to go," she said, standing from the bed clutching the sheet across her, "I'll be in touch."

She noticed a photograph of Courtney and me on the nightstand and picked it up before looking at me with pretend sympathy. She placed it face down and gathered her things to get dressed. I went downstairs to prepare something to eat, and she hugged me from behind.

"Can't wait to see you again, Sean," Kat whispered provocatively in my ear before biting my earlobe softly.

"You too, Kat," I smiled.

I walked her to the front door and watched her jog down the street into the distance. It felt good to have someone to confide in and talk about what had been going on with me. I wasn't sure about her plan, but what options did we have? They knew where I lived, and they had proven that before. I couldn't risk them returning if I ever patched things up with Courtney. But I couldn't shake the feeling that Kat had some dark secrets of her own that she didn't want to tell me. She certainly wasn't repulsed by the violence; if anything, she seemed to be turned on by it. Part of me wondered if I was being used by her for some nefarious purpose, but the bigger part of me didn't care.

I carried on making dinner, if you could call it that. Some grey matter, marinaded in grey sauce, irradiated to perfection by the microwave. I looked around the kitchen, and it was a mess. I had let the place go since Courtney's departure. I couldn't bear the sheer monotony of household chores when I could be out there instead. I barely made it through half of the washing up when my phone beeped.

Got home safe xxx

	Good.

When shall we meet again?

	Soon.

> *Tomorrow night?*

> *Okay, meet me at mine.*

> *Can't wait xxx*

I couldn't wait either. This was exhilarating. I don't know what excited me more, this bizarre relationship I'd found with Kat or the thrill of fighting for my life. Either way, it wasn't something I wanted to end. I didn't even care about the legal ramifications of what we were doing; I only cared about how it made me feel. These people weren't innocent. They were killers. I was providing a public service, if anything.

And the sex. It was incredible.

I continued washing up, lost in a Kat-themed daydream. I am interrupted once again by knocking on the front door. Had they come to my house to try and take me again? I took the lock knife with me as a precaution. I opened the door and saw DS Banks standing there.

"Hi, Sean. Can I come in?"

"Sure. Tea?"

"No—"

"Not a social call, got it," I interrupted.

"How have you been?"

"I thought it wasn't a social call? Has he been locked away yet?"

"No, we actually had to release him this morning."

I couldn't believe my ears. Just as we got rid of one, baseball-bat man returns. I had neatly packaged him up with a raft of evidence and handed him to the police. And they released him back into freedom. It just proved to me that as impulsive as our actions were that morning, it was the only chance we would deliver justice to these creeps.

"What? How does that even happen?" I shouted.

"The man must have some friends in high places. Word came down that we had to release him. Lack of evidence, apparently."

"He tried to kill me. On multiple occasions."

DS Banks shrugged. "Lack of evidence. We can't put him on the canal at the time of your attack or at Jordan's murder."

"So, what now?"

"We are keeping a close eye on him. He didn't give us anything to go off, just replied 'no comment' to every question. The attacks have stopped for now, though. We haven't had a report for weeks. Probably because we had the perpetrator on remand."

"Have they?"

"They haven't come after you again, have they?"

"No," I lied.

DS Banks saw through my facial expression with ease. He was a seasoned detective, and it probably wasn't wise to be dishonest with him. But my body count was racking up now, and the last thing I needed was another stint in the cells and a long interview. It would just be my luck that they would find a way of prosecuting me, but the actual villains get to walk away free.

"Listen, Sean, it isn't for me to tell you what to do, but there is a dangerous man out there, and he has very good reason to come and find you. You need to be careful."

"I am being careful."

"If anything happens, no matter how insignificant you think it is, you need to get in touch with us. Let us do our jobs."

"I will."

"Good."

DS Banks returned his hands to his pockets and left the house without a further word. For a moment, I thought they had found the body on the canal we left, but considering I wasn't in cuffs, they couldn't know about that. It's likely the masked men have cleared it up to keep the police out of it. I took the lock-knife upstairs to bed with me. I couldn't take any chances now that baseball-bat man was out. They could strike at any moment, no pun intended.

Coconut and vanilla. Her scent lingered in the room sweetly. A single blonde strand of hair decorated Courtney's pillow mockingly. I upturned the photograph of us on the nightstand and returned it to its rightful position.

What astounded me was that I only felt guilt about Kat at that moment. Courtney was pretty adamant it was over, so was I wrong for doing what I did? I was still married, legally, at least. I knew I couldn't resist Kat, though. Not after the night we had. She definitely had her claws in me. I stripped the bed and threw it all straight in the washer. The smell had turned sour. I wouldn't bring her here again. It was an insult to Courtney, and she deserved more than that.

I tried to fall asleep on the bare mattress, clutching the blade in my fist. I was thrown back to the paranoia of months previous. With every crack and creak the house made, I thought they were there. I expected the sound of a baseball bat tapping at the front door, but it never came. I lay there in a semi-unconscious state, trying to stay alert at rest. The sun slithered through the crack in the curtains, and it was the start of a new day.

I had to get my run in, and it was the safest time to do it. The sun had literally just risen, so I could see, but the canal path would be quiet. Paranoia was getting the better of me. I wanted to check out the bridge from the day before to check we hadn't left any evidence. I decided to treat the daytime runs as training for the nights with Kat. I had barely got a mile down the path when the thudding of the app was interrupted by beeping. I awkwardly checked my phone as I ran to see a stream of notifications.

> *Are you out on a run now? X*
> *Do you need help?*
> *Sean, are you okay?*

I didn't reply; I just continued. She must have seen my name on the leaderboard go green. I could tell she was just trying to be helpful, but it did strike me as a bit of an intrusion. A flurry of message notifications kept beeping in my ear. With each one, I grew more agitated. I paused for a moment to send a reply.

> *Yes, just going to clear my head. x*

I put my phone back in my armband and continued running. The messages stopped. I approached the scene of the brutal beating I had delivered the day before and could still see the blood stains on the stone, but the body was gone. The red of the blood had been baked black by the constant sun hitting it. At the sight of it, my bruised knuckles swelled and tingled. They remembered, too.

I crouched down to inspect the blood stain closer. When I reached it, something splashed against the water's surface beside me. I stood up and peered over into the water when I heard something impact the stone of the bridge. A tiny crater had formed with a small whisp of smoke emanating from the centre. Inside, a small, crumpled ball of lead. I didn't immediately recognise what it was at first but realised it was a bullet hole. Still confused about what was happening, I took refuge underneath the bridge, and a third shot struck down at my feet. I looked towards the previous bridge in the distance, and a glare from something reflective blinds me for a second before a fourth shot was fired.

I scrambled beneath the bridge away from the shooter's line of sight and hastily got my phone out. I didn't know whether to ring the police or get in touch with Kat. I barely knew her, but I knew what her opinion would be on the matter. But it had escalated dramatically. I hadn't been shot at before. Even in my frenzy, I decided I couldn't involve the police because I was afraid of being caught myself.

> *Someone is shooting at me.*
> *I'm at the bridge from yesterday.*

> *Sit tight, I'll be 5 minutes.*
> *Run to the next bridge.*
> *I'll meet you there.*

I ran through the exit side of the bridge and kept going towards the next one. Kat said she would be there. The first hundred metres or so, the line of fire would have been obscured by the bridge I was under, but as soon as I was clear of it, the storm started. The rounds kept coming and hitting the gravel like hailstone, obliterating the gravel into dust. I meandered down the path erratically, trying to avoid them. The further I got from the shooter, the less accurate and regular the shots became. I saw a posh-looking white sports car screech to a stop on the bridge, and Kat got out of it, gesturing me to hurry up. The shots had ceased by the time I got there, but I wasn't taking any chances. I took the steps three at a time and immediately got in the car. Kat returned to the car and threw it in reverse.

"Are you okay?" she asked.

"No, they were shooting at me," I said, catching my breath, "where are we going?"

"To the other bridge."

"What! Why?"

"To get them, it's obviously one of them."

"Kat, they've got a rifle. Your taser isn't going to do much."

"I'm not using the taser."

The car ripped around the corner towards the upper level of the bridge the shooter was firing from. It was a single-lane crossing designed for light vehicles to cross the water. About fifty metres further up the road, one of the masked men was sprinting in the opposite direction with a rifle over his shoulder. Kat slowly put her seatbelt on, and I did the same. She reached the fleeing masked man and ploughed straight into the back of him, sending him soaring over the bonnet and landing face down in the middle of the road.

Kat got out of the car first and walked over to the man. The rifle had separated from his shoulder in the impact, and he was crawling towards it, desperately trying to reach it. He coughed and spluttered as he struggled onwards. Kat beat him to the rifle with ease and picked it up.

I hadn't seen a rifle like this in person before; I had only ever seen them in films or on television. Just the sight of it made me shiver. It was fitted with what looked like a silencer on the end of the barrel. What was Kat going to do with it? Surely, she wouldn't shoot the man. She turned it over in her hands for a few seconds as if she were working out how it worked, then offered it out to me.

"Do you want to do the honours?"

"Er, I don't know—"

"Fair enough. It is my turn, after all."

She turned the rifle on the masked man on the ground and fired a single round into the back of his head at point-blank range without a moment's hesitation. The silencer lived up to its name; with a dull pop, the masked man became lifeless. I stood staring at Kat in astonishment, at a total loss of words.

"Another one bites the dust," she laughed, "Oh my god, that felt amazing."

She threw the rifle at me for me to catch it and opened the boot for me to throw it in. She then went to the front of the car to inspect for damage. There was barely a dent. She patted the bonnet and got back in the car hastily.

"Are you coming, Sean?" she said through the window.

"Are we just leaving him here?"

"Yes, I don't want to get blood in my boot. We need to get out of here!"

I entered through the passenger side, not knowing how I felt. Seeing Kat put a bullet in that man's head was simply breathtaking. I didn't know if I was terrified or euphoric. She just took charge of the situation and, without hesitation, came out on top. She had her own darkness in her, too. That's what attracted me to her. Kat was amazing in the most deeply dangerous way. Her hands gripped the steering wheel as we sped off down the country lane ahead of us.

"Kat, I don't know what to say," I mumbled.

"Well, a 'thank you' goes a long way." She said, half giggling.

"Thank you. How are you feeling after that?"

"Incredible. How did you feel yesterday?"

"The same."

"Sean, is there something wrong with us?"

"Probably."

"But these people are killers, right? We can't be bad people if we kill killers." She bargained.

"I think we are bad people if we enjoy it. He was barely alive after we hit him; we could have gone to the police."

"What, and casually mentioned we killed one yesterday, too? Think ahead, Sean, how would you explain that to the police?"

She was right, of course. I couldn't afford to be caught at another scene of a murder. DS Banks suspected I wasn't telling the whole truth as it is. If he saw me with Kat and another dead body, I was going down. Kat terrified me to my core. I had caged my darkness away for so long, only calling on it recently in an emergency, but she had lived side by side with hers. She wasn't afraid to fight for what she wanted or to kill if someone crossed her. I was jealous in a way, but she was perilous. She was infectious.

She pulled up outside my house and gripped my thigh sensually, using her other hand to pull my head in closer for a kiss. Her lips sealed against mine for a few moments before she pulled away slightly and nipped at my lower lip. She sat back in her seat with her eyes closed, making noises of satisfaction.

"Am I coming in, Sean?"

"I'm not sure. I feel weird doing it again in the house. I'm still married, after all."

"Doing… it?" she jeered.

"You know what I mean."

"I thought you said it was over with her?"

"It is. Or at least I think it is."

"Well, you should probably tell her that." She said, pointing towards the house.

Courtney was standing in the window, witnessing the whole thing. Our eyes locked for a moment. And at that moment, I saw profound sorrow cross her face. I knew that I had just broken her. All of her insecurities and accusations had just been proven to be true. She couldn't bear to look at me any longer; she stormed off out of view. I couldn't believe I had been so stupid. I turned to look at Kat, and she gave me a wry shrug before patting me on the leg in jest.

"Have fun with that."

RUN FOR YOUR LIFE

11

AN OLD FRIEND

I ducked and dived from every plate we owned, which was being thrown at me at high speed. When she ran out of ammunition, she came at me, beating at my chest with her fists. I tried to restrain her lightly, but she was strong, fuelled by the rage of what she had just seen. Her wailing was deafening. It wasn't even words anymore. The broken pieces of ceramic and clay on the floor perfectly symbolised our marriage, smashed and broken beyond repair. She slumped back on the only standing dining chair in fatigue. She could barely look at me without gritting her teeth. I had never seen her like this before.

"How could you do this to me? To us? To Dylan?" she bellowed.

"You weren't here, Courtney, I tried, and you weren't interested."

"You tried? You rang my phone a few times; big deal. You never even came round to try and see us."

"I didn't think you wanted me to."

"I didn't, but you should have tried."

"Listen, I can explain."

I couldn't explain. I couldn't even begin to explain. Was I capable of reciting anything other than cliches? She had every right to be absolutely furious. I had screwed up royally. Her fit of rage had paused for a moment in response to what I had just said. Another meaningless evasion of the truth coming out of my mouth. I felt ashamed.

"Oh really? I don't think I need an explanation, Sean. It's pretty plain to me. It looks like you were snogging some blonde tart in her sports car on our doorstep."

"Yeah, that happened. But you don't know why."

She laughed madly. "Why?"

"Yes, why."

"Go on then, enlighten me. God, this is going to be good."

This was it. The moment. I stood at the crossroads once again. I wouldn't be given the chance to tell her the truth ever again. I needed to be honest. Fully lay bare who I am and what I've become. If she accepts me, we have a chance. Otherwise, it's definitely over.

"Jordan died."

"Who the hell is Jordan?"

"Jordan from work, who I went for a run with."

"Okay?"

"He was murdered whilst we were on the run."

"What? Why didn't you tell me?"

"I don't know. I'd lost my job. I found that app, and I thought if you found out about Jordan, you would stop me from using it. It is the only thing that has been keeping our heads above water."

"Okay. That's terrible, obviously. But what has that got to do with the slapper outside?"

"I carried on running. And I got kidnapped by the same people who murdered Jordan."

"You got kidnapped?"

Her anger subsided for a moment. A part of her obviously still cared about me, I could tell. You can't turn off 12 years of marriage like a switch. I just needed to continue being honest and tell her everything, and it would be okay. We can build on it.

"Yes. And the only way I escaped is I killed one of them."

"Sean, you've killed someone?"

"It was him or me, I promise you. They had me tied up in this room with loads of knives. They were going to torture me and kill me."

The anger in her returned. The switch was flicked. Concern turned into deep grief. I desperately wanted her to believe me. Everything was hanging by a thread. But even as I told her the story, I didn't believe it myself. It was farcical.

"Honestly, you must think I am stupid. How am I meant to believe any of that? And even so, how does it explain her?"

"I met her on a run–"

"Fantastic."

"– and the same things were happening to her. She was getting chased by the masked men, but they never caught her. We went on a run together to look for them, and we got attacked."

"The masked men?"

"That's what we call them."

"Fun. So, you have been going on runs together?"

"Yes, and we got attacked."

"I suppose you killed him too."

"I did."

"Why haven't you gone to the police?"

"I did with Jordan, but since I killed the first one, I can't."

"Right, so let me get this straight. You nearly got killed using that stupid app. Your friend got murdered. You got kidnapped, you became a serial killer, and now you are going for runs with that whore outside? Have I missed anything?"

"That's about the size of it."

"And she's the one sending your little love notes, I presume?"

"No, that was the masked men."

"The masked men got it." She mocked. The story had become so farfetched that Courtney stopped crying and actually laughed. Her grief had reached such a point that she was numb to it.

"It's the truth."

"Have you slept with her?"

"What?"

"Have you slept with her?"

"Yes. But only once."

"Only once! Fantastic. In that case, I'll move straight back in."

"Courtney, please listen to me."

"No, Sean, you listen to me. Do not contact me again. Ever. I will get the paperwork together."

"Courtney, I love you."

"No, you don't. You never have. All I ever wanted was for us to be a family. And for you to be honest with me."

I knew deep down that it was definitely over. I had just witnessed the last shred of her love for me die in her eyes. I don't even think she was angry anymore; she was just done. For different reasons, but I'd been in that same pit of despair she was now trapped in. She looked so exhausted. We both did. Should I just accept it as the end and continue on with my life? The fight in me had died, too. We had grown apart so much as people we barely recognised each other. But Dylan, I didn't want him to grow up without a father like I did. I couldn't let that happen.

"What about Dylan?" I murmured.

"What about him?" She scorned.

"Can I see him?"

"You have to be joking. He barely knows who you are. Neither do I! You are never here. I don't know if you have had a mid-life crisis or something, but I can't take it anymore. I hope you are very happy with her."

With that biting critique, she pushed her house keys into my chest and left my life, possibly forever. She was right, as always. I didn't recognise myself either. I heard Courtney's car drive off, and I have to admit my first thought was Kat. I checked outside to see if her white sports car was still there, but it wasn't. I hoped she hadn't heard the screaming match between Courtney and me and thought it was too messy to get involved with me. I'd spent so long worrying about how to work things out with Courtney that when it came to a head, it just left me feeling dull.

I didn't feel guilty for thinking about Kat, either. I saw my relationship with Kat as less complicated, if you can believe it. In only a few short days, we had somehow neatly compartmentalised our relationship, separated into lights and darks, both holding equal value. Kat was new and exciting. It felt easier to start afresh than try and fix my broken marriage. In my head, I had done everything I could to try.

I sat down in the rubble of the kitchen. I felt like the sole survivor of a battle; debris and shrapnel from Courtney's plate onslaught almost completely obscured the floor. I needed to tidy it up, but I couldn't face it. Instead, I took out my phone and opened the 'B-Run' app. I hadn't even had time to check all the summaries for the past few runs. It didn't really matter to me anymore. A message came from Kat, and I hesitated to open it, thinking she could be breaking it off.

> *Well, that was intense xxx*

> *Very. x*

> *Do you want to meet up?*

> *For a run?*

> *Christ, no. For a drink x*

> *Okay, where?*

> *I'll pick you up. I know a place. Dress nice. I'll be there in an hour x*

I didn't even know what 'dress nice' meant. I didn't feel like going out either, but I needed something to take my mind off everything, and Kat would fit the bill nicely. I browsed through my wardrobe, looking for something nice; the best I could come up with was the suit I was going to wear to my interview at TPL. I barely got out of the shower when Kat had arrived outside. She was brazenly beeping her car horn for me to come outside. When I didn't come out within a minute, she knocked on the door melodically.

I opened the door and saw Kat standing there, leaning provocatively against the doorframe. She had a black silk dress elegantly draped across her soft, radiant skin. Her bronzed leg extended out of a waist-high slit, with her leather high heel pressed into the front step. The neckline of the dress almost reached her navel, showcasing an expensive-looking necklace nestled deep in her cleavage. Her hair was pristinely curled but unforced; they bounced in the breeze with sophistication. The dark, smoky eye makeup lured me into her bright blue eyes without reluctance as I stood there, awestruck.

"Well, what do you think?" She said daringly.

"That's a nice necklace."

"Like you are looking at the necklace. Is that it?" She joked.

"You look absolutely stunning," I looked down at myself, "I think I misunderstood the brief of dress nice."

"You look very handsome, Sean. It's good to see you out of those running clothes. Are you ready?"

"Oh yeah. I'm ready."

"Follow me."

She tempted me towards her car, patting the passenger seat gently and urging me to enter. I didn't think twice. I was fully ensnared by this woman; she knew exactly what to say and do. And definitely what to wear. Like pheromones, the coconut and vanilla of her scent enraptured me. I should have been at home mourning the destruction of my marriage, but what can I say? I'm only human. Then again, maybe I'm not. Not anymore.

"So, you like the necklace then?" Kat said, pulling away from the curbside.

"Yeah, I don't really know anything about that kind of thing, though. I was just making a joke."

"My husband bought me this necklace."

"Husband?"

"Don't worry, he isn't with us anymore."

"Oh, I'm sorry."

"Me too."

I saw a glimmer of Kat's fragility; it was weirdly refreshing. I thought she was invincible, but it turned out she did have a heart. I didn't want to ask her any more questions about her husband, and she clearly didn't want to talk about it. We fell silent for a minute or two because of the awkward exchange. I decided to change the subject.

"So, what do you do for a living?"

"This and that. Why?"

"Well, the posh car, the fancy jewels, just wondering, that's all."

"Finance. But no business tonight. I am all about the pleasure."

"I'm sure you are. Where are we going?"

"A little place I know in the city. Do you like Italian?"

"Yeah, who doesn't?"

"Then I was thinking we could get a hotel for the night. What do you think?"

"Sorry to ruin the mood," I awkwardly began, "I can't really afford that."

"Sean, I'll take care of it. Just relax."

Kat pulled the car over by the curb of 'Massimo Lusso', a luxurious-looking restaurant with a valet outside. It was housed in an old 18th-century building with a red rope containing a queue outside. The queue was filled to capacity with well-dressed restaurantgoers eagerly waiting to enter the eatery. Kat stepped out of the car and casually threw her keys to the valet, who carefully drove the car out of sight.

"I think there might be a wait Kat."

"Not for us."

The man on the door greets Kat with a kiss on each cheek before inviting us in warmly, to the disdain of the queue dwellers. This was Kat's world; I was just lucky enough to live in it. The stunning architecture inside complements Kat's beauty as we are led through a litany of tables to some booths on a raised platform at the back. Grand chandeliers hang from the ceiling, illuminating the fantastic hand-painted artworks spanning it. The place was absolutely buzzing with activity. The clinks of glasses and laughter surrounded us. A string quartet harmonises the atmosphere into sophistication. We are led to our table, up a few steps and behind a rope. It lends a higher view of the entire restaurant. Kat smiles at me with expectation, waiting for my opinion on it all. I'd never stepped foot in a place like it.

"Wow, this is a nice place," I mused with glee.

"Yes, the lobster ravioli is to die for."

"I never thought I'd eat somewhere like this."

"Why?"

"Because we are broke?" I laughed.

"Oh, sorry. Well, you don't have to worry about that tonight."

The waiter makes his way over, wearing white gloves and a bow tie. He placed the wine list in front of Kat with a welcoming smile, and she perused it nonchalantly. I'm glad he didn't put it in front of me. I wouldn't have had a clue.

"Will we be drinking wine tonight, ma'am?" He asked.

"Yes, and a lot of it. We will take a bottle of… Lafite '64, please." She requested.

"Certainly. Excellent choice."

"And you know about wine? What other secrets do you have, Kat?"

"You don't know the half of it."

I broke from the conversation for a minute to just take it all in. I see the people down below, filling their faces with food and wine, not a care in the world. I spent so long worrying about being able to pay for the basics, but it seemed so trivial here. I checked the list; the bottle of wine Kat flippantly ordered cost more than half of my usual monthly salary at TPL. The waiter returned with the wine and poured it into our glasses to sample. Kat slowly wrapped her lips around the glass, allowing the liquid into her mouth, before pulling away from it with a smile. I attempted to replicate it, but I was taken aback by the taste. Was she pretending to like this?

"Fine. Fill her up." She instructed.

"Kat, can I ask you something?" I enquired.

"Sure, of course you can."

"Why are you interested in me?"

"We are having fun, right?"

"Yes, but we are from different worlds. You are clearly used to the finer things in life, and I just don't know where I would fit into all that."

Kat looks at the waiter, patiently waiting for him to leave the table with a smile. She turns to me when he leaves with a look of slight pity in her eyes.

"Why would I care about money?" she began, "we have a connection. I'm not sure what it is, but I want to explore it. You know things about me that no one else will ever know. That's got to count for something, right?"

"I agree. Same."

"Well, don't ask stupid questions then. I've not felt this way for a while, and I'm not going to let anything get in the way, alright?" She lectured.

"Yes, ma'am," I quipped.

Happier for the affirmation; I felt like a weight had been lifted. Maybe this wasn't just a weird relationship built on the darkness we shared. It could be more than that. For the first time in a while, I looked forward to the future. I didn't know where this would lead, but it was exciting. I hadn't forgotten about Courtney, but Kat was right. We did have a connection. And it was worth exploring.

Since the dust had settled on the argument with Courtney, the guilt was creeping in. It didn't feel right that I was here, out enjoying myself, without her. We could barely afford to keep food on the table, let alone splash the kind of cash Kat was doing on wine. I couldn't help but think everything would have been different if we had the money. Our erratic finances always left a grim backdrop on our relationship, and it was hard to enjoy each other with so much worry.

Kat was looking at me with anticipation, aware that I was daydreaming. She smiled when my eyes focused on her. She was beautiful. I felt torn by the decision, but it had already been made. I was sitting here, after all. I just had to go with it and deal with the hand I'd been dealt. My attention was drawn from Kat for a brief second when I vaguely recognised a figure leaving the restaurant below.

"I don't believe it," I uttered.

"What?"

"That's my old boss, Neil. Right there. Paying the check at the counter. He must be meeting clients or something."

"Do you want to go and say hello?"

"God no, he is a wanker."

"Oh right, that kind of old boss." She said, laughing.

"Also, he is probably looking for me; I left a big, deep scratch in his car when he sacked me."

"You keyed his car?"

"Yep."

"That's a bit juvenile, isn't it?"

"I suppose it is, but I was angry."

"Well, between us, I think we can come up with something better than that."

Kat threw some cash down on the table and stood up. I stared up at her, bemused, as she beckoned me to follow her. We made our way down the stairs, stalking Neil through the tables. He left through the main entrance, waiting for a taxi to come and collect him. The valet radioed through some instructions when he saw Kat, and her car was delivered seconds later. We got in, watching Neil on the street.

"Kat, what are you planning here?"

"I don't know yet, but this is more fun than chain-eating bruschetta, right?"

"It depends. As long as you don't go too far."

"Too far? Me?"

Neil's taxi arrived, and Kat followed them a few cars behind. She weaved in and out of lanes, trying to keep line of sight on the taxi. I was panicked at first. I had no idea what she had planned. It quickly turned to excitement; Kat was so spontaneous and carefree. She giggled in anticipation as we travelled through the city in the hunt. We slowly made our way out of the city into a suburb largely filled with big, detached houses donning automatic gates. The taxi pulled up outside a house, and I could see Neil's pride and joy, his offensive red sports car, sitting in the driveway. Neil staggered his way up the driveway, obviously drunk. Kat slowly drove up the street, directly facing Neil's house, which was an unlit, private road. She drove down it and turned the car around to face the front of Neil's house.

"Come on, get out. I have an idea," Kat said.

We both exited the car, and she popped the boot open with a click of her car key. To my shock, the masked man's rifle was still in the boot. She put it over her shoulder whilst kicking her high heels off and climbed onto the top of the car. She aimed the rifle at Neil's house, taking her eye away from the crosshairs to gauge my reaction.

"Shall I do it?" She queried.

"Do what, exactly?"

"Take the shot, of course. Don't go all soft on me now."

"Kat, don't. Yes, he is a wanker, but he doesn't deserve this."

I genuinely didn't know if she was joking or not. There was being spontaneous, but this was erratic. I knew the thrill of killing someone all too well, but it was always in some level of self-defence. This would be crossing a line that we wouldn't be able to come back from. Neil was largely innocent; he certainly didn't deserve a bullet between his eyes. Kat looked at me with a huge smile on her face, willing me to give her the go-ahead. She was so hard to read she could have pulled the trigger at any moment. I hoped it was the single glass of red wine talking and it was all bravado.

"Come on, Sean, he deserves it."

"He really doesn't deserve it, Kat. Please, don't."

Something in her face changed. I saw the light fade from her eyes, overtaken by the darkness. Her glazed expression and furrowed brow terrified me. She wasn't joking, and I was too far away from her to physically stop what she was about to do. She returned her eye to the scope, inhaled deeply, and pressed the trigger firmly. Every mechanism in the rifle clunked and moved in preparation for firing. The barrel popped, followed by a flash. The bullet sped towards its intended target, and the casing landed tentatively at my feet.

"Bullseye," Kat whispered.

12

COLD TURKEY

I stood breathless, staring at Neil in his sitting room. Seconds had passed since Kat fired the bullet, but he was still sitting there, drinking beer. Kat was stifling a laugh as I turned to look at her.

"Did you miss?" I gasped.

"No," she laughed, "I wasn't aiming for him."

My eyes darted around Neil's property, looking for the impact, until I noticed the cracks on the windscreen of his car, originating from a perfect hole in the centre.

"Come up here," Kat requested.

I obliged. I made my way up the back of the car, and she handed me the rifle pointed directly at Neil's car. I looked through the scope; the bullet had travelled through the front and back windows, leaving a smouldering hole in his double garage door.

"Take a shot." She dared.

"I don't know, Kat; he might have kids in the house. I don't really know the guy."

"Ten points for hitting a headlight." She joked.

Despite my objections, her jovial pressure had worked. I, too, was feeling the effects of the glass of wine; I hadn't touched a drop in so long. I was definitely tipsy; my inhibitions dulled. I lined up the shot. I had only ever fired an air rifle when I was a kid, and I never thought I would be taking potshots at Neil's car. I pulled the trigger and watched the headlight shatter into pieces through the scope. She was right, this was fun.

"Now, the other one."

I took another shot at the remaining headlight. A second or so after the impact, the car alarm broke the silence of the street. It alerted Neil, who stood in his bay window, looking at his car from behind the glass. I followed his movements through the scope of the rifle. He set down his beer and broke into a lame jog towards his car. Neil noticed the damage and held his head in his hands, spinning around in circles, looking for the culprits. But we were hidden, shrouded in the darkness, just far enough away to be invisible.

Kat lay on the roof of the car next to me; I could hear her breathing become deeper and faster, so much so it made me back away from the scope to look at her. She was biting her own lip slightly, her hand mindlessly stroking the small of my back as we watched Neil frantically try to work out what had just happened. She inhaled deeply and turned to me.

"Put one between his eyes," Kat jested.

"No… I can't," I protested feebly.

Whilst maintaining eye contact, Kat had managed to worm her hand in between my thigh and the roof of the car and was suggestively snaking her it up my leg. She had me in the palm of her hand now, literally. It's pretty pathetic, but I probably would have done anything she asked at that moment. With every movement of her hand, I felt my trigger finger tighten, closer to firing. My heart was pounding so heavily it banged on the car like the beating of a drum. Tighter. The scope was still trained on the back of his head, but I was barely paying attention. Tighter. I felt the trigger mechanism creak slightly as it reached the brink. Kat's hand started moving faster.

"Do it, Sean." She whispered in my ear softly. I couldn't resist any longer. All my inhibitions had gone, and I pulled the trigger.

Click.

"Unlucky Sean, it looks like you are firing blanks." She teased.

"What just happened?" I gasped.

"The rifle only had three rounds left in the clip."

"Did you check?"

"Yeah, of course. But you did it. You pulled the trigger. Just to please me."

"I wasn't thinking straight."

"I've got to say, Sean, you looked real good pulling that trigger."

Neil was standing in his driveway on his phone, most likely to the police. We needed to get going. We couldn't be here when they arrived. He clearly had no idea we were here; he still had a gormless expression on his face, looking for the vandals. He didn't know how lucky he was to be still breathing. If Kat had miscounted the rounds in the clip, the contents of his head would have been splattered all over his ridiculous motor.

But I did it. I took the shot. The fact there were no rounds left in the rifle didn't change that. I was willing to kill him in cold blood. I flirted with the idea back in his office months before, but I never actually went through with it. All because Kat was urging me to do it. My moral compass was spinning out of control, and I couldn't decipher right from wrong. It almost felt like I had killed him; I must have intended to.

My actions that night marked a change in me; the darkness within me had grown in strength and influence. With every corpse I left and every selfish decision I made, I fed it. It was plump and strong. The balance in my mind was tilting in its favour. The darkness was taking over. I could have blamed Kat for goading me into it, but I wasn't strong enough to resist her.

"We should get going; the police will be here soon," I advised.

"Get back in the car." She ordered.

We sat back in the car, but Kat didn't start the engine. Her hand continued to snake up and down my thigh suggestively. I knew what she wanted to do, but it was dangerous; the police would be here any minute. She looked at me achingly but didn't make a further move until the police arrived. The blue lights cavorted across her face and chest, her late husband's necklace sparkling coldly. She bit her lip again slightly and lowered her head into my lap.

It was safe to say my attention was diverted somewhat from watching the police. They were just speaking to Neil and assessing the damage. It was nowhere near as interesting as what was going on inside this car. Just as Kat was about to read me my rights, a torchlight beamed through the windshield. A police officer in a high visibility jacket was slowly making his way up the private road to investigate our car. We were about to get caught.

"Kat, stop, there is someone coming."

"Shh."

The police officer made it to the car window just in time to see me scrabbling about, trying to get redressed, and Kat laughing. He knocked on the passenger side window with his torch, signalling me to open it.

"You do know it is an offence to do that in public, sir." The officer said.

"I know, I'm sorry."

"Private road. Not in public," Kat interjected.

"Even so, you shouldn't be doing that here."

"We are sorry, officer, we'll leave," I stated.

"Before you go anywhere, did you see what happened to that gentleman's car whilst you were… here?"

"No, officer, we were a bit indisposed," Kat answered.

"Do you mind if I take a look in the vehicle? It looks like a firearm was involved."

"Do we look like the kind of people to have a firearm, officer?" Kat charmed.

"I don't know. Please get out of the car. We need to take a look, and then you can be on your way."

Kat and I both got out of the car; on my exit, I noticed two of the round casings still on the ground, subtly shimmering in the blue of the police lights. I kicked them underneath the car whilst the officer poked around. He tried the boot, but it was locked.

"Ma'am, can you open the boot?" The officer asked politely.

"Sure," Kat responded.

"Kat?" I gasped.

She went over to the boot casually and opened it in front of the officer. I walked over to see the boot completely empty.

"See, nothing there. Are we free to leave, officer?" Kat asked.

"Don't let us catch you here again." The officer warned.

"You won't, officer," I assured, "we will be on our way."

We both got in the car, and Kat slowly drove down the private road. Once we got onto the main road, she started laughing uncontrollably.

"Where the hell is the rifle?" I questioned.

"I threw it in the bushes, relax," Kat deflected.

"What if they find it? It will have our prints all over it."

"I wiped it down first. You worry too much."

"I just don't want to get arrested; we have both killed people. God knows how many lives that rifle has claimed."

"Did you not think it was exciting?"

Did I think it was exciting? To me, the act alone was enough, but Kat seemed to need something beyond the vanilla. I must admit, I had acquired a taste for it too. She was slowly easing me into her world. It was exciting and lawless. Everything in it was caught in Kat's gravitational influence. It was scary, but I could feel myself almost becoming dependent on it.

"Yes, it was exciting. Mainly, I think I am just excited by you."

"Wow there, Sean, don't be catching feelings."

Maybe I was catching feelings. I didn't know. Was Kat a rebound? Probably. I had met her in the worst time of my life, and she was the polar opposite of what I was used to. My mind raced just thinking about the journey we had been on together in such a short time. But where did that journey end? I took a leaf out of Kat's book and lived in the moment. The dark secrets between us had formed a bond like no other. There hasn't been a label invented for the kind of relationship we were in. The faint line between the dark and light in our relationship was becoming blurred, and the darkness leached into the light and visa-versa. We were stuck in the huge grey area between them, and I didn't know right from wrong anymore.

"I won't," I hesitated.

"Good," she replied, looking slightly miffed, "I won't either."

We were back in the city. Kat pulled into the entrance of the car park for a fancy-looking hotel. The entire building was made of glass, and warm, welcoming lighting poured through it onto the street below. Huge sandstone statues stood outside like security guards, stopping anyone without at least a six-figure income from entering. I had never stayed in a place as nice as this. We parked up, and Kat walked through the revolving doors like she owned the place. For all I knew, she could do. She walked straight over to reception to arrange a room.

I intentionally stood at a distance, watching her. She was truly stunning. I couldn't believe she was interested in me. She had taught me so much about myself. Sure, it was mainly to do with murder or sex, but deep down, I had already caught feelings. I felt ludicrous for feeling that way, but the way we met was so intense I couldn't be blamed for how I felt.

Kat's offhand comment about catching feelings made me think. The thought pierced the veil of the fantasy I had lived that evening. My moral compass steadied, and I knew what I had to do. I couldn't let it go any further. A causal affair was wrong enough, but I couldn't fall for her. I flicked a switch in my head; it was painful, but I couldn't see her again. Not in this context, anyway. I needed to patch things up with Courtney. I needed my family back. That was the best thing for me, and my current course would only end badly. I made my way over to Kat and delicately put my hand on her arm.

"Kat, I'm sorry, but I need to go."

"Oh, why?"

"I just need some time to clear my head. Things are moving really fast. I'm sorry."

"Are you not having fun?"

"More than I ever have in my life, but it's not about that."

"Then what is it about?

I hadn't lied to Kat before, not about anything serious, and I shouldn't start now. I had already made that mistake with Courtney. She deserved the honesty; I did have feelings for her. But I couldn't understand them. They shouldn't be as strong as they are. That's what scared me more than anything. I was going down a path I shouldn't be travelling down.

"Before, I said I wouldn't catch feelings, but I already have. I haven't even processed what has happened with Courtney yet, and this is moving too quickly for me. I'm sorry," I explained.

"Okay, I get it, Sean, I really do. And I feel the same way. I know I make jokes, but let me be serious; when you find a connection like ours, you grip it with two hands. And you don't let go. You never know when it might be taken from you." She said with tears in her eyes.

"I appreciate you saying that. I feel the same. But I need to think about it before we go any further. I hope you understand."

"I do. Do you need dropping off?"

"No, I can make my own way home."

Kat gave me a restrained kiss on the cheek and an ardent hug. I left the lobby. It looked like I wouldn't be staying in a place that nice after all. I held my hand out to hail a taxi. The lights of the city at night were dulled without Kat next to me. Colours turned to greys. Kat was addictive, but I had decided to go cold turkey. I knew it was the right thing to do, so why did it hurt so much to do it? We were at the beginning of something dark and beautiful, but the intensity scared me off. In the end, it was my own feelings that had terrified me the most.

By the time I returned home, I was completely miserable. I should have stayed with Kat. But I reminded myself assertively I'd made the right choice, possibly for the first time since all this began. The house was cold and empty. I shivered my way up the stairs and fell flat on my face in bed. Courtney looked at me from the photo frame on the side of the bed. It was a photo from our honeymoon in Spain. I barely recognised either of us; we were so happy.

It was nine years ago. If you took the photo and compared it to us now, you would see every single day of those nine years etched into our faces. I gripped the photograph tightly, hoping to somehow get sucked back into it so I had another shot at making it work. The glass cracked under the pressure of my thumbs, leaving an ironic split in the glass between us.

I woke the next morning, still clutching the photograph. I had a few minutes of clarity outside of Kat's influence and knew what I had to do. Courtney said it was over, and I believed her. But I had to fight for her. I had taken the easy way out and let her leave. I needed to fight for her with the same vigour as when I had fought the masked men. I had learned in the last few months that I was capable of far more than I realised. If I channelled the darkness into the light, I could use my inner strength for something good. Something right.

I got a shower, trying to wash every drop of Kat's scent from my skin before I prepared to find Courtney and win her back. I stared into the mirror in preparation. I was nervous about seeing my wife for the first time in years. It felt amazing but made me sick to my stomach. This was what she wanted, after all. To be fought for. It took me a while to realise it, but I was ready to finally give her what she needed.

I got in the car, and the radio came on halfway through the breakfast news. I pulled out of the parking space and made my way down the road towards Courtney's mum's house. The radio was turned down quite low, but something piqued my interest, so I turned it up to listen.

"—were called to the property earlier that evening to investigate some damage done to the victim's car," the radio said, "unfortunately, after reports of a further disturbance at the address, officers returned to the scene to find the man beaten to death in his home. City Police are yet to make an official statement."

I slammed on the brakes, forcing the car behind me to swerve onto the other side of the road to avoid my car. He beeped as he passed me, and I sat there entirely still. The explained scenario was almost identical to what Kat and I did to Neil last night, but they hadn't mentioned his name in the report. It couldn't have been him, but it was too much of a coincidence. I turned in the road in the direction of Neil's house. Before I saw Courtney, I had to check for my own sanity.

I barely got down his street before I saw the mass of police vehicles and press vans. The entire street had been taped off. I parked at the curbside in shock, hoping to see Neil making his way through the crowd. Even though I hated the guy, he didn't deserve this. A few smashed headlights were one thing, but the police would have combed the area for evidence if there was a body. They would have found the rifle, probably with mine and Kat's prints on it.

I got out my phone to message Kat. I needed to speak with her urgently; Courtney would have to wait again. We were still using the 'B-Run' app to communicate. I never thought to ask for her number.

> *Neil has been killed.*
> *You aren't involved, are you?*

Don't speak on here.
We need to meet.

> *Okay. Where?*

Where we first met. x

I turned in the road and made my way to the bridge where I first met Kat. I honestly had no idea if she was involved or not, but I knew she was dangerous. Did she see it was some twisted way of garnering my affection after my rejection last night? I didn't think she would be physically capable of the brutal beating the radio had described, but who knows what she was truly capable of. I arrived at the bridge and found Kat's car already parked there. I parked nose-to-nose with her car and made my way down the steps onto the canal. She stood there, as beautiful as ever, with a bright smile. She walked over to give me a hug, which I accepted hesitantly.

"What's happened, Sean?" She asked calmly.

"Neil has been beaten to death in his house. A few hours after we were there."

"That's awful," she began, "do the police have any leads or anything?"

"I don't know, I haven't spoken to them."

"That's good."

"It's not good, Kat. Please tell me you weren't involved."

Kat stepped back, incredibly offended by what I just said. She placed her hand on her hip and shot me a patronising look, waiting for me to recant what I had just said. I didn't think it was much of a jump from what we did to him to actual murder. She did want me to pull the trigger on him for a start.

"No, Sean, I wasn't involved."

"Well, who the hell did it then? It's too much of a coincidence."

"Really? You even have to ask that?"

"I'm not following."

"It's the masked men."

I hadn't even considered they could have done something like this, but it was their modus operandi. But we weren't followed. I must have checked that private road a hundred times before we even started firing the rifle. Why would they target Neil? They could have been watching us the entire time, following us from the restaurant. It made me feel sick knowing we were being watched.

"No one followed us. And why would they attack Neil? They have been after us."

"Think about it, Sean. You had a motive. He sacked you. You were at the scene hours earlier; they are setting you up."

"There is no way they could know all that."

"Sean," she sighed, "they obviously know a lot more than we think."

Maybe she was right. They had been ahead of us at every turn. This was a definite change in tactics, but for now, they hadn't worked. I hadn't touched the app the night before, though, so they must have been following us physically. Kat looked at me with a deep sadness on her face. She wasn't one to mince words; I rarely had to wonder what she was thinking. She took a deep breath, and a wry smile spanned her face.

"When I saw your name on my phone, I thought you wanted to talk about us." She explained tenderly.

"No, I'm sorry. And I'm sorry about last night."

"Have you thought about us?"

"Yes, but I need more time."

"I can wait, Sean, but I won't wait forever."

"I know. Thank you."

Kat started to kick at the gravel with her feet idly. I hadn't seen her so emotionally frail before. I wondered if I had made yet another mistake. The darkness inside me was already in love with her, but she was luring the light side, too. The dichotomy of our relationship was the most terrifying and beautiful thing about this. And as warped as it was, it kind of worked.

"No more advances. I'll take it slow; I promise. But we need to deal with the masked men before they deal with us." She reaffirmed.

"I know. I'll send you a message later."

"Give me your phone," she asked, "here is my number. Stop using the app to message; we shouldn't use it to talk."

Kat put her number on my phone and then put both of her hands on my cheeks; she leaned in to kiss but remembered her promise only seconds earlier. She playfully tapped me on the nose and sullenly trudged up the steps to her car. Great, now I was upsetting two women.

13

UNLUCKY FOR SOME

Neil's death had rattled me. When I got home and put on the television, it was all over every news channel. The beating sounded absolutely gruesome. There still wasn't a police statement. I stood in the kitchen watching the door, waiting for the familiar knock of DS Banks waiting to arrest me. They had taken my prints after Jordan's death, so if a single print remained on that rifle, I was done.

I must have spent weeks staring at the door, only leaving the house for the occasional run to keep my bank balance healthy. I went a few times with Kat, but we didn't encounter the masked men again. They were waiting silently in the shadows, watching their plan play out. In some ways, it was even more terrifying than them just chasing us. Kat and I had both given up hope that we would find them again; they had a different game plan now. I got the impression that Kat was using it as an excuse to see me, but I could see the desire fade from her eyes on every visit. It had definitely cooled off.

Part of me thought this was their plan to drive a wedge between me and Kat. After everything that had happened, we had become close, but my rejection had definitely dampened things. Kat didn't seem fazed by Neil's murder and wasn't worried about it getting pinned on us. They hadn't announced they had found the rifle; the masked men probably cleaned up after us once again and removed it from the scene. It was theirs, to be fair.

I still hadn't spoken to Courtney. Neil's murder had thrown a spanner in the works, and I couldn't risk the masked men following me to her mum's house. For now, I had to suspend my efforts to win her back. I wouldn't be able to live with myself if anything violent happened to them. I was still trying to protect them, even if they didn't know it.

That's half true. In all honesty, I didn't know what I wanted. Or who I wanted. I had imprisoned myself slap bang in the middle between both women, both worlds, waiting for a way of somehow merging the two. I wanted Kat's excitement and spontaneity with Courtney's normalcy and steadiness, but that combination couldn't co-exist. It was an impossible decision; I was waiting for it to be made for me without my input.

I managed to arrange a few awkward phone calls with Dylan, supervised by my soon-to-be ex-mother-in-law. All contact was to be through her; Courtney didn't want to see or speak to me. It was pretty rough. The closest thing to contact I received from her was seeing the monthly deposits drop into our joint account to help cover the bills. I actually started to look forward to it. I used to check the reference to see if she had left a message for me, but she never did.

The divorce papers had come through. They sat there on the kitchen table, still enclosed in the brown envelope they arrived in. I hadn't signed them yet; putting pen to paper felt like accepting defeat. But I was so exhausted by it. My wife became an elusive figure; I knew her less than I would know a stranger. She wasn't pressuring me to sign the papers, though. A part of me saw it as a hint, and I hoped we could still somehow rekindle what little we had left.

Spring had turned to summer. Running in the heat was a different beast entirely, but we had many more daylight hours. I had taken to running on my own again. It was a different flavour of solitude to that of staying in the house on my own. Less bitter. I had lost my love of running, too; my senses had been overstimulated by the events of the past six months. Kat looked the same; whenever we shared the canal together, she looked almost bored. And boring Kat was a cardinal sin. Her messages were less frequent now, too. She was losing interest.

I got ready for my early morning run on what would be the hottest day of the year. I started going at the crack of dawn to avoid being baked in the sun. The daybreak beauty of the canal was the only thing that gave me a slight mood boost. Watching the sun dance on the water as I jogged past. I usually made it to Jordan's bridge and stopped. The thud of the app in my ears only added to the boredom. Its monotone rhythm dulled my other senses. I ran on autopilot, with no desire to go faster or farther. I did the bare minimum to cover our bills, and that was it.

I reached the final approach to Jordan's bridge fairly quickly. My pace was still improving, even though I wasn't trying. I could see from a distance that a bunch of flowers had been left there. This was the first time I had seen anything left there in his memory. Somebody missed him. I felt a pang of guilt when I saw them, another preventable death at the hands of the masked men.

The flowers were propped up against the wall with a card attached. It was a vibrant bouquet of greens and purples, not in the same league as the petrol station flowers that I often got Courtney at the last minute before some occasion. I crouched down to inspect them. Part of me didn't want to read the message that had been left for fear it would have brought everything back up. But the card wasn't addressed to Jordan or his family.

It was addressed to me.

'Sean' was written on the envelope in ornate, calligraphic writing. There was no one I passed on the canal and no one beyond the bridge. I had no idea how long these flowers had been there, but they had been left for me. I opened the envelope slowly, not knowing what to expect from its contents. The envelope was heavier than I initially expected, much heavier than a standard card or letter. I opened the flaps of the envelope, revealing a grainy, black-and-white photograph.

I barely recognised her at first. It was a long lens shot of a woman casually eating dinner at a restaurant. Her dining partner was obscured by the foliage outside. She was smiling. Gripping a half-finished glass of red wine, enjoying herself.

It was Courtney. She had moved on.

It was like staring through the window of my own life years prior. I remembered that smile. I hadn't seen it in a while, but I knew she was happy. She had her hair done like she had when we first met. Silky brunette curls thrown back in laughter. Just seeing her like that made me smile initially before I realised it wasn't me sitting across from her, but someone not known to me.

To be clear, I knew I had no right to be angry. We were separated. But the darkness snarled in the pit of my stomach, battling to be released. It bared its teeth, pleading with me for liberty. I wanted to rip apart the next person I saw. My wrath only grew when my attention turned to who had left this for me. The thought loitered in my mind, left just out of reach of my howling rage. I emptied the rest of the contents onto the ground beneath me. A blood-stained steel scalpel and a single bullet casing. It was a calling card. The masked men had been watching my every move since the beginning and continued to do so.

They no longer wanted to just kill me. They wanted to obliterate me. They were now operating from the shadows; we had dwindled their numbers, but they still played their sick game without relenting. On the back of the photograph was a scrawled address. I recognised it; it was the warehouse I had been held captive in. The intention was surely two-fold: they wanted to rattle me about Courtney moving on, and it was a threat. A personal invitation to an esteemed ambush, and I was the guest of honour. They wanted to knock me off balance and make me act compulsively, and it worked. I wanted to tear them asunder.

The anger fizzled away back into sadness as I continued to study the photograph. Courtney had made her decision. She was loyal, and she wouldn't have taken the decision to see someone else lightly. It wasn't a revelation, but she deserved better than me. She always did. Dylan deserved a father figure. Every time in recent memory she asked if we could go out for a meal, I gave her some excuse about money. She deserved someone who would look after her in ways I couldn't. I needed to let her go. I still loved her, and this was the best thing for her. Courtney needed to be far away from the chaos I had become. I called her to give a warning, but she didn't answer; it went straight to voicemail.

"Courtney, I know you don't want to speak to me, so just listen. I will sign the paperwork, but you need to get out of town for a few days. I can't explain why just now, just trust me," I warned.

Even after what I just saw, I needed to know Courtney and Dylan would be safe. The rage I felt towards her was misplaced. This was my fault. Everything was my fault. Every death or bad thing that happened to me that year could be traced back to my terrible decisions. I needed to speak to Kat, but I'd already asked so much of her. She would know what to do.

> *Kat, I need to see you.*
> *Urgently.*

> *Are you okay?*

> *Yes, I'm near the bridge.*

> *Give me ten minutes. xxx*

I stood at Kat's bridge, holding the envelope and flowers, waiting for her. I hadn't realised the connotation until I saw her beaming face when she pulled up on the bridge. She left the car, arms stretched out in a hug and threw herself into me.

"Sean, I'm so glad you messaged," She gleamed, "I've missed you."

"I've missed you too, Kat."

"Are these for me?"

"Oh god, no, sorry," I said awkwardly.

"Oh?" She said, deflated.

"It's a lead. They were left for me on the path with this."

I handed her the items, and she looked so saddened. She had likely been waiting for that moment, the cheesy moment in a film where the guy realised what he was missing and turned up with flowers and a boom box. Her face changed to a puzzled expression. She studied the items closely, but she was not sure what to make of them.

"That's Courtney," I pointed out, "that is the scalpel I used when I escaped the warehouse, and that is the bullet casing from when we shot up Neil's car."

"This is the scalpel you used to kill that man?" She asked tentatively.

"Yes, I dropped it there when I escaped."

She almost stroked the scalpel, feeling how sharp it was, examining it, deep in thought. I could see the cogs turning in her head.

"So, this is from the masked men. Is that an address?"

"Yes, it's the warehouse."

"Well, it's obviously a trap. We can't go there without some kind of plan."

"We?"

"Of course, we. I wouldn't let you face them alone, Sean." She reassured.

As anarchic as Kat was, I knew I could depend on her. I felt like I was somehow manipulating her, but this was as much her fight as mine. At this point, I didn't know who had corrupted who.

"I see Courtney has moved on too. Does that mean you are back on the market?" She half-joked.

"I wanted to speak to you about that, too," I confessed.

"Oh, so as soon as she is out of the picture, I'm the next best option?" She scoffed.

"No, you were never second best. I was just confused. But I know now that it's over between Courtney and I. Kat, you are the best thing that happened to me at the absolute worst time of my life. You kept me going. I've made some awful choices, and the way I've gone about things was terrible, but I know what I want now."

I barely identified the words coming out of my mouth as my own. I had never been this open with Courtney. Kat and I had a connection forged in darkness but strengthened in the light. In only a few short months, she knew every corner of me. She knew my soul. I couldn't ignore that. It was time to accept Courtney was gone for good.

"Say more nice things," Kat smiled coyly.

"You are scary. You are amazing. I have fallen for you," I uttered nervously.

"I've fallen for you too."

Kat gripped me lovingly in a tight embrace, a toast to our gorgeously toxic relationship. Coconut and vanilla. The smell of her golden hair wafted in my nostrils and satiated the darkness within me. The sun, now in full radiance, highlighted every pore of her immaculate complexion as she leaned back to look into my eyes. I had never seen her look so happy; her eyes became dewy as they glowed into mine. The desire was back, definitely.

"But first," she said, her tone turning serious, "we need to deal with this. We get rid of them, and we can finally be happy."

"I can't wait."

We both got in the car so Kat could drop me off to get changed. During the entire car journey, Kat barely took her eyes off me, smirking at me. It was a miracle we didn't get into a car crash because she was barely paying attention to the road. It felt good to have her affections again; it was something that I had been missing. The period of going cold turkey was over, and I was back on the hard stuff. There was so much tension between us the past few weeks, largely because I had called it off. My own feelings vindicated the decision to choose Kat; I felt happy and comfortable I'd done the right thing.

When we arrived home, I could see she wanted to come in; the same burning desire before our first encounter crackled in her eyes. I saw her holding it back. We needed to take care of business first and keep our minds on the task at hand.

We had arranged to meet at the industrial estate where the warehouse was situated later that evening. Kat suggested that we should both get a taxi there under false names to avoid an evidence trail; she was smart like that. Kat got out of her car and was dressed entirely in black.

She had a large duffel bag with her; she dropped it on the ground in front of me with a heavy thud and gave me an impassioned kiss. We waited for the taxi to disappear onto the main road before speaking.

"Fancy seeing you here." She smiled.

"What a coincidence," I jested.

"Are you ready to do this?"

"Yes, what's in there?"

"A rifle."

"I thought you got rid of it?"

"I got another."

"Why?"

"Oh, I don't know. Maybe because they have been trying to kill us, Sean, we need to protect ourselves."

"I suppose it can't hurt to have it in case of an emergency."

"This is an emergency, Sean. We are ending this tonight." She asserted.

It always gave me butterflies whenever she was so serious. She was right, of course. This was the final showdown. It was them or us again. We had no idea what waited for us in the warehouse, but we had no other recourse than to face them head-on. Kat was the ace up my sleeve; they wouldn't be expecting her, and certainly not when she was armed to the teeth.

"We will scope the place out. You walk through the front door, and I'll find another entrance to cover you." She planned.

"So, I'm the bait. Fantastic."

"It's worked before. Don't worry. I won't let them lay a finger on you. I have been practising."

"All I have is this knife."

"Here," she said, handing me the taser, "take this too."

I was walking back into an obvious trap with a butter knife and a glorified bug zapper. I trusted Kat to protect me, but I was still shaking. I didn't know if I was trembling in fear or in excitement for it to be finally over. We skulked outside the warehouse for a few minutes, and there were no comings and goings. The for-sale sign had been ripped off the fence and lay deserted on the ground. There were lights on in the warehouse, but they didn't illuminate any signs of life.

I felt sick seeing the warehouse again. It brought back the painful memories of being held there. I could have quite easily never walked out of that warehouse. God knows what they had planned for me. It reaffirmed what we were doing was the correct course of action. I couldn't have been the only victim; they were going to keep doing this until somebody stopped them. We silently walked through the empty car park, where we both splintered off in different directions. Kat pointed to the left; she had spotted some ladders leading to a door on the upper level. It would be a perfect vantage point. I tried the reception door; it had been left unlocked for me. It was definitely a trap, but knowing Kat would have my back gave me the confidence to enter.

What happened to this place? The couches had been slashed to pieces in some apparent fit of rage. The expelled stuffing from the upholstery rolled around the ground like a tumbleweed in the breeze from the open door. The desk had been smashed up into firewood. The once spotless décor was now dominated by a huge mural spray painted onto the plaster. It was the bleeding foot logo from the 'B-Run' app.

I was standing at the door to the warehouse, with my hand firmly gripping the handle. I turned it slowly, with my eyes half closed, expecting an immediate ambush. The emergency lights in the warehouse were the only ones illuminated; the eery glow they produced barely allowed me to see a few metres in front of my face. I was convinced I could see movement all around me, but it was a trick of the light. I walked aimlessly through the dim walkways the gaps in the racking provided. At every crossroads, I expected to be jumped and dragged into the shadows. I prayed that Kat had reached some kind of vantage point and was tracking my movements.

I reached the approximate centre of the warehouse floor, and all the lights illuminated dramatically. Three of the masked men stood in front of me, dressed for the occasion in their usual garb. Baseball-bat man had obviously rejoined their ranks since his release from police custody. He batted at his free hand with the bat threateningly, pacing on the spot. The other two stood still in front of me, not speaking a word.

"Well, I'm here just like you wanted. Now what?" I shouted, gripping the meagre arsenal concealed in my pocket.

The man in the middle walked forward a few steps, breaking the line. I prayed that Kat had found a suitable place to cover me. The man reached into his pockets and pulled out a bundle of zip ties.

"Well, Mr Miller. We are here to resume what we started before you so rudely escaped from here." He calmly threatened.

I vaguely recognised his voice from my previous stint in captivity here. He must have been the leader. They were down to three of them now. We had killed three of them, what's three more, I thought. Baseball-bat man was itching to come at me; he could barely keep still. The leader turns to him and holds up his hand, gesturing for him to calm down.

"I'll come quietly, but I want answers first. And you need to leave my family out of this."

"Fine, not that it matters. You will be dead soon. What do you want to know?"

"Who are you?"

"My name is Victor. I'm in charge."

"Why me?"

The man laughed through his balaclava before pulling it up slightly to expose the bottom half of his face. The question had obviously amused him, so he turned to his associates to get a response from them, but they remained entirely emotionless.

"You were on the list." Victor sighed.

"What list?"

"Your precious exercise tracking app."

"I was chosen at random?"

"We live in the digital age, Sean. You would be amazed what any teenager with a laptop could hack into. We steal that data and sell it to the highest bidder."

"To do what with?"

"Whatever they like. Your pal Jordan, for instance, would have been a decent earner if you hadn't intervened. We connect rich psychopaths to their victims. They let us know of any 'special requests', and we are happy to oblige. The weirder the request, the higher the price."

"You are sickos."

"True. But we get a lot more money in return for your life than the crumbs you collect on your runs. And this one is personal. You and your little bit on the side have killed some of my associates. We are going to sell you and sell you cheap, to the sickest one we can find."

They knew about Kat. I prayed that this man's head was in the centre of her rifle scope. I willed her to pull the trigger. I held the taser in my pocket tightly. The previously unarmed masked man had revealed a pistol from his inside pocket and had it trained on me. Victor was making his way over to me, preparing the zip ties. I believed every word he said. This would be the end of me if Kat didn't come through.

Pop.

The man holding the pistol dropped it to the ground, blood erupting from his chest. He slumped to the floor almost immediately with a wet thud, prompting Victor to turn and look at him.

Pop.

Blood sprays across my face from Victor's back. I can taste the iron content as the mist hangs in the air before falling with him to the floor. The bundle of zip ties he was holding scattered across the concrete in every direction.

Pop.

Baseball-bat man got hit right between the eyes. He propelled backwards in the air, landing flat on his back like a dead weight. I stood there, inhaling the cocktail of the men's blood suspended in the air, staring at the trio of corpses in front of me. The smell should have been disgusting, but it tasted sweet. It was finally over. Kat had managed to take them all out inside a few seconds.

I owed her my life.

14

A NEW CHAPTER

K at came running towards me from beyond the cadavers, ignoring them completely and slamming into me in an embrace. The blood from my face tainted her blonde hair, staining it pink. She grabbed my head, frantically kissing me, not dissuaded by the blood. I remained frozen, unable to process what had just happened.

"We did it, Sean." She gasped in between kisses.

"You did it."

"We both did it. I'm just so happy you are safe, and it's finally over."

"Are they really gone?"

"Yes, they are gone."

The men were almost gliding in the pool of blood behind Kat. The image itself was harrowing and something I wouldn't forget. Three men had lost their lives that night, all because of a bit of money. Baseball-bat man wasn't much older than Jordan. What decisions had he made which landed him dead on this warehouse floor? Part of me felt bad for them and for the choices they had made to put them in Kat's sights. But these men had terrorised us all year, threatened my life, Kat's life and my family's lives. They deserved what happened to them, right? It could have quite easily been us on the ground, our blood leaching into the porous concrete, before being shipped off to God knows where. We weren't their first victims, but we ensured we would be their last.

Regardless of how I felt about it, the threat was finally extinguished; the proof lay dead on the floor before us. I convinced myself that they weren't human. We had simply slain the monsters pursuing us. If I hadn't done that, I would have probably been sick right there and then. Kat didn't seem too bothered about taking the lives of these men, and maybe I should have taken a leaf out of her book. She seemed more concerned that I was okay, gripping me harder than anyone had ever done before.

We remained embraced before the realisation dawned on us: we were standing at a crime scene. There would be no explaining this away to the police, considering there were three blood-soaked dead bodies on the floor.

"We need to burn it," Kat said calmly, "to the ground. We can't leave a trace."

"You are right."

We desperately searched around the warehouse to find something to set it ablaze. There was a small fuel depot that hadn't been completely emptied, used for fuelling up forklifts. We both took a canister, distributing the fluid everywhere we could. With each drop that hit the floor, it gradually cleansed us of our sins. We were going to survive this. Kat emptied one of the canisters on the dead men she had left, and the petrol left a thick rainbow-coloured film on the stagnant pool of blood underneath them. It was deeply cathartic, eradicating the past year's worth of fear and anxiety with a couple of gallons of flammable liquid. We created a stream leading outside, where Kat produced a fancy engraved lighter.

"I didn't know you smoked," I mused.

"I don't. It was my husbands." She said dryly.

"Sorry."

"Do you want to do the honours?"

The lighter was a lot heavier than I thought it would be, ornate and meticulously well-crafted. The casing had been engraved with skulls and hearts surrounding the inscription, 'Kat'. She had obviously gifted this to her husband. I looked at her, and she had tears in her eyes, avoiding eye contact with me. She was using this as an opportunity to say goodbye to her husband again, and this was way more cathartic to her than me. She had so much anger in her, layered with an overwhelming melancholy. I held the lighter in my palm as she avoided eye contact with me, just gazing at the profile of her face.

"Are you sure you don't want to, Kat?" I asked.

"No, do it, please." She mumbled.

I cast the lighter through the open doors of the reception area into the combustible stream we had created. The fluid ignited blue, racing through the doors, igniting everything in its path. It obliterated everything that it touched, decimating it quickly back into ash. We stood there for a moment, and I watched the wall where the bleeding foot had been sprayed set ablaze. The flames danced around the mural for a minute before the paint surrendered to the heat and started to bubble and crack.

Kat and I rushed out of the car park as plumes of thick black smoke exited through the broken windows of the warehouse. My survival instinct urged me to sprint all the way home, but I needed to see the warehouse burn to ashes. I needed to know it was definitely over. We retreated to the distant safety of the canal path and watched it burn; the skyline glowed red in the flames.

With a huge bang and a fireball emanating from the now collapsing roof, the warehouse began to crumble in on itself. The spirals of thick black smoke blacked out every star in the sky as it travelled upwards into oblivion. Kat's sombre expression broke into a slight smile as we heard the approaching sirens. We broke out into a casual jog down the path towards home.

I thought about her husband, a man I'd never met or would ever meet. I didn't know anything about him, but we shared something in common: we both loved this woman. Did he see the darkness in her, too? Or was that born in his death? Kat had an unfathomable depth to her;

I had merely breached the surface and was looking into it, unable to see the bottom. Behind the lewd comments and confident exterior was a profoundly sad woman. I didn't know what I could do to help her feel any better, but I knew I never wanted to ever make her feel that way.

Kat's black ensemble gave her the appearance of a panther, eloquently striding through the darkness. Breathtakingly beautiful but incredibly dangerous, I admired her form at a slight distance, effortlessly gliding through the night with each footfall. I owed her my life and probably the lives of my family. I was worried the foundation of the peculiar relationship we had built was solely based on the fight against Victor and his masked men. Hopefully, there would be enough left for it to still work between us. I psychically shook the insecurities from my head. I didn't need to think about that now. I had to live in the moment, like Kat had taught me.

We arrived home, and Kat gave me a look. I knew what she wanted. She didn't need to say words to me anymore. The silent bond between us was louder than ever. I took the driving seat this time, tenderly pulling her inside and upstairs to the bedroom. We were so desperate to consummate this new chapter in our relationship we didn't even wash away the grime and blood. I had noticed a change in her that night; maybe it was an imperceptible microexpression or a subtle suggestion in her eyes, but she had let go of something. She was reinvested in us, and in this strange connection we had found, it felt good to be on the receiving end of it.

The next morning, my eyes opened to see Kat's eyes staring right back at me, smiling. I could hear birds singing outside. I had no idea what time it was, but there was nowhere else in the world I would rather be. Everything felt right again. Normally, I would wake up and have a glorious sixty seconds before I remembered the threat we were facing, but this morning, to my delight, my mind was clear.

"Good morning, sunshine," Kat warmly said with a smile.

"Morning, what time is it?"

"Does it matter?"

"It really doesn't."

Kat's smile had temporarily wiped any memory of the night before from my mind. I gazed longingly into her blue eyes, lost in time and space. But the usual sensual scent of her hair had been replaced by the smell of the smoke from the night before. The memories of the night before flooded back into focus, bringing the nausea with them. I felt like I was recalling the actions of someone else. That morning was a stark contrast to the evening before it.

"Shall we talk about last night?" I asked.

"Which part?"

"The bad part."

"There was a bad part?" She joked.

"Do you think it's really over?" I asked.

"Yes. We got them all and burned the place to the ground. It's definitely—"

She was interrupted by the sound of my phone ringing. It was Courtney. I started awkwardly at Kat, showing her the name on my phone screen. The smile slipped from her face into an eye roll, but she got out of bed to give me some privacy. I had forgotten about the frantic voicemail I had left for Courtney.

"Hi, Courtney," I said gingerly.

"What the hell was that voicemail last night? Are you trying to scare me to death?" She screamed.

"I'm sorry Courtney… I'd had a bit to drink."

"Oh, date night, was it?"

"Something like that."

"So, you and that fancy woman are just having a drink and leaving me terrifying voicemails together?"

"No, it wasn't like that."

"Sean, I don't even know what you are trying to do anymore. Just stay out of my life." She scolded as she hung up the call.

"I will," I whispered.

I would have explained to her the real reason, but what was the point? She wouldn't have believed me anyway. The only thing that mattered was that she was safe. Our marriage may have been over, but I needed to give her the warning, at least. I was walking a new path now with Kat; Courtney and I were both moving on. I heard the shower running. At least Kat didn't overhear the awkward exchange. I was debating whether or not to join her when there was a knock at the door. I recognise the tune. I hastily put some clothes on and ran downstairs to open it. DS Banks, sweating profusely in the sun but mysteriously still wearing his peacoat, stood there waiting for me to invite him in.

"Can I come in, Sean?"

I nodded and ushered him into the kitchen. Kat joined us seconds later, wearing one of my long t-shirts and a towel wrapped over her hair. DS Banks looked alarmed at first but quickly realised what was going on and gave me an awkward, knowing look.

"There was a fire last night. Did you hear about it?" DS Banks questioned.

"No, we've just got out of bed."

"I can see. The rubble is extensive, but we have recovered a body. It's the man you caught on the canal."

"Oh?"

"Do you know anything about that?"

"Nope."

"We were a little busy last night, officer," Kat interjected, running her fingers up and down my neck suggestively. DS Banks actually started to blush.

"Well, with the only suspect now deceased, we will be closing your case. And the case for Jordan."

"That's good," I said thoughtlessly.

"Good? A man is dead, Sean. And you didn't get any justice."

"Well, if he was responsible for Jordan's murder and my attack, it sounds like justice to me. Good riddance."

DS Banks looked shocked by my response; it threw him off guard. I didn't care anymore. The charade was over. This was the new me. I wouldn't be seeing him again, so it didn't matter. Any evidence pinning us to the fire or any of the deaths of the men had burned to ash. In a split second, I'd made my decision; I didn't feel guilty about their deaths. Not one bit. It couldn't have gone any other way. Kat gave me a knowing look; we were finally on the same page about it.

"Fine," he muttered, "well, I was just letting you know." DS Banks stood up from the table and moved over to the door to leave.

"I'll leave you to… whatever this is. Send my regards to Mrs. Miller." He said, exiting the house. Kat stared at me, stifling a laugh, until she heard the front door open and close, and then she finally released it.

"Send my regards to Mrs. Miller," Kat mocked, "what a self-reverential prick."

"He is only doing his job, Kat," I defended.

"Yeah, right. If he was any good at it, there wouldn't be three bodies in that warehouse."

"I suppose."

"We did the right thing, Sean. We can relax now. Focus on us, I'm excited."

"I know. Late breakfast?"

"Sorry, Sean, I'd love to stay, but I have to go and take care of something."

"Like what?"

"Don't look so worried. Work thing."

"It's crazy that we did all that last night, and I still don't even know what you do for a living."

"I've told you…" she smiled, "finance. It's boring. Listen, are we back to normal then now? No more taking it slow?"

"No more taking it slow," I smirked.

"Good," she said, leaning in to kiss me avidly, "send my regards to Mrs. Miller."

Clearly very proud of her quip, she skipped off to get dressed and ready to leave the house. It was the start of something beautiful, I'd hoped, but Mrs. Miller still loitered in the back of my mind. I was surrounded by fragments of our marriage. Everywhere I turned was a constant reminder of what had happened between us. The divorce papers sat unsigned on the kitchen table, patiently waiting for my autograph.

I impulsively scribbled my signature on the pages without reading a single word. Whatever she wanted from the divorce, it was hers; I just wanted a clean slate. Kat had stuck her neck out for me on a number of occasions, and I had to do the same. I sealed the completed forms in the envelope, and Kat returned just in time to see me throw them back on the table. They were completed.

"So, you are a free man now?"

"Not yet, but I will be."

"Wrong, you are mine." She teased.

"I know," I smiled.

"Be good while I'm gone, Sean, don't do anything I wouldn't do."

"Wouldn't dream of it."

I followed her out of the house to go and post the papers. I had to get rid of them before I changed my mind. Kat pulled me back almost aggressively to stick a kiss on me before she got in her car and drove off with a smile. She was clearly happy I had decided to sign the paperwork; it was another step closer to us being together properly. At least I wasn't making her miserable anymore; I couldn't bear the thought of upsetting her, not after everything we had been through together. It felt good to be finally moving forward in my life in a positive, somewhat healthy way.

I made my way around the corner to the post box. I'd love to say I didn't hesitate, but I did, for a minute. Putting pen to paper had a level of finality, but I hadn't considered I'd have another chance to change my mind. I never thought that something as simple as letting go of a letter would be such a huge decision. I dropped it into the void; it clattered against the sides as it hit the bottom.

It was done. Kat and I had come too far for me to fall at the last hurdle.

When I returned, I could almost hear Dylan laughing from outside and Courtney's feet chasing him up the stairs. It felt different looking back on it now; the hardship had been stripped away, and I only remembered the good times. In hindsight, I don't actually think we were that miserable. We did have fun, and we were in love for over a decade. But the man Courtney married didn't exist anymore. He died in that warehouse. Whatever emerged from the flames wasn't her husband. I didn't know if I had changed for the better or the worse. Only time will tell.

In the end, I just wanted her to be happy. If that meant her moving on with her life with somebody else, then that was what she should do. I couldn't stand in the way of this new relationship she had found; I was setting her free. As well as myself. I still needed to be there for Dylan, and maybe we could hash together some kind of relationship from the rubble of our family. Maybe I could even introduce him to Kat when the time was right. I finally had enough free time to be there for him; it was just unfortunate it was after his family imploded. He was the true innocent in all this.

But I was starting a new chapter with Kat. And I was excited. Every time I saw her, I felt my feelings grow more intense. She was everything I wasn't, but it worked. We were two sides of the same coin. There was still so much that I didn't know about her, but I was determined to know every part of her. She felt the same, too. I knew it. Although Courtney definitely wouldn't agree, it was the best decision for her, too. I came back into the house and called Courtney again, and it rang, so she hadn't blocked my number after the last heated exchange. I could tell by the way she was breathing that she had been crying again, but I was bringing her good news, I thought.

"What now?" She said hoarsely.

"Listen, I have signed the papers. I've just put them in the post now. I just wanted to say I'm sorry for everything."

"Okay."

"I've had a lot of time to think, and I want you to know that I won't stand in the way of you two now. I want you to be happy."

"Me and Dylan?"

"No, you and whoever you are seeing."

"Sean, I'm not seeing anyone else. That's you who's doing that, remember?"

"I know about you going on a date with someone. Honestly, it's fine. I'm happy for you."

"Sean, I haven't been on a date in about ten years, and that was with you. I've honestly no idea what you are talking about."

She sounded like she was telling the truth, but I couldn't be sure. Still, it didn't matter. She had no obligation to tell me anything anymore; it was her business. If she wanted to keep that part of her life from me, I understood. I wasn't itching to talk to her about Kat either. I just wanted to clear the air slightly so I had a chance to see Dylan again.

"Fine. Listen, when can I see Dylan?" I asked.

"Oh, Sean," she started, "I don't think he wants to see you. We will have to see."

"Why? What has he said?"

"Nothing. But he knows what's going on."

"Right."

"I will speak to him, I promise. But let's just get all the paperwork out of the way first, and then we can sort Dylan out."

"Okay. Thank you, Courtney."

"Take care, Sean."

"You too."

It felt good to not have her screaming at me for a change. I meant what I said. I wanted her to be happy. We were through the worst of it; surely, we could at least try and be friends, for Dylan's sake. I didn't know if I was emotionally mature enough to pull that off, but I would try. I couldn't let him be without a father; it didn't do me any good.

I couldn't shake the image of her going on that date from my mind, though. I didn't know if it was some lingering jealousy, but something felt off. She was adamant she hadn't been on the date. That grainy photograph was the whole reason I decided to let her go in the first place, but I couldn't bring the photo up, not without the context. I wondered if I would have chosen Kat without seeing it; the photo did tip me over the edge. It was one last masked man riddle from beyond the grave; they were burned to ash but still manipulating my life. Before I managed to lock my phone, I had a text message waiting from Kat.

I miss you already. x

I miss you too, Kat.

And I did miss her. But I missed Courtney, too. Kat was the single worst influence on me, but also the best. I had done things with her I wouldn't have ever dreamt up in my worst nightmares, but she was teaching me so much about myself. Courtney represented safety and comfort and, to be blunt, normal. In one moment, I bitterly regretted posting those papers, and in the next, it was a huge liberation. I never thought it possible to love two women at the same time, but they sat on opposite sides of the scales, perfectly balanced.

I thought that it was my decision, but in reality, I knew that I didn't have any right to choose, not after how I'd acted. I could feel myself splitting in two, the darkness dragging me towards Kat and the light pulling me back towards Courtney. Regardless of how I felt, I'd chosen the path now, and I had to walk it.

15

TAG, YOU'RE IT

Me and Kat spent the back end of the summer mostly running together. I retired from solo runs. With the threat of the masked men extinguished, each week, we moved further up the leaderboard, running farther and farther. The thrill wasn't the same, but being with Kat helped. I became totally enamoured by her. We spent pretty much every day together, getting to know each other beyond the physical. I was falling head over heels for her, and I was sure she felt the same.

The only days we didn't spend together were when she had to work, which was fairly infrequent and irregular. It had always bothered me why she was still using the app when she was obviously very well off. But deep down, I understood she yearned for the thrill of the chase like I did and the threat of danger. Our bodies became impossibly fit while the darkness within us grew fat and slothful.

The divorce still hadn't been finalised, but Courtney and I agreed through our solicitors that I would take the house and buy her out. She stopped contributing to the household funds, and I ran to make up the shortfall. I was earning more than I had ever done in my life. I still had a deep respect for her, but the love had faded. Every reminder of her sat in a cardboard box underneath the stairs, waiting for her to collect it. We hadn't had a big chat again; the resentment between us was left unsaid, which was my preference, to be honest. It was useless dragging it all back up, and I was so exhausted from worrying about whether I'd made the right decision or not.

Dylan had still refused to see me. Courtney said I just needed to give him time, and I did what she suggested. I missed his little cheeky quips. But I have firsthand experience on the matter, and I know that watching your family break apart at such a young age was devastating. I would have loved to sit him down and try to explain it to him, but if Courtney didn't understand my rationale, neither would he. The only thing that truly mattered was that he was safe.

Kat and I were good, but I felt like there was something between us that was left unsaid there, too. The high-octane way we met had given way to a kind of tepid normalcy. We had become 'that couple' people saw jogging up and down the canal together or going out for a meal. It was enough for me, but I could tell Kat missed the thrills. I constantly searched for ways we could inject a little of our previous iteration into this new relationship, but there wasn't really anything quite like it.

It was date night, and I was meeting Kat at 'Massimo Lusso' in the city. We hadn't had a chance to eat there since the Neil fiasco, and she had pleaded with me that we had to return. I made my own way there; Kat said she would meet me after work. When I arrived, she was waiting there at the front door, dressed in a satin floor-length dress. Every time I saw her dressed up like this, I couldn't believe she was ever interested in me.

"Hi, lover." She smirked.

"Wow. You look incredible," I gasped.

"I know. Are we heading in?"

"Sure, I'm excited."

We were led through the tables to the exact table we sat at before Neil's murder. The waiter came to take our order, and I already knew what I was having.

"Lobster ravioli, please," I asked.

"Me too," Kat smiled, "and a bottle of Lafite '64, we didn't get to finish it last time."

"It feels good to be here," I started, "during the summer, we were constantly looking over our shoulders, but it's nice to relax. Don't you think?"

"I agree," Kat said whilst looking at her phone.

"Work?" I asked.

"Yeah, I'll be all yours in just one minute."

"You've never actually told me what you do."

"I said. Finance. Boring."

"I know," I sighed, "but I'd like to know more about you."

"Why are you so interested all of a sudden?" She asked, getting agitated.

"I just don't get why it's a big secret, that's all."

"Secret… right. After how we started?"

"Okay, you are blowing this out of proportion now. I was only asking the question."

"Fine." She snapped.

The waiter arrived at the table, and Kat emptied the small amount he put in the glass and tapped the table, demanding more. She drank deeply until the glass was almost empty again. I had seen Kat's dark side before but never directed at me. I had just got a glimpse of it through the curtains. Something had clearly irked her. From my point of view, we had an amazing summer together, but it had been relatively uneventful. I felt closer to Kat than we had ever been, but I could feel her pulling away slightly. We rarely spoke about the divorce; it was an undiscussed topic that I assumed was at the forefront of her mind a lot of the time.

In my quest to get to know her better, I realised that her job was a bit of a taboo subject. We had shared so much with each other, but she always clammed up whenever work was mentioned. I took it at face value, though. Kat hated being bored, so I decided not to press the issue further. She knew everything there was to know about me, and I didn't have any secrets from her. But I felt like she was withholding an obviously large part of her life from me, and I didn't understand why.

I didn't enjoy dinner. The lobster ravioli wasn't to my taste. Neither was the wine. I would have much preferred a greasy cheeseburger and a lager. There was an atmosphere; I had touched a nerve, and it was awkward. We stood outside in the early Autumn breeze, waiting for Kat's car to be returned from the valet. I could see her getting more and more agitated, obviously regurgitating our little spat.

"I'm a broker," she said, "I connect buyers with sellers. That's it. It's boring. I hate talking about it."

"Okay, that's all you needed to say."

"I just don't like how you are with money."

"How I am with money?"

"Yes. You are obsessed with it. From what you've told me, it was that obsession that started all your problems in the first place. It's only money."

"With respect, Kat, the only people who say, 'it's only money', have money. We barely had anything."

"We?" she asked,

"You know what I mean."

"I know *who* you mean."

"Please don't bring Courtney into this."

"I didn't. But that's all I am to you, isn't it? A distraction from her."

"No, it's not like that. I chose you."

"Yeah, conveniently after she divorced you."

"It wasn't like that, no."

Kat was deflecting. I could tell. My insecurities grew like a tumour. The start of our relationship was so intense and filled with excitement, but the 'honeymoon period' was over, if you could call it that. We had become vanilla; a few months ago, I was watching her from behind a rifle, and now we were organising date nights. Without constant threats looming over us, we had become boring in comparison. When I looked into her eyes, I realised the truth. We had been running, constantly trying to go faster and further, as a weak substitution for the thrill and danger we had felt at the hands of our pursuers.

Just like the leaves of the canal gradually turning from greens to browns, I hadn't noticed the distance growing between us. The light inside of us was still in love, but the darkness had been starved. What was left was a shrivelling bony beast waiting impatiently for its next meal. I wondered if we were broken, unable to feel any form of catharsis without violence or threat involved. She knew it, too; I could tell by the way she was looking at me.

"Do you miss it?" She tenderly asked.

"Miss what?"

"The hunt."

"Sometimes. But they are gone, Kat."

"I know. Maybe we can find something else."

"Like what?"

"I don't know."

Kat's car arrived, and she stood there in silence for a minute before getting into it. It was awkward for the first time. I didn't want to lose her like I'd lost Courtney. She stared at me, waiting for me to say something to make it all better. But there wasn't anything to be said.

"Listen, I think I'm going to head home." She explained delicately.

"Okay. I'll see you tomorrow?"

"Yeah, maybe."

She got in her car, and I watched her drive off. I had a very pensive taxi ride home. I didn't know what I could do to bring back the excitement in our relationship. I was desperate not to let it fail like my marriage had. Money wasn't the issue anymore. Kat certainly had plenty of it, and thanks to my running, so had I. Maybe we just had a deep-seated incompatibility, and there wasn't anything we could do about it.

I returned home and got straight into bed. I had struggled to get to sleep for a long time, plagued by the memories of the last year. I would often wake up in a cold sweat, screaming. I could still hear the three dull thuds as the men's bodies hit the floor. I never took the time out to process it, and Kat always trivialised it as a victory, but part of me was left in that warehouse, too. My routine was a few hours of sleep, followed by an hour awake, on repeat.

PHILIP ANTHONY SMITH

That night, I was woken up in the early hours of the morning by my phone beeping. I reached for it on the nightstand with my eyes still half shut. I expected a message from Kat; she often sends messages through the night for me to wake up to, but it wasn't. Instead, it was a text message from an unknown number.

> *Tag. You're it.*

Still half asleep, I stared at the message, not knowing what it meant. A second message appeared a few seconds later. It was a picture message. I opened it but couldn't make out what I was seeing through my squinted eyes. My heart stopped, and I was jolted fully awake. It was Kat's car, wrapped around a lamppost in a crumpled mess. The airbags had deployed, and the car doors were still open. I studied the picture frantically, looking for any sign of her, but she wasn't in the frame. I immediately rang her, but she didn't answer. I thought she had been taken; I had no idea what to do. I paced in my bedroom, calling desperately. No answer. I was just about to ring the unknown number when Kat started ringing me back.

"Kat, are you okay?" I asked franticly.

"Sorry, this isn't Kat. This is a nurse from the hospital. Kathryn has been in an accident. Are you her next of kin?" The nurse said.

"Yes, my name is Sean."

"She is going to be fine; she just has a concussion. She is currently in a room recuperating."

"So, she is safe?"

"Safe? Yes, she is safe here."

"Can I see her?"

"Of course, but she is resting."

"I'm on my way."

I hung up and shot out of the house straight into the car. The nurse had described it as an accident, but I knew better. The owner of the unknown number that had sent me the picture was responsible. I knew they were all dead, but it had to be them, somehow. They had waited just long enough for us to stop worrying about them, and they struck. I sped through the night in my car, racing to the hospital. They would never leave us alone.

I had never seen Kat look like this before. From what I had seen of the crash, she had been very lucky. She was sleeping when I arrived; her right eye was so swollen and bruised I could barely see the opening. She had a deep cut on her head, and the blood stuck her golden blonde hair to the side of her face. Her left arm was in a sling, pinned up against her body. She looked so fragile.

I sat there, waiting for her to wake up. I watched her for hours; I didn't know when they would strike again. I held her hand lightly as I sat in the chair next to her. The darkness roused from its slumber, pacing backwards and forwards, impetuously waiting to pounce. And I would let it. I would find the people responsible for this and kill them with impunity.

The sun had risen, and Kat finally woke up, disorientated. It took her a minute to come to, but she smiled wearily when she recognised me and gripped my hand tightly.

"How are you feeling, Kat?"

"It was them, Sean."

"It can't be them. We killed them."

"I know, but there must be more of them than we realised."

"Are you sure?"

"Yes. They rammed me off the road."

Kat tried to get up with a groan before a nurse came in and gently guided her back down. Kat nodded at her, knowing she needed to rest. The nurse left; Kat started stroking my hand to get my attention as I stared into space.

"I'm so glad to see you, Sean, I thought after our last conversation—"

"Kat, I love you," I interrupted.

"What?"

"I love you. That's why I am here."

"I love you, too."

"We are going to get through this, and we are going to find the people who did this to you. And you know what happens next."

Kat's facial injuries did little to stifle the expression on her face; she was happy. I didn't know if it was because of my declaration of love or because the hunt was back on. Right then, I didn't care. I needed to find the people who did this to her. The doctor entered the room and picked up Kat's charts. He didn't seem too concerned about what he saw.

"You should be able to go home tonight, Kathryn. You have a slight concussion; you've been incredibly lucky."

"Thanks, doc." She said.

"Try to be more careful in the future. I'm sorry, sir, but Kathryn needs to rest now. You will have to leave." He said, returning the chart to the end of the bed and leaving the room.

"I'll take care of this," I grimaced.

"No. We will deal with this together. Promise me you won't do anything yet."

"Okay, I promise."

"I love you, Sean."

"I love you too, Kat."

I gave her a prolonged kiss on the forehead and left the room. It felt odd saying those three little words to her, but they were true. I didn't want to tell her about the text message I had received, not whilst she was recovering. I had a direct line to those responsible. I needed to lure them out in the open so I could end this, finally. I returned to the car and immediately tried calling the number, but it was disconnected. It was obviously sent from a burner phone.

I wanted to be close to Kat, so I sat in the car, waiting for her to be discharged. I felt disgusted in myself for thinking it, but if this was the masked men, I should send them a 'thank you' note. I had felt her slipping away; in a twisted way, their return to our lives might be just what our relationship needed. Don't get me wrong, I still hated them for what they had done, and I would make them pay, but their actions had unintended positive consequences.

I fell asleep in the car, lost in my own thoughts, but awoke to a faint tapping on the glass. It was Kat, and she was on her feet; I jumped out of the car and gave her a besotted hug.

"Ouch." She groaned.

"Sorry."

"It's okay. I'm just a bit sore. Can you take me home?"

"Sure, but should you be there on your own?"

"Maybe not, I guess. Can you stay?"

"Of course."

It was strange, I know, but I actually hadn't been to Kat's place before. She had spoken about it in passing, but I hadn't actually stepped foot in there. I knew it was just outside of the city, and it was a bit awkward asking the woman I loved where she lived. She put the postcode in the navigation and slumped back in her seat.

"How are you feeling?" I asked delicately.

"Angry." She grunted.

"Me too. Listen, the reason I found out was because they sent me a text message."

"Why didn't you mention it before?"

"You were resting. I didn't want to upset you."

"What did it say?"

"It just said, 'Tag. You're it,' and it had a picture of the crash."

"Can I see it?"

I handed Kat my unlocked phone, and she studied the picture. She looked shocked by the image, obviously not recalling how close she was to being killed. I could see her in my peripheral vision, zooming into it, trying to see any details I had missed.

"Well, that's the mystery over."

"What is it?"

"Pull over, look at this."

I pulled the car over, and she zoomed into the reflection of her open car door. It was grainy but unmistakable. It was the figure from behind the camera, wearing a black balaclava. I couldn't believe it. I watched them die. All of them. Like weeds, we ripped them out, root and stem, and more arrived in their place. It felt never-ending.

"So, they are back. But we killed them all?" I asked.

"Obviously, not all of them."

"I can't believe it. I thought it was over. What do we do?"

"Just get us home for now; we will work it out later."

I started driving again; when we arrived, Kat directed me down a ramp into an underground parking structure for a huge apartment building. She looked exhausted while she was getting out of the car. We got in the lift, and she hit the top floor. We emerged in a short hallway with two doors. She took her keys out and entered first, ushering me through the door behind her.

"Make yourself at home. I need to wash the hospital off me." She said, undressing as she left.

The place was incredible. I initially thought the grand entrance hallway was the entirety of the apartment. Rich oak parquet flooring softly sheened in the warm lighting from above. The walls were littered with artwork and paintings, tastefully selected to perfectly complement the rustic brick interior. It was all open plan, and each room flowed into the next effortlessly. Every single surface was immaculately pristine. But there wasn't a single family photograph or personal memento to be found.

"Wow," I whispered to myself.

I poked my head around one of the only doors in the apartment. It was Kat's bedroom. The décor was dominated by blacks and reds; a dramatic four-poster bed sat in the middle of the room, with huge glass windows letting in the city behind it. It reflected Kat's personality flawlessly, dark and mysterious.

Kat got out of the shower and sat on one of the three huge couches in the living room. She clearly felt better after having a shower and sat there with her head back, staring at the ceiling. She rested for a moment, then sat up to beckon me over.

"Shall we call them?" She asked.

"I've tried to, but the number is disconnected."

"What if we try texting? It might get through."

"Give it a try."

I sat next to Kat. She typed a message to the unknown number and hit send.

> *We need to meet.*

We sat there in silence, waiting for a reply. After a minute, the bubbles started to appear, indicating that the recipient was typing.

> *Is Blondie out of the hospital?*
> *We should all catch up soon.*

Kat looks at me expectantly, waiting for me to suggest a response. Her breathing was fast-paced and heavy. She was enjoying this. She was snaking her hand up and down my leg. I knew we couldn't give any information away that would leave us vulnerable, but we needed to lure them out in the open.

"Tell them to meet me at the bridge where they killed Jordan tomorrow night," I suggested.

> *Meet me where Jordan died.*
> *Tomorrow night. 10 pm.*

"Sent." She said.

"Have they replied yet?" I asked.

"No, what's the plan, Sean?"

"Same as before. I go in as bait, and you sit at the next bridge with the rifle."

"I need to get some rest if we are doing this tomorrow," she yawned, "do you want to stay here?"

"Yeah, I'd love that."

Kat led me into the bedroom; even though she was totally drained, I saw the spark in her eyes again. A treacherous cocktail of the anticipation of the hunt and the three words. I felt close to her again, and she wasn't slipping away anymore. She fell asleep almost as soon as her head hit the pillow. I stayed awake for what felt like hours, just watching Kat sleep.

The darkness within me so far had been living off a diet of anger and lust alone, but I had given it something far more nutritious: love. It would dutifully rip apart anyone or anything that stopped it from getting what it desired. She was the only thing that mattered to me now. I would do anything for this woman, and I would gladly give my life to protect hers.

16

CHOOSE

We woke up the next day after midday. I don't know if it was sleeping in Kat's bed or pure fatigue, but it was the best night's sleep I'd had in months. Kat's swollen eye had gone down overnight; she opened it cautiously as her gaze met mine. The bruise on her eye had gone darker, but she was so beautiful, even after what she had been through. The cut on her head, still held together by the sutures, had dried and already started to heal.

It felt like I had woken up in somebody else's life. Kat, inexplicably rejuvenated from her injuries in a single night's sleep, made us breakfast. Poached eggs on toast with a side of bacon. We then jumped in the shower together. Afterwards, we brushed our teeth in the matching his-and-hers sinks in her bathroom. I looked at the reflection of us in the mirror; we looked like a married couple, living the high life. I saw a glimpse of what our lives could be if we made it through the night.

We lounged around her apartment all day, laughing, joking, and fooling around. The rest of the city looked tiny from the 50th floor of the apartment building. Aside from Kat, the best part of the apartment was definitely the view. The people in the city resembled ants, all playing their roles in society, diligently walking the streets for crumbs. But we existed outside of society. As the daylight started to wane, we were reminded of the brutality of our evening's task and the fact that we had no idea what we were facing.

Kat started to get ready. Her demeanour was as if she was going for a night out, brushing her hair with a smile, humming some tune she had heard on the radio. She looked happy and excited. For her, this was the perfect end to the day. I didn't feel excited; I felt numb to it now. I just wanted it to be over so we could get back to our lives. I wasn't even that worried, particularly. I knew that between us, we would be able to take care of anything they threw at us.

She was a fan of wearing black and had plenty of options on what to wear. Kat found some clothes for me, and I didn't ask where they were from. I didn't want to bring up her husband again just before we left. She retrieved the rifle, and sat at the dining table, loading the clip with round after round. Kat took the rifle to the window and looked through the scope, pretending to aim it at the pedestrians below. She imitated the sound of it firing and turned to smile at me. If the context of what she was doing wasn't so menacing, I would have probably described her as cute.

We made our way down to the parking level in the lift without saying a word. It felt like business as usual, just another day at the office. A couple got in the lift as we descended, obviously going out for the evening. They laughed and flirted with each other, unaware Kat had a rifle in the bag at their feet. When they left the lift, Kat rolled her eyes and smiled at me mockingly. She clearly disapproved of the vanilla evening they had planned.

I reciprocated the look to Kat, but part of me would have swapped lives with them in an instant. They looked happy. I still liked vanilla. I would much rather have been going out for a nice meal with Kat or going to the cinema, rather than the night we had planned. But we had made our decisions, and it landed us here, and we had to complete the journey. I just hoped the return to vanilla would be enough for Kat when this was all over.

We got in my car and set off towards Jordan's bridge. Kat's excitement built; I could tell by the way she was breathing. She aimlessly touched my leg and gripped it as I drove out of the city. We didn't physically say a word to each other the entire journey, but the darkness inside of us communicated better than we ever could. I have to admit, part of me felt good to be on the hunt again after our hiatus. I always felt closer to Kat somehow whenever we found ourselves in these situations.

I stopped near the bridge after Jordan's, and we got out of the car. The bridge had a good, clear view of the meeting point. If I got into trouble, I just needed to stay on the correct side of the bridge. She tackled me and kissed me passionately like it was the last time she ever would.

"I love you, Sean." She whispered.

"I love you too, Kat," I smiled.

"Don't worry. If there are any wrong moves, I'll start shooting. Just like we planned."

"I know. I trust you."

"Good luck," she whispered in my ear before biting it playfully, "I'll be watching."

I got back in the car, leaving Kat at the roadside with the rifle, and made my way to Jordan's bridge. I parked near the farm that it connected and walked down onto the path. The sound of my shoes hitting the stone steps was the only sound to be heard. Once I was on my own on the dark canal, the reality of the situation hit me. My heart was pounding, and it started to bruise against my rib cage. The canal path was full of shadows, and the contrast in the lighting at the street level made it almost impossible to see what was lurking in them.

I entered the shadows cautiously. I could see in both directions if I stood under the bridge, out of the influence of the street lighting above. It was a few minutes before 10 pm. No sign of them yet. With every passing second, my heart raced faster. I expected them to be already waiting for us, but there was no sign. Every movement in the shadows, I thought, was the end. Each flutter of a slumbering duck nearly sent me into a panic attack. It was almost five past the hour now. They were late. The tension in the air was suffocating me, and it was impenetrable and viscous. I worried that the plan, hastily drawn up the night before, was ill-conceived and rushed. I was an easy target.

I started to think they wouldn't come, but then I had an idea. I opened the 'B-Run' app on my phone and put my earphones in. If they got close, the thudding would warn me by speeding up. But it made the tensity worse. I threw my arms in the air in Kat's general direction, hoping she would see through the scope and give me some kind of forward warning or non-verbal encouragement.

The thud started to speed up. They were close. I heard a car approaching the bridge above at slow speed. The thudding reached a frenzied frequency, and I removed the earphones to listen. Car doors opened. Once, twice, three times, four. They shut in unison. I was outnumbered. But they didn't know about Kat, lovingly waiting with her scope trained on me.

I heard feet heavily making their way down the steps. I returned to the nearside of the bridge, in the safety of the light, waiting for them to arrive on the canal. There were four of them in their classic suit and balaclava combination. They lined up on the canal in front of me conveniently like targets, waiting for Kat to take the shots. The plan was actually going to work. I could almost see the smile span Kat's face as they stood in order like a living shooting range.

Their formation put me at ease, and I knew Kat would be able to take them out quickly if things went sideways. But what was she waiting for? I thought she was probably giving me the opportunity to get some more information from them. The anticipation got the better of me, and I broke out with a smile.

"You wanted the catch-up, let's catch up. How have you all been?" I jested sarcastically.

One by one, each of the men produced a weapon from inside of their jackets. Behind door number one was a masked man armed with a pistol. Door numbers two and three pulled out hunting knives. Door number four started putting on knuckle dusters, punching his own hands to get the fit right. They started walking towards me slowly, flaunting their weapons theatrically. They weren't interested in speaking this time. They would let the violence do the talking for them. I slowly retreated down the path backwards, with my hands up in submission.

Still no shots from Kat.

They were getting very close to me now, and I started to back away further, giving Kat more time to line up the shots. I turned to look at the bridge in the distance, and I couldn't see anything in the darkness.

"Kat, a little help!" I shouted.

I waited for the pops, but none came. Number four swung at me with the steel wrapped around his knuckles, striking me in the left side of my head. I started to plummet towards the gravel. I felt the impact, but the pain was delayed by the sheer force. A high-pitched ringing deafened me as my face hit the ground. The blows kept coming, I barely put up a fight, and I fell unconscious with my face in the dirt.

I was out for a few minutes. Or it was hours. It was impossible to tell. My eyelids had stuck together thanks to the blood streaming down my face. Any immediate memory of what had just happened had been beaten right out of my skull. I vaguely remembered sustaining some injuries, but I wasn't really in any pain. My senses activated again, one by one. I was still on the canal path where I had been beaten, but the masked men had long gone. The pain came a little later, like an explosion inside my skull, forcing me back down to the ground, holding my head to keep it from erupting. The pain brought back my memory. I clearly had some kind of concussion; I could taste my own blood that had pooled in my mouth whilst I was knocked out.

"Kat," I gasped.

I aimlessly paced around, trying to get some of my faculties back. I decided to walk back underneath the bridge to recuperate under some cover. The stench of strong solvents amplified my headache. The smell was deeply unnerving. I looked around for the source of the smell. Once I had my phone torch on, you couldn't miss it.

Sprayed onto the old rocks of the bridge were two huge red arrows. Underneath the left arrow, 'Kat' had been hastily sprayed. Below the right arrow, simply read 'Court'. I didn't know what I was looking at, but it was the most sinister thing I had ever seen. I called Kat, but she didn't answer. Courtney's phone went straight to voicemail. My brain felt bruised and swollen; I couldn't make sense of the painting before me.

My phone beeped. It was a text from the same unknown number that had brought me here.

> *Choose.*

My situation became apparent. They had taken them. They had Kat and Courtney, and they wanted me to choose between them as a part of their sick game. It was an impossible decision between the new love of my life and the mother of my son. My head snapped between left and right. It was most certainly a trap either way, but I had to react and choose one of them, at least. Another message.

> *Choose. Now.*

To make matters worse, they were clearly watching me and saw me stationary under the bridge. I needed to decide; there was a chance that I could lose both of them. I started running one way and then back the way I came. I couldn't decide. I didn't feel like I was saving one of them but condemning the other. I had Kat in my left hand and Courtney in my right.

I made my choice, returned my earphones, and started running. The sudden jolt in my heart rate made my head wound bleed faster, and I constantly wiped my brow to keep it going in my eyes. My head was absolutely pounding, and I couldn't tell if it was the metronome of the app or brain damage. Nothing mattered. I just had to get there and quickly.

They had created some macabre scavenger hunt with spray-painted arrows on the ground. I was obedient, following the arrows at speed. Nothing else mattered; I just had to get there. I couldn't save them both. I already felt intense remorse for my decision; a simple left or right had split my life into two. It was obviously a trap, too, but if they wanted me dead, they could have easily finished me off when I was unconscious. I didn't know their motives anymore, and it petrified me.

I could see Courtney's face on our wedding day. I had never seen her so beautiful. I turned from the altar to see her, and my heart became liquid. Her chestnut eyes locked onto mine as she ambled towards me like I was the only man in the world. I fixated on the little details. She had little flowers delicately weaved into her perfect hair, and they bounced slightly as she walked. Courtney looked absolutely flawless, but what I really remembered was the way she made me feel by walking down the aisle to marry me.

I remember the first time I took Kat back to my house. The unbridled raw passion and chemistry between us. Whenever I saw her, it felt like my body had been set on fire. She was the definition of desire and exhilaration, but we had since built on that. We were building a life together out of our crazy beginning. I loved her, and she loved me.

I couldn't let either of them die.

I took out my phone as I was running to make a call. I knew it would have dire consequences for me, but I had to stop thinking selfishly for once. I scrolled down to DS Bank's number on my contacts list and hit call.

"DS Banks. It's Sean," I said.

"I've got caller ID, Sean. What do you want? It's almost midnight!"

"Tony, I can't explain it all now, but Kat and Courtney are in danger. The masked men are back."

"Sean, where are you right now?"

"Just go to the bridge where Jordan died and follow the arrows north. I'm going south."

"I don't know what is going on or what you are planning, but whatever it is, just stop. Let us do our jobs."

"I can't. They are watching me. They made me choose between them. Just hurry, please."

I abruptly hung up the call, and I continued to follow the arrows on the floor. I passed bridge after bridge; I had felt like I had run miles. I reached the next bridge, and there was an arrow pointing left; it was sprayed onto the concrete, pointing up the steps. I sprinted up them, and a further arrow on the wall directed me down a rarely-travelled dirt track.

The track was treacherous and riddled with holes and dips in the ground, making speed difficult. I struggled to see anything in the darkness and was almost running blind. I hadn't seen an arrow for a while, and my panic grew, thinking I had missed one and I was lost.

I saw a dim light in the distance. It illuminated an old concrete utility building next to a nearby stream. The building didn't have windows; it was made of stone slabs stacked and screwed together. The building had clearly not been entered for a very long time; the steel exterior door leached rust into the concrete on either side of it. On the steel of the door was a fresh spray painting of the bleeding foot, the logo from the 'B-Run' app. This was the place where I had been led, like a lamb, to the slaughter.

I had run so far down that path there was no chance of getting any extra help. I was on my own. I just prayed that she was alive. The door had an open padlock clipped into the housing, allowing me to unhook it and gain entry whilst not allowing anyone inside to escape. I unhooked it slowly. The rusty scrape of metal on metal broke the ghastly silence. The steel door creaked and cracked as it opened. I expected an ambush as soon as I was inside.

Instead, I heard her. The muffled whimpering, which in itself would normally be harrowing, but it was a welcome noise. It meant she was alive. I crept around the dusty room, following the stifled cries until I saw her. Her bare feet were protruding from beside some crates. They had been frantically slashed open and sat in a small puddle of their own blood.

Ignoring the threat of ambush, I ran over to help her. I untied her hands first; they were damaged and dirty, obviously in her attempts to escape. She went to remove the gag whilst I untied her ankles; her legs were adorned with fresh bruises and cuts. I helped her with the fabric forced into her mouth, and she gasped for air when it was released.

"Sean, I'm so sorry. I love you." She cried.

17

THE RIGHT THING

D S Banks hadn't skipped the cuffs this time. I can't say I blamed him. He fastened them tight, too; I could feel my hands going numb behind my back. The once-abandoned building was receiving a lot of attention. Police were combing every crevice, looking for any scraps of evidence. They mummified the structure in police tape, only allowing entry to officers in forensic suits.

I was left in the back of a police van cell; I watched it all unfold through the chain link doors. I could see the ambulance through the grate, and she was inside it, getting medical attention. DS Banks flitted from officer to officer, directing the scene. He came over to the cage I had been placed in, gripping the side as he looked at me.

"Have you been read your rights, Sean?" He asked plainly.

"Yes. Did you find her?"

"I can't discuss that with you, Sean. It could compromise the investigation."

"Tony, I need to know, please," I pleaded.

"I'm sorry, Sean," he started reservedly, "she wasn't there, and it doesn't look good."

"What do you mean it doesn't look good?"

"I could get sacked for even showing you this, but look."

DS Banks got his phone out of his peacoat pocket and showed me a photograph. My whole world shattered into pieces. I had made some depraved decisions this year, but the consequences of this one would haunt me forever. The photograph was in a similar room to the one I had just been in, with a huge pool of blood on the floor. In the centre, her violently hacked-off ponytail was stained by the blood it sat in.

Kat's ponytail.

The last trace of her beauty was discarded in a pool of her own blood like a rag. I broke down, pulling at the handcuffs behind me until they cut into my wrists. I screamed so loudly that every single police officer in a mile radius turned to look at me in shock. I had done this to her. Whatever grim end she faced, it was by my hands. I would likely never see her again, taken by the men who pursued us and sold to the highest bidder.

"I'm sorry, Sean, we just didn't get there in time." DS Banks sympathised.

"I'm going to kill them."

"Easy, son, I'm still a copper." He warned, leaning in closer to the grate.

The ambulance doors opened, and I saw Courtney on the bed inside. She was alive, she was okay. The paramedics beckoned DS Banks over to give him an update. I couldn't see her face, only her mutilated feet that had been wrapped up in bandages. DS Banks returned to me with his hands in his pockets.

"She is okay, Sean. They are taking her to the hospital, under police guard, just to be sure."

"What about Dylan?"

"We will send officers there too."

"I need to speak to her."

"Not possible."

"Tony, they did this to her to get to me. It's my fault. I need to speak to her," I begged.

DS Banks huffed, "two minutes."

He took me out of the van and handcuffed himself to me. He marched me over to the back doors of the ambulance. Courtney was inside, awake but clearly in tremendous pain. I had never seen her in this much pain before, and it was entirely my fault. I felt unfathomable guilt. I should have been there to stop this, but I didn't know what I could have done differently.

"Court, I am so sorry," I cried.

"So, you were telling me the truth." She sobbed.

"They made me choose between you and her, but I chose you. I couldn't bear the thought of anything happening to you or Dylan."

Courtney half smiled, "I have missed you."

"I've missed you too."

I thought it was done between us, but the emotion of the evening had affected us greatly. I never thought I would hear those words from her again. I didn't know how to feel. I didn't deserve her or Kat. It should have been me on that gurney or my severed hair in that building. What grave injustice had I inflicted on these men for them to want to destroy my life in this way? I only ever defended myself and those around me. And Kat. She was gone, likely dead.

"Please don't do anything stupid, just talk to the police, tell them everything. Do the right thing."

"I will."

"Come on now, Sean, we need to get you to the station." DS Banks interjected.

"Do I have a choice?" I asked.

"No." He replied.

"Sean, we need to talk when this is all over," Courtney said.

"We do," I replied as DS Banks ushered me away from the ambulance and back to the police van. He uncuffed himself from me and marshalled me inside. The van doors shut, and the engine started, taking me to the police station.

I wanted to rip the cage doors off their hinges and find the people who did this to us. But I couldn't. The dichotomy of darkness and light was now the deepest black. Every single molecule of light inside me had been extinguished. Profound anger ruled over me; I kicked and roared in my cage. It did nothing to free me. Even in the obvious futility, I continued, imagining the anonymous faces of the men who had tormented me for the best part of a year.

Meeting Kat changed me forever. I'd never felt love like it. Beautifully destructive and exquisitely poisonous, she had contaminated every single cell and thought. Kat had a smile that could collapse empires and blue eyes that could turn a man into solid stone. Lavish lips that crushed dreams. She was the most unique woman I'd ever met or loved, and that loved me. And I had to come to terms with the fact I would never see her again.

The decision I made to end her life swelled in me like a cancer, warping and perverting me. The regret started in my throat, crushing my airways and leaving me struggling for breath. It moved down like a brick hitting my stomach, the lining surrendering to the weight as it tore under the strain.

I was stood at the bridge again. I imagined what would have happened if I had run in the opposite direction. Kat would still be breathing, and Courtney would be gone. I would have had to explain to Dylan what had happened to his mum, watching the light die in his eyes as I explained he would never see her again. In the end, that's what confirmed my decision. Dylan's name should have been written on that wall under Courtney's.

My heart felt black and heavy, like dark matter. Broodingly pushing the jet-black syrup of vengeance through my veins. I didn't care about the consequences anymore; I was absolutely driven by the fantasies of revenge. As soon as I was out of this cage, I would find them and destroy them all for taking Kat from me. The game they were playing didn't matter to me. My own life didn't matter to me. I just wanted to kill every last one of them.

The van stopped shaking violently as we left the dirt track and back onto the tarmac. The ride became much smoother, and I felt the van speed up. I had no point of reference in the van because of the lack of windows, but I could feel it speeding up further. The tyres squealed around every corner as I was tossed from side to side in my cage.

I heard the commotion from the cabin. They were inaudibly shouting down their radios. I tightened my grip on the cage as I was thrown in every direction. A huge bang at the back of the van crumpled the doors, warping the cage with me in it. I backed away from it as much as I could, not knowing what the danger was. Another impact. With each collision, the van became inches smaller, crushing the grate into my skin. The gravitational forces of turning a corner at high speed sent me careering into the opposite side of the cage. The van flipped on its side, leaving me pinned against the wall as it abruptly became the floor. The van became totally stationary as I felt it crash into something solid.

I writhed and struggled in my chains to try and get upright. I heard car doors opening outside, and after a few seconds, something started striking at the van doors. A dozen hits later, the van door flung open on its side, and two of the masked men were standing there. I heard dull thuds and muffled shouts from the officers in the cabin and then silence. The other two masked men returned to join their colleagues.

I bared my teeth at them almost in a snarl. I was no longer capable of speech; I had become a creature consumed by rage. I wanted nothing more than to rip the chain between the cuffs in two and rip them apart. But the chain held firm. They loomed over me in total inaction, gazing down at me. One of them threw something into the cage: a mobile phone with some wired earphones attached. Another threw a small set of keys.

They returned to their vehicle without a word; I heard it reversing down the road into the distance. I squirmed my way around to try and get the keys in my hand. I could feel the steel of the cuffs cut into my hands and wrists as I tried to rotate my hands to unlock them. I finally got the key in, and they opened with a click. I made my way out of the van; both of the officers escorting me were unconscious but breathing in the cabin.

I picked up the phone and earphones; it wasn't password-protected. The background image was a picture of Kat, beaten half to death, in the same room as the image DS Banks had shown me. The phone screen almost shattered under the sheer pressure I was putting on it. The phone had one app installed, the 'B-Run' app. A text appeared from an unknown number with an address enclosed.

> *Clydebank Industrial Estate.*
> *Now.*

This was my opportunity to get my revenge. I could run to this address right now and kill every single one of them. But the image of Courtney strapped to that ambulance gurney cut through the darkness. A glimmer at first, growing into an explosion of light. The darkness cowered in the corner, blinded by it. I heard Courtney saying, "Do the right thing," but what was the right thing? My sense of right and wrong had been completely warped, and I didn't know what to do.

My head was still pounding, and I could barely think straight. The evening was filled with choices I didn't have the brain capacity for. I was so lost in myself. I had been grateful for the darkness within; it had saved my life. But there was a price. And now it was clawing it back, one piece at a time. Depending on my decision, there was a slim chance I could go back to my old life and to the old me. The Sean who wouldn't stand up for himself, who had a steady job and a struggling family. Or I could continue down the path the masked men had set out before me, one born of blood and retribution.

I wanted justice for Kat, but I had been blinded by the rage. Maybe I should rejoin society and finally put my trust in the police to do their jobs. As flawed as DS Banks was, I could see he cared about the case. But he was restricted by the law, and I wasn't. Not anymore. I knew what Kat would have wanted me to do: pick up that phone and give them what was coming to them, but she wasn't there. And it was because of me.

I didn't care what happened to me; that didn't even come into it. But I think Courtney would have cared. Even though Dylan hadn't spoken to me in months, he would have definitely cared.

I dropped the phone where I found it.

I stumbled to the cabin. The officers were still unconscious from the crash, but they were still alive. I took one of their radios from their vest.

"This is Sean Miller," I said, "the van has been hijacked, and the two officers are unconscious. Send help."

"What is your location?" a voice responded.

"I have no idea. Bring an ambulance."

I sat on a nearby rock, waiting for the cavalry. We hadn't travelled for more than ten minutes, so they couldn't be far. The masked men had changed up their game plan, and I didn't know what they wanted with me anymore. They were systematically destroying every part of my life. The only way to win this game was to not play at all. If they wanted me at a certain address, that was the last place I was going to go. I had to trust the police to do their jobs from now on. I couldn't afford to lose anything else.

Maybe there was another reason I had chosen Courtney. I felt almost unfaithful for thinking it, but subconsciously, I must have been holding out hope that we could fix everything. She didn't know the importance of her telling me to do the right thing. If she hadn't, I would have been running to that address right now. She believed me now, and she wanted to talk about it, but I didn't think she would get the opportunity, not without bars in between us.

The police were involved now, and Kat and I had left a trail of bodies behind us. It was only a matter of time before they linked some of them to us. I could see the blue lights approaching from the distance, growing closer quickly. It wasn't alarming; it was comforting. With me in police custody and Courtney under guard by the police, it would be the safest we have been for a while. A seemingly unending stream of police vehicles arrived, coming to a screeching stop behind the upturned van.

"Sean, keep your hands where we can see them, and walk towards us slowly." A voice shouted.

"It wasn't me. I'm coming," I said calmly.

"Turn around, get on your knees, and interlock your fingers behind your head."

I complied. Officers replaced the cuffs on my wrists and dragged me to the back of another police van.

18

FRIENDS IN HIGH PLACES

I did the right thing.

And it landed me back in the cage of another van, being escorted to a police station. I had lost so much to the masked men, but I wasn't going to lose anything else. Or anyone else. I wasn't playing their game anymore. I was going to tell the police everything. Every single detail. If it landed me in prison, so be it. It was better than giving them the satisfaction of me being their puppet once again. I had to tell them everything; it would give the police the best chance of finding them. And hopefully, to get some level of justice for Kat.

I braced myself in the van the entire way there, expecting another attempted breakout, but we arrived without incident. DS Banks was waiting for us when we got there, a lit cigarette poking out of his mouth. He stubs it out on the wall when he sees me and comes to collect me from the cage.

"We appreciate what you did, Sean." He thanked.

"It was the right thing," I said, jangling my cuffs in the air, "still didn't get me out of these, though."

"We will definitely take what you did into consideration, though. The only reason you have been arrested is because the whole thing is so confusing. But we will clear it up."

He marched me through the doors again into booking, and I was left in the same cell as I had been in months earlier. They still hadn't fixed the light. I sat on the cot bed, picking at the dried blood on my face and hands. The headache had subsided, but the left side of my face was bruised and inflated. I pressed it lightly, and the searing pain helped stop me from thinking about what I was about to tell the police.

I didn't know if it was the concussion, but I could see Kat sitting on the cot next to me. She was still with me, even though I was responsible for her losing her life. She put her hand on my thigh and gave me a look of disappointment. Kat would have loved to watch me rip the men who did this to her limb from limb, but violence bred violence. This was the right decision; I was sure of it. I was snapped out of my trauma-induced trance when DS Banks came to collect me. I was only in the cell for a few minutes. He must have been eager to hear my story.

"Are you ready, Sean?"

"I'm not doing anything else."

I knew the drill. He led me to the padded interview room again. I picked up the water that had been left but set it down; I didn't know how long it had been there. The long beep of the recording machine filled the silence as DS Banks stared at me intently. This was it. I was about to spill my guts and tell them everything. This was the only possible way of getting rid of the masked men for good. I just hadn't realised it before. They were professional killers; I was stupid to think I had any chance against them. Any time I gained the upper hand, it must have been sheer dumb luck.

"Okay, this is a police interview with Sean Miller with DS Tony Banks in attendance. We are investigating the disappearance of Kathryn, her last name unknown, and the attempted murder of Courtney Miller. We also would like to ask some questions regarding the incident tonight where your transport to this station was hijacked. The time is 2:42, on the nineteenth of August. Sean, you are waiving your right to a solicitor. Is that still the case?"

"Yes."

I had only just realised I didn't even know Kat's last name. It just never came up. We had skipped the usual formalities of meeting someone and straight into going out killing together. I thought I knew her deeply, but I didn't even know the basics. It made me laugh slightly; DS Banks pulled a face in response.

"For the benefit of the recording, I would just like to thank you for your actions this evening regarding the two officers escorting you."

"Anytime."

"I'd like to start, if I may, with an open question for you, Mr Miller. What can you tell me about the events tonight?"

I didn't feel anxious; what I felt was absolute apathy. I'd saved Courtney's life, but I didn't have the energy to save my own from incarceration or otherwise. If I were put in prison, at least I wouldn't have to keep running from the masked men. They clearly wanted me for themselves, and I was determined not to give them what they wanted. More than anything, I was just exhausted. The mental and physical toll that had been inflicted on me was massive.

I couldn't even bear to toe the line with DS Banks. I just wanted everything out in the open so they could deal with me quickly and concentrate on the real villains.

"I've killed two people," I stated.

The shock almost split DS Bank's face in two as he leant forward in his chair in disbelief.

"Sorry, Sean, can you repeat that?"

"And I was involved in the death of four others. But they were all in self-defence."

"Sean, at this time, I need to urge you to reconsider getting a solicitor. If you can't afford one, one will be provided for you. Would you like to take a break?"

"No. I want to talk about what I've done. What Kat and I have done."

I went through every single detail from the beginning. I could tell DS Banks was struggling to believe me, but I started seeing the puzzle pieces forming a picture in his head. Just retelling the story made me realise the journey I had been on; I was a completely different person now. I didn't feel guilt, and I wasn't even worried about the repercussions. By the time I had finished, I felt like I had lost half my body weight; it was finally out in the open.

Once you plotted the story out in the open, it was hard to believe. The journey I had been on to get from there to here was astounding. I was so wrapped up in the moment that most of the time, I didn't take a step back to think about it. I described myself as a feral animal, ripping through the night and stalking my prey. But I didn't care as long as the men responsible were caught.

The look on DS Banks face was completely different now. My arrest was necessary to clear up the confusion of what had happened, but now he thought he was staring down a cold-blooded killer. My story had definitely rattled him, but he snapped himself out of it and returned to his professional demeanour.

"I appreciate you being so forthcoming, Mr Miller. Obviously, you have given us a lot to investigate." DS Banks thanked.

"You are welcome," I responded.

"You have made some pretty shocking admissions to some serious crimes."

"I know."

"I have no further questions at this time, and I will be terminating the interview there. The time is 04:12."

The beep fills the awkward silence once again. DS Banks, clearly exhausted from the night's events and admissions, slumped back into his chair, staring at me with uncertainty.

"Sean, off the record, why have you just told us all this? You could have easily got away with it. Half of these bodies we didn't even know about."

"I wanted to tell the truth. I am sick of lying. And I wanted to give you the best chance of finding these people."

"Fair enough. You are going to go back to your cell, and we will give you a charging decision in the morning. I strongly suggest you think about getting a solicitor."

"I'll think about it. Thanks, Tony."

"You are welcome."

DS Banks stood up and ushered me back to my cell. It didn't feel like a cell anymore; it felt like a fortress. I was safe in here, at least for now. The masked men wanted my blood, but I wasn't going to give it to them. I had been awake for over 24 hours, but I didn't feel tired; I felt wired. Although it would likely land me in prison, I was finally a step ahead of them. I would rather neither of us win than them.

I trusted DS Banks to do his job and get justice for Kat. I didn't like the person I had started becoming; I wasn't cut out for it. Before this journey, killing someone was an incomprehensible act to me, but I had become all too comfortable with it. Kat was partly responsible for that transformation in me, but she was also responsible for a lot of the positive changes. I had fought for what I believed in, right or wrong, and I will always be grateful for that gift she gave me.

I just wanted to see her again. Just one more kiss. But she was gone. I still didn't have any designs for sorting things out with Courtney; it would be impossible with me behind bars. The night's events proved that they were always better off without me. I would bring nothing but chaos and danger into their lives. They were the true innocents in this, and the more distance I could put between us, the better.

I managed to get a few hours of broken sleep before the clunking of the cell door woke me up. It was DS Banks, seemingly powered only by nicotine and caffeine. He looked at me for a minute in thought, tapping some paperwork against his own chest.

"Mr Miller. You are free to go."

"What?"

"You are free to go. CPS came back, no bodies, no crimes."

"You are kidding me. I've just confessed to two murders."

"That's what I told them. You must have some friends in high places."

"Not friends."

"That's what I thought. You need to be careful, Sean. I'm not sure who you are messing with."

"Me either."

DS Banks returned all my possessions and escorted me outside. In a matter of minutes, I had gone from looking into the abyss of spending the rest of my life in prison to being as free as a bird. It didn't feel right. I always acted in some level of self-defence, but there should be some legal repercussions for me.

The early morning heavy rain was sobering. Every drop that hit my face teased and taunted me. I had tried to do the right thing, at great personal cost, but there was no escaping them. They were far more influential than I ever thought possible. DS Banks was absolutely correct; I didn't know who I was messing with. And they weren't going to stop. I was now forced to play their game; they wouldn't let me just bow out. They must know I had just told the police everything. They were watching my every move.

The darkness within me sniggered as I came crawling back for it. Deep down, I don't think I ever wanted to do the right thing. I craved this too much. This brutal game of cat and mouse consumed my life and the lives of the people around me. Seeing Courtney beaten and tied up in that dusty building made me question the strategy, but Kat had the right idea all along. She knew what people like this were capable of and the only way of stopping them.

I didn't get a taxi home. I walked. I was in no rush to exact my revenge, and I had to be patient. If I ran head-on into another ambush, it's likely I wouldn't survive it. I just had to wait for them to make a mistake. I would do this for me, for my family, and for Kat. I meandered through the masses of people rushing for shelter in the downpour like a ghoul. The disappointment of trying to do what was right and failing had left me feeling empty and alone. The path I walked was chosen for me, and I didn't have free will anymore. I was being dragged along for the ride.

I got home without incident; the downpour had removed all traces of the evening before from my skin. The long walk did little to clear my head. I was simply waiting for the next set of instructions on where to go next. I had only been out of the shower for a few minutes before I heard my phone beeping again. It was them; it had to be. Was this the mistake I was waiting for? Or mine? I unlocked my phone.

> *Two Pines Trading Estate.*
> *10 pm.*

I had a few hours to prepare. How generous of them, I thought. I placed my hand on the darkness inside and shook it violently awake. I needed it. I had to throttle myself out of the numbness. I didn't know if I would come out on top, but it was my last line of defence. It roused from its slumber, and I let it devour me from the inside out. My knuckles cracked under the pressure I was putting them under. My teeth crumbled to dust under the force of my jaw, clenching them. My vision became narrow and focused.

My car had been left on the canal. I had no choice but to run to the trading estate. But I had a final opportunity to centre myself before the showdown, but I didn't take it. With every step closer to my oppressors, I seethed; the blood in my veins could melt steel. My skin was hot enough to evaporate every drop of autumnal rain instantly on impact. Every inhale of the cold, wet air returned fire. The ground trembled with every foot strike; the gravel shuddered in fear. Every muscle twitched and pulsed in anticipation of the fight ahead.

I could hear footsteps on the track behind me. Kat's footsteps. I didn't turn to look at her; it would have broken the spell. I imagined her in her last moments, beaten but beautiful. It did nothing but spur me down the path faster. There was a chance I would be joining her, but it didn't deter me. One way or another, it would end that night.

The thudding of the app remained steady as I arrived at the trading estate. The streets were sparsely lit and looked dramatic. The rain continued to pelt the tarmac without yield. It hit the tin rooves of the industrial units in a sustained attack. The road ahead was devoid of life, and I had no idea which unit they would be in. I cautiously inspected each one.

The thudding started getting slightly faster. I was moving in the right direction. The units were encircled by tall steel fences and gates. I spotted one in the distance that had been left open. I approached it; it was one of the smaller units. It was most likely operated as a car repair business. The shutters on the outside had been left slightly open, maybe 12 inches, allowing the incandescent white light to leak into the car park.

I bent over as far as possible to look inside but couldn't see anyone waiting. The opening was too small for me to make my way under stealthily. I would have to pull the shutter open, alerting anyone here to my presence. Screw it, I threw the shutters open and looked inside. My instincts were correct; it was a mechanic's unit. The floor was decorated with past oil spills and grime. A half-disassembled car lay suspended in the air, gutted of its innards.

I navigated the mass of scrap metal and tools on the floor, trying to stay as quiet as possible. The app thudding became unbearable. This was definitely the right place. I took the earphones out and heard laboured breathing behind a large steel toolbox. I picked up a lump hammer from the ground. At least I was armed. When I turned the corner, there was a figure tied to a chair with a bag over their head. They were wearing a baggy black tracksuit, but it was quite clearly a woman.

The masked men had obviously ensnared another victim, another innocent, in their malicious games. I placed the lump hammer down silently and went to remove the bag from her head. The bag had stuck to her face because of the injuries she had sustained, and I tugged at it to release it. She turned her head to the side in a futile attempt to protect herself from me. As I removed it, I could hear subdued weeping. I couldn't believe it.

It was Kat.

She was alive.

I raced to remove the gag in her mouth. No longer being subdued, she wailed almost deafeningly until I placed a single finger on her lips to calm her. It took her a minute to recognise who I was, but when she did, I saw the hope return to her blackened eyes.

I untied her feet first and then her arms, and she threw them around me as soon as she was free.

"You came," Kat whispered.

"We need to get out of here," I muttered softly.

I helped her stand, and we made our way through the minefield of tools that had been left on the floor. We got maybe 6 feet away from the door before Kat started faltering, likely exhausted from the hell she had been through. I turned to look at her, being propped up underneath my arm, and she looked up at me with a half-smile.

I didn't see it coming. I didn't hear it coming. I barely felt it at first; it was just a weird feeling of pressure in my right thigh, like I had been punched. Followed by an almost pleasant feeling of a warm, viscous liquid running down my leg. It was blood. My blood. Kat backed away.

As soon as I saw the wound, the pain arrived fiercely. A searing hot agony like a thousand needles being stuck in my thigh from the inside out. The pain made me drop like a dead weight to the floor with a loud thud, clattering the discarded tools around me.

I couldn't see who stuck the knife in me. They must have been waiting in the shadows for the perfect opportunity to stick me with it. I thrashed my head around, looking for the perpetrator, but I couldn't find them. I had expected a fight, but I had been struck down before I could even react.

I had clearly lost a lot of blood, and quickly. I felt so lightheaded I could barely lift it a few inches from the concrete floor. My eyesight started to fail me, and the objects surrounding me turned into nothing but a blur of colour and shapes. I could see Kat standing over me, mouthing some words that I couldn't understand. I could hear them, but they sounded distorted and blurred. I wanted desperately to return to my feet and get us out of there, but the wound and the blood loss left me entirely incapacitated.

The last image I was left with before I fell unconscious was the masked men encircling Kat as I feebly reached out to warn her.

19

EVERYTHING

I'd never been woken up with a bucket of cold water before. It isn't an experience I'd recommend. Firstly, I experienced the initial shock, and then afterwards, I was left with confusion as to why I was in that situation in the first place. I started to remember, and not for the first time, I found myself tied to a chair. The stab wound had been bandaged up, but the blood was slowly soaking through, forming droplets on the surface. I felt awful like the worst hangover I'd ever had, magnified by a force of a thousand. I was still in the garage, with a bright light pointed directly into my eyes. I could feel the heat coming off it, and it had already started to dry my clothes.

"What have you done with her?" I screamed.

No one replied. Not words, anyway. I just heard a chorus of laughter from behind the light. The laughter fell silent, and I heard footsteps approaching the light. The light was turned off. It took a few seconds for my eyes to adjust, but five of the masked men were standing in front of me.

"Well, Mr Miller," one of them said, removing his balaclava entirely, "we have unfinished business."

The image of the men we killed in the warehouse was seared into my mind forever. Especially Victor, who had spoken to me. But he was dead, shot in the back by Kat, and buried in the rubble of the warehouse we burned to the ground. But it was him, definitely. The way he formally said my name sent a frozen shudder reverberating up my back. How did he survive? I stared at him in disbelief as he made his way closer to me. He only smiled in response, patiently waiting for the penny to drop.

"You died," I reasoned.

"No, I didn't. Actually, quite alive and well, and we are here to collect what is ours."

"What have you done with her?"

"You will find out soon enough, Mr Miller."

Three of the other men also removed their balaclavas. They were not concerned with anonymity anymore. I studied each of their faces, but I didn't recognise them. The last masked man walked over to me, still wearing the mask, and menaced over me.

"Sean, meet the person who gave you that little stab wound in your leg. We couldn't have you running away this time."

"I am going to kill you all. Starting with you," I threatened, turning to the masked figure above me.

"I love you, Sean." They whispered in my ear, biting my earlobe suggestively.

It was Kat.

She removed the balaclava; all the injuries on her face had completely disappeared. She loosened the tie on her suit with a cheery grin across her face. I sat there, tied to the chair like a wounded animal, with my mouth wide open in absolute shock. I couldn't think of a single possibility that would place her behind that mask. She looked at me with heavy expectation, willing me to put it all together. After a minute, when I hadn't formed any words, she pressed the wound on my leg sharply. It sent searing pain through my entire body, and I tensed every muscle like I had been electrocuted. A small amount of my blood had ended up on her thumb, and she wiped it on my shirt with disdain.

"What's up Sean, Kat got your tongue?" She jested maliciously.

"Kat, what the hell is going on?" I pleaded.

"As if I would ever fall in love with someone like you. A bottom feeder. You should have seen this coming a mile away," she began, "you are pathetic."

"What have I ever done to you to warrant this?"

"You took *everything* from me!" She screamed.

The spittle from Kat's rage sprayed against my face, forcing me to turn away in futile avoidance. She pressed her forehead into the side of my head, pushing me with enough force to almost topple the chair. It rocked on two legs, confirming that I was truly at her mercy.

"You were just meant to be an easy job, a low ranker, easy catch. But no, you just had to kill him, didn't you?"

"Kill who?" I asked.

"My husband," she shrieked violently, "Peter."

Just uttering the word husband sent her spiralling around the room in a fit of rage. I never asked how her husband died, and she barely ever talked about him. I just assumed it was a long time ago and didn't want to reopen that wound. She started to kick over anything she could reach. The unmasked men stood there in silence, not breaking their eye contact with me. Her rage boils down into despair, and she returns to me so close that I can feel her breath on my face.

"He was literally bringing you some water. A kindness. And you thanked him by sticking a scalpel in his neck." She hissed.

All the times I had wondered about Kat's husband, and it turned out I had met him. I stood over his lifeless body after I had watched him bleed out by my hands. It was the birth of the darkness in me, or at least its release. Once the connection was made, I almost felt some guilt for ending his life until I remembered the threat I was under.

"It was him or me," I uttered.

"It should have never been him. You should have just accepted what was coming. You played the game, and you lost."

"So, you and your thugs hack the app, and I should just sit back and accept that I am going to die?" I argued.

"We didn't hack the app, Sean. We created it. To lure in suckers like you who think they can make a quick buck from something as trivial as exercise."

I could feel my face crumple in on itself in confusion, and I couldn't accept what she was saying. I could see the words leaving Kat's mouth, but I didn't understand them. I didn't even recognise her. It was like she had been possessed.

"The whole thing is designed so you tire yourself out," she continued, "running through the night makes for an easier catch. The hilarious thing is you agreed to the whole thing when you clicked accept on the terms and conditions. It was right there in black and white. It helps weed out the intelligent ones who actually stood a chance of escaping."

"You made the app?"

"Yes, keep up. When you clicked accept, you gave us permission to track you whenever we liked. We literally heard every pathetic argument you had with your wife and every awkward conversation with your kid. I must have listened to your sacking about fifty times. Hilarious."

"But why? Why do any of this?"

"The oldest reason in the world, Sean, money. I didn't lie to you when I said I was a broker. There are some filthy rich people out there with very dark and expensive habits. They pay a fortune to be delivered a fresh victim."

My heart refused to accept what she was telling me. I loved Kat in a way that I had never loved before. Even though she was telling me it was all a lie, I couldn't believe it. Or I just didn't want to. It would soil the memory of what she was before. It just wasn't possible for me for someone to fake those feelings for revenge.

"But we fell in love," I reasoned.

"You fell in love. When you killed Peter, a quick death at the hands of one of our clients became too good for you. I needed to take everything from you, like you did to me. I wanted to destroy every part of you, a piece at a time."

"Kat, I don't understand."

"I needed you to fall in love with me, so you would break things off with your whore of a wife. But you wouldn't. It didn't take much, though, a doctored photograph and a cheap bunch of flowers. Sure, it would have been easier to kill you, but to watch you destroy your own life for a few quid was worth the effort."

"We actually killed people together! Your people! Are you the kind of person who would sacrifice your own just to get one over on me?"

"Oh, absolutely. But I didn't. You didn't kill anyone other than Peter. The man you beat on the canal is standing right there; you barely gave him a black eye. The sniper? Right there next to him. He switched the bullets to blanks after he intentionally was shooting at your feet. He was hurt when I hit him with my car, but he was well compensated. You even fell for our little stunt at the warehouse, a few remote-control blood packs, hook, line, and sinker."

"We did actually kill Steve." One of the men reminded.

"Oh, I forgot about Steve," Kat recalled with a laugh, "well, he was useless to us after you got him arrested. He had to go. The best part was when you literally helped me burn down all the evidence after."

The unmasked men smiled slightly but still remained perfectly still and silent. Kat had stopped pacing and was staring at me intently. The entire year had been a lie. The darkness in me was deflated. Even that was a lie. I didn't know if I should be relieved or bitter. But the worst part was that Kat was a lie. I felt heartbroken. I felt ludicrous. And she was rubbing it in my face.

"I forgot about Neil! Oh my god!" she exclaimed, "You were right, he really was a wanker. When I sent the boys to go and remove the bullet casings we left, he actually came over to confront them. Can you believe it?"

"That's just the way the cookie crumbles." One of the men said dryly.

"What about Jordan? He was totally innocent," I interrupted.

"Jordan? Oh, 'Jordy', he would have made us a pretty penny if you hadn't been hot on his heels. We were just getting him ready for transport when you got there."

"The car crash? That was fake, too?"

"I loved that car, Sean. I really loved it. And you made me crash it because you started getting all emotional and lovesick. I had to snap you back into reality."

"You are vile."

"You know what your worst mistake was?" Kat said, leaning in so close I could taste her breath on my tongue.

"What?" I uttered.

"You didn't pick me," she whispered bitterly, "after everything, you still picked your boring fucking wife. After the nights we've shared? You still picked her."

"I'm going to kill you."

"No, you aren't," Kat laughed, "how is the Mrs anyway? Recovered from the beating my boys gave her?"

Kat watched with a sick smile as I gave everything I had, trying to break away from the chair I was tied to. The wood started to bow and creak under the pressure but refused to give way. I slumped back into it, exhausted, and Kat laughed right in my face. She had won; no one knew I was here, and I was too injured to escape. I wouldn't feed her sickness any longer by allowing her to enjoy watching me squirm. I had to accept that this was the end of the road.

"What happens now?" I asked calmly.

"After all our runs during the summer, you actually made it quite far up the leaderboard. There is a very nice prize on your head, and a lot of prospective clients want to do some very disturbing things to you. It's unfortunate because none of them are getting you. You are mine."

"Cut to the chase, Kat."

Kat gripped the wound on my thigh with malice; I fought the initial reaction of screaming in agony and kept eye contact with her. A glimmer of pain must have made its way onto my face, as a sick smile crosses her face as she leans into my ear with a whisper.

"I am going to find Courtney, and I'm going to bring her here. Then, I'm going to stick a scalpel in her neck while you watch. So, you have to go through exactly what I had to go through. Then I'll start cutting pieces off you until you beg me to end it all. And only then I might consider killing you."

In a bizarre way, this was the least terrifying Kat had ever been. This was Kat, unfiltered. I finally knew her like I always wanted. Her plan had succeeded, spectacularly, of course. She had destroyed me. She destroyed my family; she even destroyed my own sense of who I was. I thought I was a cold-blooded murderer, but I wasn't. I just got put into an awful situation with no way out. I was backed into a corner and reacted.

I had fallen in love with her. Even then, a part of me thought it would all be some elaborate joke, but she was a true psychopath. The man behind the mask was finally unveiled, and it wasn't a man at all. It was the new love of my life. In a single moment, I questioned every single decision and what Kat's part in it was. She was wearing me like a puppet, effortlessly tricking me from one destructive event to the next.

But I couldn't let her hurt Courtney. Not any more than she has done. But I didn't see a way out. I was tied to this chair, heavily outnumbered, and had a pretty serious knife wound in my thigh. I let out a blood-curdling scream internally, but my facial expression didn't change even slightly. I couldn't let her see my weakness again. That was what she was doing all this for, after all.

Two of the men replaced their balaclavas and left to go and get Courtney. Kat was standing in the corner, very loudly sharpening a knife. She was enjoying this prolifically. She stopped every now and again to give me a wink or blow a kiss. It made me feel sick to my stomach. A car started outside; the men set off to collect her. I heard the engine make its way down the road before coming to a screeching halt and a thud.

"Check what is going on," Kat ordered.

Without a word, the rest of the men ran outside, replacing their balaclavas. Kat had broken character and started to look nervous. Not wanting to leave me alone, she stood at the roller door, waiting for them to report back to her. Before they could, blue light started to flood the inside of the garage. Kat let out a panic-inducing roar at the sight of it before picking up the knife and pressing the blade flat against my throat.

"No!" she screamed, "I had you. I had you exactly where I wanted you. Everything went exactly to plan."

"Do it, then," I threatened.

Kat pressed the blade further into my throat, cutting into the skin slightly. I could see the internal battle within her. She never wanted anything more in her life. One more slight push with her arm, and it would have slit my throat. But the thought of spending the rest of her life in prison wasn't something she would accept. It doesn't matter how many friends you have in high places; she would have literally been caught red-handed. The police dealing with the men outside would buy her some time, but would it be enough for her to kill me? She bitterly made her decision, dropping the knife on my lap and running through the back of the garage.

I managed to get the handle of the knife between my teeth, and I sliced open the bonds on my left arm. I got free quickly, taking the knife with me and giving chase. The pain in my thigh was unbelievable; my entire leg felt like it was combusting. I could barely walk, but the promise of revenge kept me going. The adrenaline kicked in; it numbed the pain. I was losing blood by the bucketload, but I planned to spill more.

Kat never created the darkness inside of me. It was always there. She nurtured it, tutored it. Even through all the lies and schemes, the one truth was my feelings. You can't fake those. Kat's admissions instantly turned those feelings into hate. Hate that she could have done this to me, to my family. She didn't see me as an equal, and she never did. I was a piece of meat she was going to sell to the highest bidder.

The rage killed the pain entirely. I managed to find her; she had used a path behind the trading estate that linked to the canal where all this began. It was a fitting place for all of it to end. She heard me coming and broke into a sprint. I couldn't let her get away, not this time. If she disappeared, Courtney and I would have to look over our shoulders for the rest of our lives, and I couldn't have that.

Kat stumbled on the cobbles underneath the bridge. Her incessant need to be dramatic and don the uniform of the masked men was her undoing. It wasn't a running-appropriate outfit; her polished shoes struggled to get any purchase on the gravelled path. Even with the wound on my leg, I managed to catch her up at the next bridge, and I pushed her to the side. She careered into the railing, barely stopping in time to avoid falling into the canal. She landed on her back on the floor, staring up at me, holding the knife.

"We both know you aren't going to kill me, Sean." She said with a smile.

"This needs to end."

"Yes, it does, but it doesn't end with me dead, unfortunately. You don't have it in you."

But I did have it in me. Kat put it there. It doesn't matter if the murders I had committed were real or staged. What mattered was how I felt about them. The darkness within begged me to do it, plunge the knife straight through her eye socket. My hand almost complied, drawing the blade closer to her face. With one swift movement, I could bring this piece of steel down and eradicate the threat forever. Objectively, she deserved to die for everything she had done. She was as evil as she was stunning; her blue eyes had almost been scorched black in the moonlight. I'd spent so much of the last year in love with this woman that I didn't know if I could do it. I didn't even know if I wanted to. It felt wrong to destroy something so beautiful, even though her heart was stone.

Kat could see the dark contemplation in my eyes, and it scared her significantly. Her expression turned from cool and collected to one of pure fear in an instant. I could see the façade she had put on in the garage break away into pieces. She had almost claimed my life and probably countless others, but she was terrified of losing her own. I gritted my teeth and brought the knife down as hard as I could.

It struck about 6 inches away from her head.

The knife was chiselled into the mortar gaps of the cobbles below, and it continued to bend and sway rapidly, still feeling the force I had just put behind it. Kat exhaled intensely, bringing tears to her eyes.

"You are going to leave us alone, Kat; if I see you again, I won't miss next time. You have done enough damage to us; I will not let you do anymore."

I whispered menacingly.

"I will. Just let me go," Kat gasped.

"I am going to tell the police everything. *Everything*. You will lose everything: the fancy cars, the nice apartment, and your sick business. I won't stop until they have dismantled your whole operation."

"I understand." She pleaded.

"Your clients aren't going to be too happy when you stop delivering warm bodies. I'll be the least of your worries."

I am interrupted by the sounds of footsteps behind me, and I turn to see a group of uniformed officers jogging towards us with torches. I looked at Kat, and I believed her fear. In the end, her pursuit of destroying my life had almost ended hers. The darkness in me obeyed; I finally had control over it since Kat's influence had faded.

"Run," I ordered.

20

THE INVITATION

Apparently, I'd lost about 2 pints of blood from the stab wound, and I almost went into shock. I could definitely believe it. DS Banks had put a trace on my phone after I had falsely confessed to the murders. Totally illegal, of course, but he decided he needed to play dirty to close the case. Technically, it wouldn't be used as evidence in the case against Kat and the masked men, so it was up to me if I wanted to prosecute. He said he would get a slap on the wrist for it, which was better than I got.

I had spent the first week in the hospital handcuffed to the side of the bed. The police were desperately trying to sort through the facts and fiction, but the masked men weren't cooperating. DS Banks visited me a few times to get more statements, but the police couldn't even find Kat's real name. All of her properties and even her car was registered in a false name. But Kat was in the wind, and no one had seen or heard of her since she split. At least Courtney was safe. She had been discharged from the hospital a few days after I was brought in, but I hadn't heard from her, and I don't blame her.

I hadn't watched so much daytime TV in my life. The tiny box in the corner of the room playing at almost an undetectable volume subliminally filled my head with its garbage. The sheer level of boredom in the hospital was actually comforting; I had experienced more than enough excitement to last a lifetime.

I still hadn't sorted through the last night I spent with Kat and her masked men. It felt like a fever dream; it came back to me in chunks when I least expected it. I still didn't truly accept her version of events, but it was definitely the worst break-up I'd been through. Top three, at least. I knew there was a part of her that was lying to herself, and she did have some feelings for me along the way. But I could categorically state I didn't have any feelings for her anymore. Only regret and disgust.

I'd had a lot of time to reflect on it, and I didn't know why I didn't kill her either. I regretted it sometimes. I had taken a massive risk in letting her live, but I don't think I could have lived with myself if it had gone the other way. I felt better knowing that I had managed to get through the entire ordeal and I had only taken one life. My silent reflection was interrupted by DS Banks entering the room; he was my most frequent visitor. In a way, we had become unlikely friends throughout the whole thing.

"Sean, how are we getting on?" He asked.

"Living the dream, Tony," I replied.

"Good to hear it."

"How is the case progressing?"

"Slowly. It's very complicated."

"What's complicated about it? You have all of them in custody. They are murderers and human traffickers."

"We still haven't even seen a peep of Kat yet. The rest of them are just saying 'no comment.'"

"Tony, give it to me straight. Is she going to get away with this?"

"No. As soon as she pops her head out of whatever rathole she is lurking in, we'll get her."

"Good."

"It was only a flying visit, and I need to get going. I'm still on desk duty for my little stunt tracking your phone."

"I never did thank you for saving my life, Tony and Courtney's. So, thank you."

"Just doing my job, Sean. Rest up, yeah?"

I nodded at DS Banks, and he left the room; he had finally come through for us. We still had to wait for the charges to drop and for them to get convicted, but at that moment, it seemed like it was over. I hadn't noticed when he was in the room, but he had left a large envelope on the drawers at the side of the bed. I reached to get it; it was addressed to me. It was quite a thick stack of papers with a letter on the top. I recognised the handwriting; it was from Courtney.

Sean,

I hope you are recovering well. Tony told me about everything. It made me sick when I found out. I'm so sorry for not believing you. I can't stop thinking about what happened that night when you found me. I was terrified. But the thing that has stuck with me the most is how I felt when I saw you again.

I know it's going to be hard, but I want to try and give things another try. I miss you, and so does Dylan. We can work through the problems between us. I know it.

I love you,

Courtney
PS I never filed the paperwork.

Enclosed in the letter were the divorce papers I'd signed weeks earlier. She was serious about it; she really did want it to work. Part of me wanted to jump straight out of the hospital bed and go and find her, but I still didn't feel good enough for her. I never was. But maybe this new Sean was good enough. At the end of the day, I was a victim in all this, and as horrific as the things I'd done were, I had to remember that. I retrieved my phone to give her a call, and the 'B-Run' app was greyed out. It hadn't been working since the masked men had been arrested. I held my thumb over the icon and pressed delete. I should have done it months before. I called Courtney, and she answered the phone within seconds.

"Sean. Are you okay?" She asked.

"Hi, Courtney. I'm good. I've just read your letter; did you mean it?"

"Yes, I did. Every word. I forgive you for what happened, and I understand. Obviously, it's going to be tough, but we can make it. What do you think?"

Hearing Courtney's voice was so incredibly soothing. She always knew the right thing to say. I wanted nothing more than to get our family back together and start afresh. The entire year had been one massive mistake, and I would work the hardest I have ever done in my life to make it right. The man she married was definitely dead, but it just meant I got the chance to make her fall in love with the new Sean all over again.

"I've never wanted anything as much in my life. I love you, Courtney."

"I love you, Sean."

"As soon as I get out of here, let's just move away. Anywhere. We need a fresh start."

"I'd like that." She beamed.

"How is Dylan?"

"He's excited to see his dad."

"I'm excited to see him too."

I ended the call with a fresh motivation to get well again and get home, and now I had my family waiting for me. The next week was gruelling. I put my all into physical therapy, and I was getting stronger. The wound had sealed, but I could still feel the knife twisted in there. The doctors said that if I hadn't run on it afterwards, it would have healed a lot quicker. But it was worth it to know Kat was on the run. She finally knew how I felt the past year.

I saw Kat everywhere I looked. Every blonde with a ponytail gave me a little fright. She had slithered her way under my skin and lived in my mind, too. She lay there, bunking with the darkness within, begging to be released. Part of my treatment included traditional therapy, but there wasn't a therapist in the world who could remove her from my head. I had to learn to live with what had happened on my own. The syndrome I most likely suffered from was so unique it didn't even have a name. I had to move on and live my life for myself and for my family.

My first breath of fresh air after the stint in hospital was incredible. I'd become so accustomed to the scents of the hospital that I'd forgotten what the outdoors smelled like. Courtney and Dylan were waiting for me when I got out, both with a huge smile on their faces.

"Thanks for picking me up," I smiled.

"You are welcome," Courtney replied.

"Hi, Dad!" Dylan shouted, "You don't look so good."

"Thanks, son."

"Are you getting in or what? We will be late." Courtney asked with a smile.

"Definitely."

I got in the car, and Courtney started driving us home. She turned to smile at me at every opportunity. I had forgotten how beautiful she was. Dylan was in the back playing some game on his tablet and kicking his feet. It was perfect. We felt like a real family again. Twelve months ago, I would have found something to complain about. But not now. I was eternally grateful.

"Don't go home, Court. Let's get something to eat," I suggested.

"Like where?"

"I really fancy a greasy cheeseburger and a lager."

"Me too." She smiled.

We pulled into the car park of a pub near the hospital, and it was riddled with potholes that were filled to the brim with dirty rainwater. We all ran inside, and it was pretty much empty. The stale smell of beer slightly sweetened the dusty air.

"Shall we try somewhere else?" Courtney whispered with a disgruntled expression.

"No, it's perfect."

We ate our meal, looking at where we could move. It was exciting; we all needed a fresh start. I didn't want to step foot in our house again. Kat had tainted it. I just wanted to leave all of this behind us and concentrate on my family. With all the running I had done, I had got us out of debt with money to spare. We could finally afford something actually pleasant.

I never thought I would be able to share one of these moments with my family again. My heart was as full as my stomach. We sat around the table, laughing and listening to Dylan talking about something he had seen on television. There was a time in the past when I would barely listen to him, just nodding along and smiling, but I took in every word intently. It was such a privilege to be in their company again.

We ended up buying a house in the countryside, a tiny cottage in a quaint little village. The windows were single-paned and leaked; you had to have the fire running pretty much 24/7 to keep it warm, but it had bags of character. We both got little jobs to keep us going, but we promised we would always make time for family. Dylan absolutely loved it there. The horses in the farmer's field behind us would lean their heads over the fence, and he would feed them apples. We were finally happy, happier than we had ever been.

Courtney and I went to therapy. We talked through our issues. Not just the obvious ones regarding Kat and the kidnapping but also the unspoken issues we had held for years. I fell in love with her all over again; we were infinitely more than we had ever been before. The cornerstone of that love was honesty, and we both promised we would hold the truth above all else. And it worked.

We spent the holidays in our new house, and it was like a scene from a cheesy Christmas film. Family time around the fire, playing board games and reading. Every day, I made a conscious effort to remind myself how lucky I was. I had become the richest man on the planet. My leg was getting stronger by the day, and Courtney's scars on her feet were barely noticeable anymore. I'd even taken up running again. There was a canal quite close to us; it was a bit daunting at first, but I fell in love with running again.

The mental scars were healing, too. I wondered if I saw Kat again if I would even recognise her. The image of her in my head became a ghost, a vestige of a life previously lived. Her grip on me had been reduced to a single claw left in my chest. She clung onto me, waiting for my inevitable bad decision to send me spiralling back to her. But I refused to let it happen.

Courtney was in the kitchen on the last day of 2023, cooking dinner. It was a little early for drinks, but we had started anyway. Dylan was sprinting around the house laughing, driving the new remote-control car we had bought him. I stood in the kitchen doorway, just watching over them with a smile.

"What are you smiling for?" Courtney grinned.

"I'm just really happy. I love you guys," I replied.

"Well, don't just stand there; you could help, you know?" She joked sarcastically.

"Yes, ma'am," I saluted.

"Dad, will you play with me?" Dylan asked.

"Of course, Son," I smiled.

Dinner was perfect. We sat around our rustic oak table, eating food, swapping jokes, and playing games. I never thought I would get the opportunity to do this ever again, not as a family. We laughed and chased each other around our little cottage. All the worries we had last year had been totally extinguished, and we could finally sit back and enjoy our little family.

We finally tired Dylan out and got him to bed, and most of the carnage of New Year's Eve was cleared away. Courtney and I were both cuddling on the couch in front of the crackling fire. I felt so peaceful and content. We both did. Courtney was barefoot, and I could see one of the scars shimmering from the light of the fire.

"Do you ever think about her?" She asked delicately.

"No. She is gone," I replied.

"I know, but you must have had good times with her. It wasn't all bad."

"It was all bad. I might not have thought it at the time, but she was manipulating me."

"I know."

"Court, I love you more than I ever have. I just want you and Dylan to be happy."

"I love you too. And we are happy."

To be honest, I did think about Kat. Not in a romantic way. I just wondered what she was doing or where she was living. If she was even living at all. Even after everything she had done to me, to us, I hoped she had moved on with her life. Grief makes people do some terrible things, and she reacted in the worst conceivable way. I wished that she could find some peace with everything and start living her life again.

DS Bank's updates were becoming more and more sparse. The last we heard, the men that had been apprehended that night had all been charged, awaiting trial. There was a mountain of evidence against them, an unfortunate byproduct of using an app with GPS to commit all their crimes. DS Banks thought there would be many more victims of the app, and they were doing their best to try to identify them and track down their families.

I was infinitely grateful that I wasn't on DS Bank's list of possible victims. I fought like hell to get here, and we did come out on top. I don't know what Courtney's and Dylan's life would be like without me here, but I knew deep down they weren't better off without me after all. I finally felt like an integral part of my own family.

We made our way to our bedroom, and we both stopped at Dylan's door to watch him sleeping through the crack in it. I held Courtney tightly. She had fought to get here, too; her fight was very different, but she still toiled for us to get to this very moment. Watching Dylan through the door was something I had always done, but it felt different now. I wasn't just an observer; I was an active part of his life. I was finally being a good father like I had always wanted.

We got in bed, and Courtney gave me a passionate good-night kiss. I won't go into too much detail, but we were like a couple of newlyweds at the time. We were rediscovering each other intimately, and it made us even closer. But not that night. We had eaten and drank far too much for that level of activity. We fell asleep in each other's arms, both feeling safe and secure.

I was generally sleeping better, but I still struggled some nights. Even though I knew it was all a ruse, I would have reoccurring nightmares about the killings Kat and I caused. I often woke up in a cold sweat, and I could still hear the popping from Kat's rifle while I watched the bodies hit the floor. My subconscious couldn't process that it wasn't real.

I generally went for an early morning run every other day so I could see Dylan off for school. I folded my running gear into a little bundle and left it at the front door so I didn't disturb them. My alarm woke me up in the morning for my run. The running helped me keep my demons in check, and I would only regret it later if I didn't go now.

I crept to the front door and noticed a red envelope sitting on the doormat. We had already done all our Christmas cards, so this was definitely a late entry. I reached down, 'Sean and Family' it read on the envelope. I ripped it open, and I could smell the contents before I even saw the card. Coconut and vanilla. In a single whiff, everything that had happened the past year was brought back in an instant. The front of the card was a fishnet stocking draped over a fireplace, with the caption 'Have you been naughty, or nice?' below it.

"Can't wait to see you again, Sean."

Kat had somehow tracked us down and obviously never had the intention of leaving us alone. On instinct, I went straight into the living room, threw the card into the fireplace and lit it. I watched the flames disintegrate the card into embers, shooting them up the chimney. She would be out there. Waiting for me in the darkness. The card wasn't a threat. It was an invitation. She must have gone to great lengths to find me; we had been very careful not to leave a trace. The fire burned the scent of the card, and it lingered in the living room bitterly.

The single claw she had stuck in me turned to two. Then three. I felt her grasp as she tried to pull me back into the darkness. I tried to shake it off at first, but the allure was too great. I should have immediately woken up my family and gotten them out of there, but I didn't. The promise I made to Courtney, to be totally honest, was discarded into the flames too. I watched the remnants of the card shrivel on the coals. As it withered, my regret for not killing Kat grew.

I dutifully accepted her invitation.

I left the house with the same lock knife I had used months before in my pocket. The scar on my thigh pulsed in the cold morning air, remembering the wound she gifted to me. I meant what I said when I last spoke to her, when I saw her again, I wouldn't miss.

EPILOGUE

I thought the first run of 2024 was going to be different. I sprinted down the path, the footsteps of my pursuer still scraping at the gravel behind me. I turned frequently to try and see who it was behind me. It had to be her or one of her goons. I arrived at the next bridge and caught a distant glimpse of my pursuer. I had spent so long studying Kat's form when we ran together that I immediately knew it was her. And she was alone.

Anxiety was drowning me. My breathing and pace were all over the place, and I didn't have a plan. I was just running. Every bridge that I passed, I expected a new set of masked men to pounce on me in ambush. Fatigue was starting to set in; I needed to form a plan and quickly. I turned to look at her, and she was gaining on me. The dead man's phone was still in my right hand, with the knife in my left. I almost lost my grip on both items because I was sweating so intensely.

It almost fell, which gave me an idea. I passed through the next bridge and immediately threw the phone down the path as far as I could and hid behind the wall. If she was tracking the phone, she wouldn't expect the ambush.

I heard the footsteps coming closer. They made the transition to the cobbles underneath the bridge, and I heard them echoing against the concrete walls.

I stepped back out onto the path.

She crashed into me at full speed, almost knocking me into the water, and she hit the floor face-first. I was no longer holding the knife; she turned on her back, and the knife was protruding just underneath the left side of her ribs. She was fighting for every breath; her chest heaved up and down as I cautiously made my way over to her to remove her hood and look her dead in the eyes.

"I told you I wouldn't miss," I said, without emotion.

"And you didn't," Kat replied.

But the reply didn't come from the woman on the ground. It came from above me. I turned my head to see Kat wearing the exact same ensemble, pointing her phone at me with a smile. I turned back to the woman on the ground, and blood was gushing from the entry wound. I hastily pulled her hood back to find a total stranger.

"What did you make me do?" I screamed.

"Well, according to this video that I have just livestreamed, you just killed a stranger."

"Who is she?"

"Don't worry, Sean, she is far from innocent. She works for me. I don't think the police will see it that way, though."

"It was an accident. I thought I was defending myself."

"There's a lot of that going around. I've had some time to think since our last meeting; death is too good for you. So, I let you have a taste of what your life could be with your pathetic little family, and now you will have to watch them from behind bars."

Kat put her phone back in her pocket and leaned over the bridge, casually watching me. I was putting as much pressure on the woman's wound as possible, but she was quickly bleeding out and struggled for every breath. The blood from the woman's wound started to dry up, and her heart was beginning to slow as she slipped unconscious. I could see the light fade in her eyes as she had taken her final breath. I was covered in her blood, almost from head to toe. I started thumping at her chest with my fists, trying to bring her back, but she was gone. Kat was slowly clapping on the bridge above me, and I turned to face her.

"You even picked up the dead guy's phone. It couldn't have gone any better. His earphones are literally in your ears right now." She goaded.

"Kat, why couldn't you have just left us alone?"

"Because you don't deserve to be happy when I've lost everything. You don't deserve to have a family when you took mine."

"It was him or me. You have to understand that."

"I understand. But I don't care. He was a hundred times the man you will ever be."

"Think about what you are doing to my family, Kat. They are innocent."

"Done. What I've *done* to your family. It's already over. And I couldn't give a toss about them. They are collateral damage in a war *you* started."

I could hear the distant sound of sirens speeding towards us; Kat must have already called the police. The whole thing was a setup. She had given me just enough time with my family to know what was possible, and then she snatched it all away from me. Kat's constant taunts and jokes made my blood boil. I removed the knife from the woman's wound and stood to face Kat head-on. She was amused by me rearming myself and had an over-the-top confused look on her face.

"Seriously? You don't hear those sirens?" She laughs.

"I don't care what happens to me. But you will pay for everything you have done."

"I doubt it, hon. Anyway, you will have to catch me first." She jeered with a wave as she started running over the bridge. I leapt up the steps three at a time and gave chase.

She had been training. The distance between us remained constant, no matter how hard I pushed to close the gap. The straight country lane in front of us was empty, but several police cars screeched onto it at the end, ripping their way down the road towards us. The impending threat of arrest encouraged me to close the gap slightly. I knew I was going to get caught, and I would likely go down for two murders, but I was desperate to make it three.

Every single muscle in my body screamed in agony as I squeezed every last drop of speed out of them. My calves and thighs felt like they were melting under the strain as I pushed them way beyond their limit. She was almost in reach, her shoulder-length hair whipping in the wind. I reached out to try and grab her, but she remained just out of my grasp.

Kat always looked the most beautiful when she was running. Her physique and form were like poetry. Each heel strike into the ground flowed effortlessly into the next. But I knew better now. Behind the thin veneer of striking beauty was her rotten interior. She had successfully achieved her goals and ruined my life. Destroyed everything about me. The worst part was that I participated willingly in it. Just before the police cars reached us with a screeching halt, Kat bounded into the thicket, disappearing in the foliage.

I was left stationary, holding the knife, and covered in the stranger's blood. The police pointed their pistols at me, ordering me to drop the knife and get on my knees. It didn't have to end this way. I could have just stayed at home; I could have rung the police. There was an infinite number of choices I could have made that would not have landed me in this very moment, but I chose this one. I couldn't resist one last expedition into the darkness. There was no doubt about it. She had won. She would be out there, continuing what she started, whilst I rotted away behind bars.

The police were clearly unhappy with my inaction and started to edge closer. I can't hear their shouting. I just thought about Courtney and Dylan and our last night together around the table. I had everything I ever wanted, and I traded it for a chance at revenge.

I dropped the knife and dropped to my knees.

A FREE BOOK

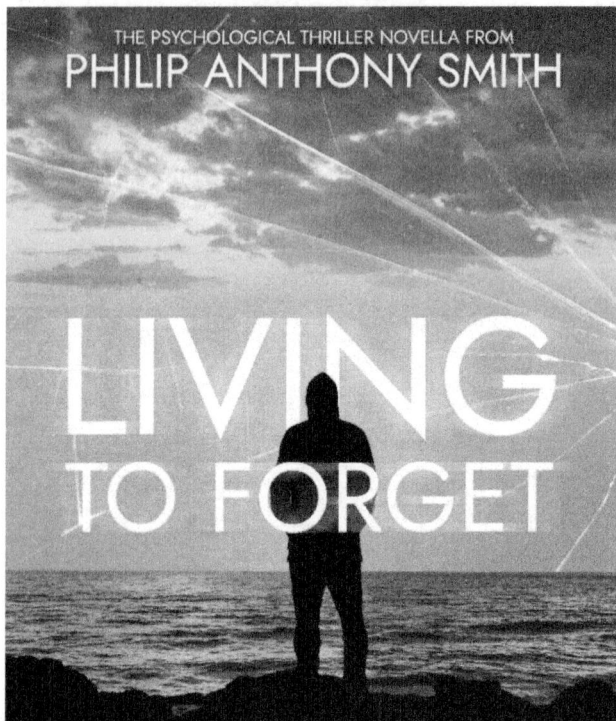

THE PSYCHOLOGICAL THRILLER NOVELLA FROM
PHILIP ANTHONY SMITH
LIVING TO FORGET

All my email subscribers will receive a free digital copy of my upcoming novella, '*Living To Forget*,' due to be released in May 2024.

Head over to my website and join my mailing list to receive it for free when it releases!

PHILIPANTHONYSMITH.COM

ACKNOWLEDGEMENTS

As cheesy as it is, my first acknowledgement is to *you*, the person who either sprinted, jogged, or even just strolled through this book. As a first-time author, I can't overstate how much it means that you made it this far, and I would like to sincerely thank you for reading! If you have 5 minutes to spare, it would be incredible to get a few words from you in the form of a review in whatever medium you feel comfortable with. In my pursuit of becoming a better writer, any comments, either positive or negative, would be invaluable in my journey.

I would also like to give a special, heartfelt thanks to the glorious people who helped me shape and refine this book. Everyone who received an advanced reader copy and sent me their thoughts is an absolute hero to me!

Rachael Willmott - @RachaelsReads – TikTok
Megan Bayes - @MegsBookshelf.x - Instagram
Esther Harman - @Esther.Reads8 – TikTok
Jen Morris - @Jen.LifeInBooks – Instagram
Lauren Bustard - @Books_withLaurenn – Instagram
Gail Kenyon - @Gales.Tales47 – Instagram
Shellie - @yorkshire.bookworm – Instagram
Katie Greenop - @katies_cosy_reading_corner – Instagram
Melina Rios - @melisbooked – Instagram
Rebekah Gleadhill-Howard - @bookish_beks - Instagram
Kammie Sue Brunswick Schutz – Goodreads

THE WOMAN HE LEFT BEHIND

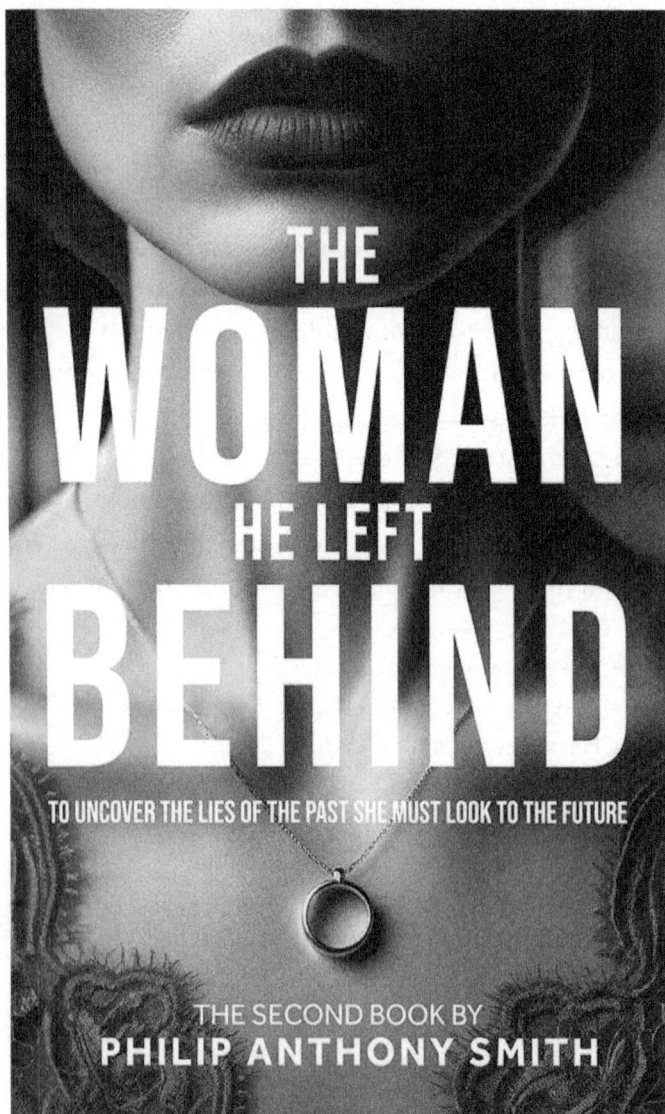

THE
WOMAN
HE LEFT
BEHIND

TO UNCOVER THE LIES OF THE PAST SHE MUST LOOK TO THE FUTURE

THE SECOND BOOK BY
PHILIP ANTHONY SMITH

Amelia and Harry are living the newlywed dream, and they are both looking forward to the future together in their blossoming romance. Harry is a terrific provider, both financially and emotionally, catering to all of Amelia's needs. She has never been more intensely in love. When tragedy strikes, and Harry loses his life on a visit to his hometown of Filey, Amelia is left broken and adrift.

Amelia enlists the services of a mysterious text psychic to help her navigate the emotions surrounding her husband's death, which quickly becomes an obsession. Feeling like she can't even make a basic decision without dire consequences, she uses the service more and more. When the psychic suggests her husband's death is more suspicious than it initially seemed, she uproots her life and moves to Filey to find out the truth.

'The Woman He Left Behind' is now available for pre-order! Visit my website to find out more.

PHILIPANTHONYSMITH.COM

Printed in Dunstable, United Kingdom